ARUMUGAM

SELECT KATHA TITLES

KATHA SHORT FICTION
One Last Story and That's It
By Etgar Keret
I am Madhabi
By Suchitra Bhattacharya
Katha Prize Stories 13
Ed Geeta Dharmarajan
20 Stories from South Asia
Asomiya Handpicked Fictions
Two Novellas and a Story
By Ambai
Basheer Fictions
Bhupen Khakhar Maganbhai's Glue ...
Black Margins
By Sa'adat Hasan Manto
Ed Muhammad Umar Memon
Downfall by Degrees
By Abdullah Hussein
Forsaking Paradise:
Stories from Ladakh
Home and Away
By Ramachandra Sharma
Hindi Handpicked Fictions
Inspector Matadeen on the Moon
By Harishankar Parsai
Masti Fictions
Mauni Fictions
New Urdu Fictions
Selected by Joginder Paul
Paul Zacharia Two Novellas
Pudumaippittan Fictions
Raja Rao Fictions
Separate Journeys
Ed Geeta Dharmarajan
The Heart of the Matter
Stories from the Northeast
The Resthouse
By Ahmad Nadeem Qasimi
The End of Human History
By Hasan Manzar
Uday Prakash
Short Shorts Long Shots
Waterness
By Na Muthuswamy

KATHA NOVELS
The Life and Times of Pratapa Mudaliar
By Mayuram Vedanayakam Pillai
Atonement and The Stone Laughs
By LaSaRa
The Heart has its Reasons
By Krishna Sobti

The Survivors
By Gurdial Singh
JJ: Some Jottings
By SuRaa
Listen Girl!
By Krishna Sobti
Padmavati
By A Madhaviah
Over to you, Kadambari
By Alka Saraogi
Seven Sixes are Forty Three
By Kiran Nagarkar
Singarevva and the Palace
By Chandrasekhar Kambar

SCREENPLAY

The Master Carpenter
By MT Vasudevan Nair

POETRY

Tamil New Poetry
Translated by K S Subramanian
Seeking the Beloved
Poetry of Shah Abdul Latif

NON-FICTION
The Epic of Pabuji
By John D Smith
A Child Widow's Story
By Monica Felton
Ismat: Her Life, Her Times
Ed Sukrita Paul Kumar
Links in the Chain
By Mahadevi Varma
Rajaji
By Monica Felton
Storytellers at Work
Travel Writing and the Empire
Ed Sachidananda Mohanty
That's it But
By SuRaa
Upendranath Ashk
By Daisy Rockwell

ALT (APPROACHES TO LITERATURES IN TRANSLATION)
Translating Desire
Ed Brinda Bose
Translating Caste
Ed Tapan Basu
Translating Partition
Ed Ravikant & Tarun K Saint

ARUMUGAM

IMAYAM

Translated from the Tamil by
D Krishna Ayyar

KATHA

First published by Katha in 2006

Copyright © Katha, 2006

Copyright © for the original is
held by the author.

Copyright © for the English translation
rests with KATHA.

KATHA
A3, Sarvodaya Enclave
Sri Aurobindo Marg, New Delhi 110 017

Phone: (91-11) 4141 6600, 4141 6610

Fax: (91-11) 2651 4373

E-mail: marketing@katha.org

Website: http://www.katha.org

KATHA is a registered nonprofit organization
devoted to enhancing the joy of reading.
KATHA VILASAM is its story research and resource centre.

Cover Design: Geeta Dharmarajan
Cover Painting: Kirann Telkar

Typeset in 12 on 16pt Lapidary333 BT at Katha

Katha regularly plants trees to replace the wood used in the making of its books.

ISBN 978-81-87649-27-4

First Reprint 2016

ARUMUGAM

W here *are* we going, Amma?"

"Don't talk, just walk."

"Can't. My legs *hurt.*"

"You're not a little baby, anymore. Walk fast. The sun's scorching as it is."

"I'll run away if you don't tell me."

"This is a wilderness. There're snakes and insects out there. You'd get bitten and die."

"I won't."

"Maybe not. Why would you want to run away? Keep walking."

"Walk where?"

She was silent.

The footpath threaded through the dry land, like a large crack in a wall.

Arumugam skipped a good two feet from it, and stared at Dhanabhagyam. She blushed as though being watched at a bride-viewing ceremony. Her steps faltered, and she ducked her head.

"Amma," he pleaded, looking at Dhanabhagyam. "Amma ..."

He hadn't understood anything, at first. He'd been playing marbles with his friends under the tamarind tree when Dhanabhagyam had dragged him to the house, put him into a clean shirt and combed his hair.

"Are we going to our village Amma? The temple?" he'd asked. "Some other village, Amma?"

Dhanabhagyam hadn't answered him. She had seemed angry instead of her usual self, and Arumugam hadn't asked her anything more.

But now, he knew. They were going to Pootthurai, and Arumugam walked briskly, his face lighting up with enthusiasm.

Shadows slid down in the east. The summer sun still burned. You couldn't look up into the sky, and the breeze lashed out like boiling water.

Red earth clung to their sticky, damp soles. The footpath meandered, like the chaotic hair-partings of children who were just learning to comb. Not a stalk could be seen in the fields. A few trees were scattered around, and cowherds rested in the shade as their cattle wandered, sniffing at one sparse patch after another. The bells around their necks jangled through the quiet wilderness.

Grandfather Muthu Kizhavar strode ahead with his walking stick.

"Amma," Arumugam turned to his mother enthusiastically. "I'll catch up with him," he announced.

Dhanabhagyam pulled him back, looking him over keenly as she did.

How tall he is! His hand, legs, face – whom does he take after but ...? I wonder if I can tuck him onto my waist? Oh, was this gangly boy really curled up in my womb like a tiny bundle of cloth? Good god above.

Dhanabhagyam smiled to herself. Of late, he'd taken to rushing about madly, and speaking saucily ... but his speech, laughter, his walk, and the build of his body – he was Raman, all over.

Arumugam had begun to stir in her womb barely three months after Raman had tied a taali around Dhanabhagyam's neck.

When had Raman ever spoken a word against Dhanabhagyam? "Enna pullay, what's up?" was his good-natured response to her every taunt. Dhanabhagyam it was, who missed no chance of yelling and shrieking abuses at him.

She slapped him. She rained blows on him. She pinched his thighs hard. Good-humoured chuckles were his only response to all her vicious pinches and punches.

Bedding her was something else altogether – for then and only then, would Raman turn into an animal.

Had there ever been a village where men hadn't yearned after Dhanabhagyam? No girl from Pootthurai had ever had her hand sought after as much.

"You won't have to shower the girl with jewellery," they would assure Kizhavar, repeatedly. "Or even give her dowry."

Nevertheless, Dhanabhagyam refused them all without exception, uncaring of the grooms themselves: "I won't." "I don't want to." "Did *I* ask to get married?" Her words might vary, but her determination never did.

Beautiful Dhanabhagyam had no rival – not even among the famed upper-caste Nayudu clans.

The old man had walked to the Koottherippattu fair, to sell the baskets

he had woven. Raman had come thither to sell his goats for money to
defray the expenses of his mother's funeral rites; within minutes of
his arrival at the fair, his goats had been sold. He had been on the
point of leaving, when fate played its hand. Why not buy two baskets?
he had thought, and found Kizhavar.

In no time, the two men had taken a liking to each other. Raman
lingered, attracted by Kizhavar's talk; on his part, the old man was
also glad to have someone to chat with. After all, thought Kizhavar,
he's from a neighbouring village; not someone from ettaapatti, living
so far away that he can't be reached.

And so, Kizhavar would turn to Raman from time to time with a
"Have I mentioned ...?" "I probably shouldn't bother you with this,"
or "There's a saying which goes, Were I to live only on water,
and lie on an earthen floor, I would still be fated to put up with
jeering villagers ..."

Kizhavar and Raman left the fair before it ended. A few baskets
remained, and Raman carried them without being told to. Kizhavar
bought dried peas, and bundled them in the flap of the veshti at his
waist. "When I reach home, my daughter's eyes will leap to my hands
to see what I've got her."

Raman met Kizhavar a month later, when he visited Pootthurai to
condole a bereavement. It was at this time that he caught sight of
Dhanabhagyam.

Definitely an eyeful, he noted with sincere appreciation. He spent a
few moments in thought, and then ventured with some hesitation, to
make enquiries about Dhanabhagyam and Kizhavar's plans for her.
Informing Kizhavar that he was an orphan and wanted a girl to look
after him, he probed obliquely if Dhanabhagyam would be given to
him in marriage.

Kizhavar had been looking at Raman ever since the young man began to speak about Dhanabhagyam, evaluating him keenly. The old man did not break his silence for a long time. Eventually, it seemed that he had come to a decision, and spoke to Raman about Dhanabhagyam.

Raman's responses to Kizhavar's queries were uniformly steadfast. "Whatever you wish." "You're the elder, after all." "I never go against my word." "You'll have to be my father, and look after my welfare." "I'd even jump into a well, if that was what you wanted." "There's no need to ask me anything." Kizhavar studied Raman's face for quite some time.

The next week saw Raman visit Pootthurai and Kizhavar again. And the next.

Kizhavar turned a deaf ear to Dhanabhagyam's protests, and made sure that the wedding ceremony was performed on a Friday, in the Mailam Murugan temple. He had the couple stay in Pootthurai for a week, and saw them off on their way to Krishnapuram.

"Chandala – traitor!" Dhanabhagyam raged at her father. She swore that she would leave her husband and return home; she would hang herself. None of these threats dented Kizhavar's determination; he maintained a stoic silence, as if he had not heard her at all. Later, he accompanied the couple to the tank-bund, to see them off. Dhanabhagyam, who could not stand the sight of him, screamed a "Paavi !" to his face, and stalked off with that last expletive. Raman brought up the rear, with Kizhavar.

"Thambi," began the old man.

"Yes?" asked Raman.

"This one kicks. You'd do well to be careful."

"I will."

"But you mustn't forget that this one yields milk. I've nurtured her like a plant for fifteen years. She's an innocent young girl – a pottapillay. She mustn't be unhappy. She never knew her mother, never knew what it was to suckle at her mother's breasts. She might be willful now, but once she's tasted the pleasure of the loins, everything will turn out well. Krishnapurathare, never raise a hand against her, no matter what."

"You may trust me," promised the man from Krishnapuram.

"Careful, now. An elder's blessings upon you."

"I'll be off, then."

"Do."

Raman cooked for them both, for as long as a week after their arrival in Krishnapuram. Dhanabhagyam took care to creep in after Raman left, eat, and scoot away to her neighbour's thinnai or porch.

"What do I care?" she would argue, to the womenfolk. "True, that man cooks. Shouldn't I eat that man's food? Or is that the way it's done in this village? If this can be called a village, that is. This is just a hamlet with four houses – no, huts. Our village and houses, now ..." Having thus delivered her scornful verdict, Dhanabhagyam would retreat to the thinnai.

Days and nights were thus spent in the homes of her neighbours. Disparaging remarks about Krishnapuram and glowing praises about Pootthurai were the substance of her monologues, all of which invariably ended with liberal curses upon Kizhavar, and her fate.

"May cholera plague him," she would fume. "There isn't a single familiar face here – what god-forsaken place has that old man chosen my husband from? What do I care for this damned village, anyway? I'm certainly not going to settle down here. That scoundrel, my father, has thrown me overboard – god help me!"

News spread like wildfire: not only was she not spending the night
with her husband, she wasn't staying at home even during the day,
whiling away the time, instead, in the houses or nearby.

The villagers made her the butt of their jokes. She could not take
their taunts anymore and muttered a wrathful, "Paaavivula, slave-
drivers," as she began to cook for Raman, the next week. Even this
she did unwillingly, scurrying away before Raman's arrival, and taking
refuge at her neighbours'. This state of affairs continued into the next
week too.

A day in the third week saw her cooking as usual, after Raman left
for work, early that morning.

Suddenly, he came back in.

Dhanabhagyam tried to run outside, but he was too quick for her.
He laughed, tightening his grip. His laughter irritated her; she was
boiling with rage.

She tried her best to wriggle out from his crushing grip,
pushing and kicking at him. "Bullheaded brute, my nose rings – my
earrings – you've torn my blouse! Murderer! Ayyo, you brute, paavi,
chandala ... cholera take you. Haven't you anything better to bite than
my nose and ears ...? Ayyayyo, my god, did that old man send me to
you for this? May he fall and break his bones – crush himself
to death. Build a paadai for him – drag him away to the burial
ground in it! Yei Maariyaayi, warrior goddess, punish him for his
sins – Ayyo ..."

Yesterday.

They had been married, yesterday. She had been living with the
mild, acquiescent Raman yesterday, and yesterday, Arumugam had
been born ... everything had happened yesterday. Raman's dead body

brought into the house, the ritual mourning through eight days and nights – everything had happened just yesterday. Watching Arumugam skipping away from the path – *that* was today. The rest belonged to the past. Could all the yesterdays ever return?

Raman's earthly possessions in Krishnapuram consisted of an old house, with four rafters holding up the roof. Close relations were practically nonexistent, and those that did exist were twice or thrice removed. Raman would go out to work everyday, and return home in the evenings with a smile on his face – a good-humoured person who knew no fatigue or anger. Never had he raised a hand against Dhanabhagyam in anger; nor had he ever spoken a harsh word to her. Dhanabhagyam's wishes reigned supreme. She did not have to work for a living unless she wished to; if she ever did, it was only because hours of idleness drove her crazy.

What she loved best was cleaning house, washing clothes, and preparing a mouth-watering array of Raman's favourite dishes as she awaited his return from work. She would lose her temper and sulk if he came in late, and tell him to serve himself for the night. She would yell at him, knock his head, punch his jawbone.

Invariably calm, Raman would chuckle at her tantrums. His laughter was infectious; she would lower her head and snigger in turn. Spotting his advantage, Raman would twine his arms around her and squeeze her tight, leaving her no room to squirm.

. "Paavi," she would shriek. "Its broad daylight, you undignified ruffian. Haven't you any shame? This village is full of brazen wretches ...!"

Raman had left for Auroville that day too, as usual. It was four o'clock in the afternoon when a few whites and local people stepped down from a jeep, in front of the house. Raman's body was lowered and placed on the thinnai. Dhanabhagyam, in the midst of cooking, heard the noise and came out. A peep from the door, and she fainted.

She recovered consciousness sometime later, but fainted three or four more times before noon the next day, when the body was taken to the burial ground. She broke down completely when Raman's body, placed in a paadai, was lifted. She sprawled on the grou before it and sobbed as though her heart would break. Her cries reverberated through the whole village. Tears of sympathy filled the eyes of those who had come to pay their last respects.

The taali, with which everyone's adorned,
Was one full sovereign, my prince did summon,
A taali for this maiden, on the eve of wedlock,
No hint of lac, pure gold, no doubt.
Crafted, with care, by the Dharmapuri aasaari,
The kundus, moulded, by the Kumbakonam aasaari.
The whole whetted, by the Sattangulam aasaari,
Its destiny weighed, by the Yamaloka aasaari.
Golden lemons we sought, and luscious berries,
My lord and master parted shrubs to capture berries,
Struck, was he, by a vengeful cobra,
He's dead, they said, and has gone afar.
That very moment I hung my head,
My fair face darkened, like a water lily dead.
Those with husbands, go northwards, go far.
Yei unwed girls, stay far away, apart,
All through the land, let bangle shops be closed.
May all of Salem District's sari shops mourn.

I shall snap my taali now, and wear a plain, black thread,
Send me to my mother, but bathe me now for death.

Three months have passed since Raman's death.

In a spirit of resignation, Kizhavar consoled himself: Nothing is in our hands, after all. All that happens is the will of the one above.

He did everything that had to be done, staying alternately in Krishnapuram and Pootthurai, in the three months after Raman's death. Dhanabhagyam agreed to shift to Pootthurai, at Kizhavar's insistence. She sorted out household articles, finished odd jobs and packed the previous night. At dawn, she set out to each and every house, bidding farewell.

"Goodbye, sister." "Aaya, I'm leaving." "My lord and master is gone. There's nothing left for me here."

When she finished, it was time for the villagers' cattle to be driven out for grazing.

Arumugam skipped ahead of Dhanabhagyam, ignoring her commands to stay with her. He came abreast of Kizhavar and began walking at his pace.

Absorbed in the landscape, he skipped along the pebble-strewn path jubilantly, stopping now and then to pick one up and send it flying. He filled his pockets with pebbles, and jingled them in glee. "Look, I've got tons of money!" and sometimes, "I've got lozenges and sweets too."

He stuffed a pebble into his mouth. He threw a stone on the pathway ahead, and ran up to it. He looked back at Kizhavar and Dhanabhagyam far behind, and yelled, "Quick, walk fast. Won't you come quickly?" He flung a stone on the path again, and ran up to it.

His irate mother's shouts and yells fell on deaf ears, as he threw stone after stone and ran to it. He tore off leaves from plants by the wayside, crushed and smelt them, chewing on a few. Veering away from the path that curved around the reservoir, he skipped along a long track that snaked through the middle of a fissure-riddled tank-bed.

Kizhavar matched Dhanabhagyam's pace as he walked. His eyes wandered, as though searching for something he had lost. Dhanabhagyam walked five or six feet behind him, diffident and withdrawn. She had never walked with him for long distances, this way.

Abruptly Kizhavar turned and looked at her. Then he resumed walking.

Eight years ago, he had come up this very tank to see Raman and Dhanabhagyam off, on their journey to Krishnapuram. The tank had been brimming then, and they had had to walk on the bund. Was this woman the same girl who had skirted the water-filled tank, that day?

She was a beauty yet. No one would guess that she had been married eight years, and was now the mother of a son. Would anybody believe it even if they were told so? But her complexion had darkened within the last three months, fading away like a withered plant. She did not speak as much as she used to, and there was no hint of a smile in her face. She spoke a few words to Kizhavar if absolutely necessary. For the most part, she moaned quietly in a corner, not even crying aloud.

Neither speech nor tears escaped her at the moment. The good god alone knew what was passing through her mind.

Searing pain coursed through Kizhavar's heart. His skin burned with it. Tears pricked his eyes, blurring the path before him.

"What is it?" asked Dhanabhagyam, and Kizhavar shook his head.

"Nothing. I was just ... looking at you." He bent his head again, and resumed walking. "Nothing."

The sun had sunk in the west. An evening breeze cooled them, wafting over the vast expanse of the tank. The shadows of palms lay on the ground, falling like long poles.

Climbing on to the bund, Kizhavar began to walk amidst Palmyra trees; the horizon and the ground below them seemed to stretch onwards, endlessly. White clouds moved slowly in the west, and a dark blue streak etched the sky, where the horizon touched land. A flock of birds flew northward. Sparrows chirped from bushes by the side of the tank bund. In the west, night descended where an undulating range of hills met the sky, matching the darkness of the ocean far beyond.

Watching the scene serenely, Kizhavar began to make conversation with Arumugam:

"Krishnapurathare."

"Yes, Thatha?"

"What're your plans for the future?"

"Let him study, Appa."

"Krishnapurathare."

"I'll do only as my amma says."

"Always?"

"Yes."

"Swear by me."

"I swear by you."

"Mustn't break your word."

Kizhavar walked on.

Arumugam's answer to Kizhavar warmed the cockles of Dhanabhagyam's heart. She felt an urge to lift and carry him; at once, she hoisted him onto her waist and began walking. He laughed bashfully. She began to cry. He slipped down and began walking.

Darkness descended in a little while, and soon obscured the path just ahead.

When they reached the outskirts of Pootthurai, Dhanabhagyam was overwhelmed with grief. Kizhavar's presence placed a restraint on her, and she sobbed softly. Arumugam asked her why she was crying. He got no answer, and so asked her to carry him. As soon as she lifted him up, he nibbled at her nose and ears.

She chuckled. "Ah, traitor that he is ... he's doing just what that other one did. Why, you son of that murderer!" she said, tickled by Arumugam's gentle nibbles.

Forgetting her woes, she began to laugh.

D awn heralded the beginning of a new day. A child cried lustily in the next street, and cocks crowed in clamorous accompaniment. People stepped out and about, while gabled roofs began to show through the dissolving mists of darkness.

Kizhavar sat up in bed. Nowadays, sleep deserted his eyes in the latter part of the night.

Great god above, why must I suffer such an ordeal? He would toss about, alternatively resting his face on drawn-up knees. My mind is a muddy pond, stirred up to net fish ... the thread holding together my body and mind seems to have snapped. What is the warp-and-woof that joins one to the other?

There were also days when, long after dawn, Kizhavar would sit rock-still, never stirring from his place.

A fatal fever carried away Sivagnanam, eight days after Dhanabhagyam's birth.

That was the month of Karthigai. No other Karthigai in the past had ever seen such rain; there was a veritable downpour, that year. The village was flooded. It took two weeks for the water to recede, after the rains had stopped. The Osutteri Lake overflowed, entering the village, and people living in two whole streets had to shift.

The rains had poured without respite on the day Sivagnanam died too. That night, Sivagnanam talked far more than usual. She tried to laugh; she looked down often at her yellow tinged body, now cold and pale. Kizhavar tried to console her in as many ways as he could, and kept by her side throughout the day.

"Yei kutti, I'm right beside you. Don't worry, little one."

"I'm going to die."

"God won't forsake you."

"He already has."

"He hasn't."

"I've forsaken him."

"Sivagnanam!"

"No one here has ever had a husband like you. Ah, god truly is blind! You'll be an orphan. What will happen to my daughter?"

"Don't think about all that. You've precious little energy left. Don't exhaust yourself."

Sivagnanam breathed her last, before daybreak. A young Kizhavar had been restrained in his sorrow.. Dear god, why have you brought me to this? he agonized, as he sat by the body silently. Despite the heavy downpour, quite a sizeable crowd had gathered to mourn Sivagnanam's passing.

Kizhavar sold Sivagnanam's taali and bought a cow for Dhanabhagyam. He could not bear his daughter to be out of his sight for a minute. He took her with him wherever he went, and brought her up without knowledge of hunger. Her every whim was satisfied; everything took place according to her wishes.

Kizhavar awoke and sat up on his bed. God is sure to lend us a helping hand, he sighed as he turned over various incidents in his mind. His will be done.

Arumugam's image appeared in his mind now, accompanying that of Dhanabhagyam. What could be done for Arumugam? What would his destiny be?

Kizhavar roused Dhanabhagyam from her slumber, informing her that he was going to cut and gather nocchi, the twigs of a eucalyptus-like tree, and asked her to bring his tools, the alakku and vaangu from the loft. Ever since Arumugam and Dhanabhagyam had arrived in Pootthurai a month ago, he had spent the intervening days staring at them dolefully; not a single basket of nocchi had been woven.

"Why don't you wait until daybreak?" asked Dhanabhagyam, as she handed the alakku and vaangu to him. "It's much too cool now. Snakes and insects would've crawled out."

Their voices woke up Arumugam, who promptly piped, "Let me go too, Amma."

"No." she refused. "Listen to me, and stay still."

Arumugam was adamant. He cried, attempting to start with Kizhavar. Dhanabhagyam caught and held him tightly. Arumugam's wails grew louder; the more she tightened her hold, the more he bawled.

Kizhavar spoke up, then. "He has to grow up. It's in your hands to make him a great man. I am a spent force now, a mere shell. He's everything to you. He's the only one who ought to be in your sight and heart, hereafter. That's all I will say. No matter what, remember that there's a god above."

He approached Dhanabhagyam, and looked at her. His heart filled with misgiving as he saw her eyes brimming with tears, and he placed his hands on her head in a gesture of blessing. She stood up suddenly, interlacing his hands with her own on her chest.

Kizhavar took Arumugam's hand in his own, and stepped down into the street.

"Appa, be careful, and come back in time for your meal. Don't get so absorbed in your work that you forget the time."

Dhanabhagyam couldn't take her eyes off her father and son. Arumugam walked along with the elder as though he were a grown-up.

Kizhavar walked with long strides; Arumugam could not often keep pace with him. He stayed alongside Kizhavar for a little distance, and began to lag behind after a few minutes. "Thatha, stop! Let me come, too. Why do you keep hurrying along, leaving me behind? I'll tell Mother. She'll scold you." He overtook Kizhavar, only to fall back after a few minutes. He lagged behind often, diverted by the scenery around, and then had to run to keep up with Kizhavar.

Kizhavar stepped down into the Vavva Canal bank. Nestled inside a depression in the bed of the canal was a pool of water, into which Kizhavar instructed Arumugam to dip the coir rope that would be tied to the vaangu. The old man then picked up a stone and honed the blade of the vaangu, testing its sharpness from time to time with his left thumb. Then, he took the rope brought by Arumugam and tied it tightly around the handle of the vaangu. Arumugam stared at Kizhavar, gaping as though at a juggler, entranced by the old man's dexterity and skill. The plant and flowers tattooed on Kizhavar's right arm, in particular, fascinated him, as did the snake with raised hood tattooed on his left forearm.

As Kizhavar walked, looking for nocchi shrubs on the banks, Arumugam accompanied him, lost in wonder at the sight of the canal. The build of Kizhavar's body, his gait, his laughter, his speech — everything delighted Arumugam. It was the canal that he liked best.

There was only one thing that he did not appreciate: that Kizhavar spoke very little to him. "Won't tell me a thing," he murmured to himself.

He had come to Pootthurai many times before this and had stayed for a week or so, but they would not allow him to even play in the street. He had not been taken to the canal even once. It was only today that Kizhavar had brought him.

The banks of the canal were a dense growth of vegetation, overgrown with shrubs and date palms, aloes, neems, babuls and kilathittus. Kizhavar's eyes seemed to gleam and his face appeared to brighten, as he came upon nocchis near a cluster of date palms. He stopped. Smiling slightly, his heavy, nail-driven sandals making a mar mar noise, he approached the cluster, and thought how best to remove the shrubs that were obstructing his way to the nocchi.

First, he lopped off the branches thrusting forward, and then cut off the wild growth around nocchi. A few shrubs he uprooted, using the vaangu to pull out aloe plants. "Stand aside," he shouted as though stung by a scorpion, whenever Arumugam tried to approach him. "Listen to me, something might get into your eyes or ears. This isn't play – you'll get blinded. How will I face your mother, then? Stay away."

Kizhavar cut down the nocchi twigs swiftly, and threw them on the dry bed of the canal. He ticked off Arumugam whenever the boy tried to collect them into neat piles. "Those sticks will split your skull. They will pierce your eyes," he warned. "You will get pricked with splinters." He kept an eye on Arumugam while throwing the cut branches on the sand-bed of the canal, lest the boy disobey him and meddle with the sticks.

What had once been dense shrubbery, was laid bare now. The debris-filled ground looked unsightly, like broken pottery. Thorny bushes lay one over the other in a crisscross fashion. Crushed aloes lay in a crumpled heap, oozing sticky sap.

When he had finished cutting from the cluster of nocchis, Kizhavar stepped down into the canal bed and began shearing the leaves from the twigs with his vaangu. The blade slashed the air in a cadence. Leaves and twigs catapulted, piling up on the sandy bed.

"Tomorrow, I'll bring a vaangu too."

"What for?"

"You cut the twigs. I'll shear the leaves."

"Indeed."

"You'll let come me tomorrow?"

"Of course."

"Really?"

"Really."

"Swear on Amma?"

"I swear."

"You won't cheat?"

"No."

Kizhavar might have been talking to Arumugam; for all that, he did not suspend his work. When he had finished shearing, he gathered the shorn twigs and tied them up into small bundles. As he hefted the bundle onto his head, Arumugam insisted that he would carry them. Kizhavar transferred the bundles to Arumugam's head, and they proceeded in search of other clusters.

In the next spot, Arumugam collected the nocchi twigs as and when Kizhavar cut and put them down. Frequently, he yelled "Thatha ...!" pointed at a tree or shrub, and shot questions about them. What were they called? When did they flower? What were their colours and smell? What about the fruits? Could he eat them?

He wanted to know about the canal too. How much water flowed in it? Where did it come from? Which villages did it flow through?

Kizhavar answered him without a pause. Nobody had ever accompanied Kizhavar on any of his expeditions to cut nocchi, starting from the early years till date. An odd passer-by might berate him on occasion, having heard the sounds of felling. "Who is it over there? What are you cutting? Can't yoù let any tree or shrub survive in the wilderness? You won't have a peaceful night's sleep unless you fell them all, will you?" But for such sporadic remarks, he was used to being alone.

Work might proceed slowly, yet Kizhavar continued to answer Arumugam's questions. Arumugam prattled on and on; his was an untiring tongue, unlike Raman, who had been a man of few words, and had always replied with polite expressions: "As you wish," "You're the elder," "Let's see," "It shall be done," "No problem."

Raman's looks had belied his temperament and manners. Those who didn't know him came to the swift conclusion that he was the worst rogue in the village, while those that did know him, wondered, Arumugam is his son, but how different is the boy from the father! He can't sit still for a whole minute ... and can he hold his tongue for even a moment? Whose was this mischievous nature of his?

Until she came of age, Dhanabhagyam had been equally spirited and frolicsome. Not a day had passed without five or six quarrels at the very least as she beat up her playmates, pushed them down, and threw sand on their heads. One threatening glare from her was enough — most boys and girls in the village fled from her, crying as though they had been trounced black and blue. There had been reports of Dhanabhagyam's behaviour even on the day of her betrothal. Boys

generally teased girls, but if they dared to subject Dhanabhagyam to
the same treatment, they were sure to pay for it. She never spared
them, and speedily earned the nickname Raakshasi, a she-demon.

"That tomboy!" exclaimed the old women of the village. "What a
sharp tongue! – this one won't bend to anyone."

Only in stature did Arumugam resemble Raman; in everything else,
he took after Dhanabhagyam. Kizhavar had observed the boy closely,
while escorting him for the last time from Krishnapuram to Pootthurai.
In the beginning, he thought that his grandson resembled his deceased
wife, Sivagnanam; later, he discerned that he had more of
Dhanabhagyam in him. Whenever Kizhavar looked at Arumugam,
the events of his life ran through his mind's eyes like a film, starting
with his setting up a home with Sivagnanam, until Dhanabhagyam
was given in marriage.

Arumugam had piled up the nocchi twigs. He handed them, one
by one, and Kizhavar began shearing the leaves. It invigorated
Kizhavar greatly to have someone to converse with and he was
jubilant, as though he had received curry and rice to feast on. Only
until the harvest would there be much movement of men about the
canal, for, once summer set in, it was usually empty of life except
for goatherds and cowherds, grazing cattle and goats, moving about
in search of water. The Vavva Canal was the only one that boasted
such movement. There was usually nobody in the vicinity of other
canals, in this season.

Kizhavar and Arumugam walked alternately on both sides of the
canal, in search of further clusters of nocchi. The sun scorched the
skies. Insects, bees, beetles and sparrows crept out of their crevices,
hovering around the trees, creating a cacophony of sounds. Both banks

of the canal were lush with foliage, like post-monsoon vegetation; the fresh fragrance of plants and flowers mingled in the breeze.

Kizhavar spied a cluster of nocchi near the jamun tree. He unloaded the bundle from Arumugam's head, made him sit on it and began cutting his way through the thicket. Barely two or three thorny plants had been cleared when he began running towards the eastern side of the canal, shouting, "Get them! Catch them!"

Arumugam was nonplussed. He too ran, following Kizhavar. He had to go through a bush on the northern side. Kizhavar did not notice Arumugam entering the bush; he was bent on pelting stones at the prey. Later, when he saw Arumugam emerging from the bush, he smiled, exclaiming, "The lord has given them a lease of life today."

"What was it?" asked Arumugam.

Kizhavar explained about the rabbits that had escaped from the thicket he was clearing. And he gave details – how many little ones, how many adults, their colour, how fast they ran, how their footprints looked, how tasty their meat would be. When they returned to the spot they had been working at, Arumugam sat down on the bundle, while Kizhavar resumed clearing his way through the thicket.

Arumugam stared at Kizhavar in wonder. He couldn't believe that Kizhavar could shout and run as fast as he had done a moment ago. He had never seen Kizhavar do something like this. Now he was lost in fantasy, his mind still fastened on how Kizhavar had chased the rabbits.

Barely moments later, Kizhavar ran towards Arumugam, shouting, "Thoo! Chee!" trying to drive away the wasps that hovered around him. Cursing the winged insects, he smeared spit where the flesh had swollen up and began to massage them. Arumugam threw fistfuls of sand on them, trying to drive away the wasps that were still fluttering around Kizhavar and himself. The boy spat into his hands and began rubbing his own spit into Kizhavar's swollen limbs, massaging them.

Kizhavar forgot his pain and hugged Arumugam tight, his eyes filling with tears that hid the canal from his vision. Arumugam moved still closer to Kizhavar. Happiness bubbled up in him as he leant against the old man, and he giggled.

Kizhavar knocked off the wasp nest with his alakku, resumed cutting nocchi twigs and threw them on the canal bed, while Arumugam collected them into neat piles.

He allowed Arumugam to shear the leaves only for a little while. "Enough. You'll cut your fingers. I wouldn't be able to face your mother. No, don't. Leave it." He took the vaangu from Arumugam's hand.

"Hungry?" he asked, occasionally. "Your intestines twisting up? Ah, it's healthy to be hungry." Kizhavar kept Arumugam engaged in conversation while he continued to work.

Finishing the cutting, he tied together the piles of twigs in one bundle, and spoke to Arumugam. "The sun's setting, let's cut the rest tomorrow. We've stayed too long. Time to leave." Hefting the bundle onto his head and the alakku on his shoulder, Kizhavar began to walk, while Arumugam accompanied him, carrying the vaangu.

"Does this path go straight home?" he asked Kizhavar.

"Yes."

"And if we go back?"

"It goes to the fields."

"All the fields?"

"Yes."

"Our fields too?"

"We don't have any."

"Why don't we?"

"We don't, and that's it."

"Can't you buy one?"

"How can I?" asked Kizhavar. "If I could, then there'd be nothing to worry about."

"Then *I'll* buy one."

"How would you?"

"When I grow up, I'll buy *lots* of fields."

"Really?"

"I swear. On Goddess Sengeniyamma."

"Krishnapurathare, your very birth was more than all the wealth in the world. It's not like that story: Wait for the race at Manapparai Manamadurai, and the white horse will fly ... that reminds me. There was a man in a village, once – do you know what happened to him?"

Kizhavar's tale did not come to an end until they reached home.

Kizhavar's plans proceeded as he had wished. He managed to weave forty baskets in just three days, with the nocchi sprigs they had collected during the past two weeks — something of a feat, given his usual pace. A great deal had been possible because of Dhanabhagyam and Arumugam's full-fledged assistance. They spread the twigs out to dry in the sun, sprinkled a little water on the dried twigs in the evening, and tied them into bundles. On the third day they spread the twigs to dry in the shade. Kizhavar went out well before dawn to cut down nocchi twigs. He went to the Vavva Canal one day, the next to Vellaikkaaran Canal, the third day to Bungala Medu Canal and so on, to Samiyaar Bungalow Canal, Kulathukkaaran Chaavadi, Oothukkuttai Moolai, Elikkunju Salai, Kanniankarai, Malamedu and Kanakaranipet Canals. A canal visited one day would not be approached the next.

His best collections were from the Oothukkuttai Moolai and Vavva Canals. Noon generally saw him back at his hut, where he would finish his meal and sit down to weave baskets. Never before had he woven baskets with such vim, vigour and enthusiasm, even though they were not as much in demand as before. The number of cattle had now dwindled considerably; the demand for baskets to collect cow dung and garbage had declined, too. Cheri inhabitants who had previously grazed all the Nayudu cattle had begun to favour other work and the Nayudus had begun selling their cattle for slaughter.

"What are we to do? Those low-caste Parayans have prospered. We can't keep our mute creatures tied up just to see them die away, can we? Might as well give them away and wallow in sorrow, instead of keeping them. All this," they complained, with bitter accusation, "is the work of the Auroville fellows. Where on earth do they get their money from?"

Families that had previously possessed an entire shed or two of livestock had had to sell their cattle, and the sheds had turned into shelters for stray dogs. There was no demand for baskets at all.

"I'll weave baskets, nothing else," answered Kizhavar, if asked why he persisted in weaving them. "Why else has god created these canals with nocchis flourishing in them? If I can't sell baskets here, I'll go elsewhere. There're clusters and clusters of nocchi just for my use." Firm in his resolve, he refrained from undertaking any other means of living.

Arumugam handed over the twigs, one by one, as Kizhavar wove. The boy was struck with amazement at how uniform the twigs were — two or three yards and as thick as a finger — and Kizhavar chuckled when Arumugam asked about this. He watched Kizhavar's nimble fingers with wonder — how deftly Kizhavar bent and twisted the twigs, one around the other, never breaking even a single one.

"Watch how my hand moves," said Kizhavar. "It's a matter of

practice. You don't have to go abroad to learn this. The hand must follow what the eye sees."

Dhanabhagyam watched Kizhavar and Arumugam intently at such times, murmuring to each other in soft tones, as though sharing secrets. She was roused to wrath, however, if Arumugam ever raised his voice against Kizhavar. "Good god, such a saucy tongue at such a young age ... I shudder to think of what he'll be like when he grows up."

Having finished his evening meal early, Kizhavar started out to go to the fair. When Arumugam spoke up that he would go with Kizhavar too, Dhanabhagyam tried to stop him. "It's too far," she protested. "Ghosts and spirits haunt the pathways. They'll catch you."

"No fear, they won't." Arumugam was adamant. "They didn't get hold of me when I went to the canal."

He began to wail in earnest, cursing Kizhavar, who had walked out to find out who else had planned to visit the fair, and Dhanabhagyam, stirring hot tamarind rice for Kizhavar's journey. He sobbed as loudly as he could, and wondered if Dhanabhagyam couldn't hear his cries.

He edged closer to her, sniffling piteously. She did not acknowledge him; nor did she plead with him to stop crying. She had to cook and garnish her tamarind rice before Kizhavar returned; her attention was on that chore, and she showed no sign of having noticed him or his wails.

Losing his temper, Arumugam leaned on her back, curving his hands around her sweaty neck, perspiring from the oven heat, and swung back and forth. She was silent. He bit her ear. She sat still, bearing the pain. Packing up food was her priority, and she finished making the packets.

Her throat ached; she dragged him onto her lap. He pulled her head towards himself, and bit her nose. She lowered her head and pressed it into his face. A whimper escaped her. He lifted her face, looked at her and laughed. She could not. He bent her head again, and bit her nose. It hurt too much; she pulled him into a crushing hug. He bit her neck this time, tickling her.

She felt a thrill of exhilaration and anger all at once. "Why, you bull-headed ..." she began to mock-chide him. "Trying to prise out my nose ring, are you? Born of a cur, that's what you are. Ah, see how this one bites. Are *you* going to make me bare-eared too? Oh, this fellow's born of Yama himself, what can I do? Ayyo, let go of me ...!"

Rivulets of perspiration flowed over her. She was sitting close to the oven – too close; her body burned. Arumugam's breath, so close to her skin, tickled her ears, awaking a wave of bashfulness in her.

Abruptly, a wave of alarm overtook her.

Why couldn't have death struck me, she lamented. What can a poor woman do, other than bear children, at the most? Even tender chillies burn hot, don't they? Why've you left me to bear this disgrace? How can I guard this body, this body that is made of salt? God above, wouldn't a body fed on salt crave what it shouldn't yearn for ...?

Dhanabhagyam began to sob loud. Perplexed, Arumugam slid down from her lap, and trained his intent gaze on her.

Kizhavar's footsteps could be heard coming up the street. Dhanabhagyam stopped weeping, wiped her face dry, and stood up. Arumugam continued to stare at her as Kizhavar, meanwhile, prepared to leave.

"Is everything ready?" he asked. "Nothing left undone, I hope." He tested whether the two bundles of baskets had been tied tightly enough. "Let Arumugam come with me. I can put him in some cart that's going to the fair."

No sooner had Kizhavar said this, than Arumugam ran in to put on a shirt. Kizhavar sat on the thinnai, waiting. Dhanabhagyam threw a look at him.

"It's been four months since I left Krishnapuram," she spoke to the roof smothered in darkness, as though addressing nobody in particular, about a matter concerning others. "I didn't bring anything with me. I don't know what the house is like, now. Won't the neighbours complain? I'd better go there once and look over what's to be done." She had broken into a sweat before she finished. She bit the words out, one by one, pushing at them brokenly.

Kizhavar gave no reply, gazing out at the street in silence.

Dhanabhagyam's ears caught the sound of Arumugam rummaging inside his trunk, and she went in. Shirts, petticoats, anklets, veshtis and towels ... she found them all scattered on the floor. "What's the hurry? Couldn't you have waited for me?" she folded them back into the trunk, and made him wear his shirt properly. She draped Raman's heavy towel also over his shoulder. "This'll be useful if it gets cold." Then, she stashed away the trunk on the loft.

"Mama," yelled Pandian, Kizhavar's nephew, as he came in. He wanted to buy a pair of bullocks. He was expecting the arrival of some North Indian breeds in the fair, and had insisted on Kizhavar going to the fair with him.

Once, the idea of giving Dhanabhagyam in marriage to Pandian had been considered. "Never think I'd give up an alliance such as that," Kizhavar's sister, Malar, had bragged.

Pandian's respect for Kizhavar lasted until Dhanabhagyam's marriage with Raman; after this event, he came and parked himself in front of Kizhavar's house whenever he got drunk, and made as much a scene as he could. "My uncle's betrayed me – I'll be damned if I leave without killing him. If my aunt were alive now, would this have happened? We're the same clan. My blood's boiling! Isn't there anyone man enough in this panchayat to protest against this?"

Kizhavar took no note of his ravings. He remained impassive, and never allowed Pandian's outpourings to sully his ears. "I see fate's hand in this. It was destined that events should turn out this way. What could I have done? If she were meant to marry him, she would have. I don't care two hoots for the fellow," he finished.

Within two months of Dhanabhagyam's marriage, Pandian chose and married a girl from Kuyilappalayam; he now had four children. The past month had seen him resume his visits to Kizhavar's house, asking that Dhanabhagyam be given to him in marriage as his second wife. He had threatened suicide if his request was refused.

Kizhavar asked Pandian to step inside for a meal; an invitation that Pandian declined. Nevertheless, Dhanabhagyam placed a plate filled with food in front of him and retreated, quaking with fear. Pandian had been the only one with the power to terrorize her, in her youth. He had been just fifteen, and even then, had threatened to abduct her.

"She's my uncle's daughter, and I alone reserve the right to seize her. I'll slash anyone who eyes her into pieces. I'm the only one who will marry her. My maternal uncle's daughter – she dare not marry anyone else!" He persisted with his threats even after Dhanabhagyam's marriage, and her subsequent departure to Krishnapuram.

She would shudder, her stomach quaking, sweating with sheer fright at the mere sight of him.

Once, when she and Raman had arrived in Pootthurai to attend a wedding, he had leered at her right in front of Raman himself: "Just you wait. One day, I'll certainly lift you onto my shoulders and spirit you away!"

Raman had merely laughed out loud. He and Pandian had struck a friendship after Dhanabhagyam's marriage; whenever Raman arrived at Pootthurai, he would visit Pandian first, and Pandian's first stop at Krishnapuram, for whatever purpose, was usually Raman's home. In the four months after Dhanabhagyam had left Krishnapuram for Pootthurai, after Raman's death, Pandian had not said a word to her. He had not threatened her; yet, she lived in fear of him. His earlier terrifying threats still rang fresh in her ears:

"Maman mavale, you might escape Yama, but you won't escape me. Remember, I'm a man who's grown up drinking the waters of Osutteri. You'd dare to escape from such a man? Call me a shameless, impotent wretch if I don't seize you before I die! I won't give up even if you lock yourself up in the famed Jenji fort, my uncle's precious daughter ...!"

Dhanabhagyam peeped at Pandian from inside the house. While it was true that he no longer terrorized her, the fear that he might yet carry out his threat haunted her thoughts.

She sat down on the floor, feeling her legs give away. A strong feeling of loss assailed her, but she could not make out what she had lost. Her eyes filled as she continued to gaze at the floor, her throat choking with emotion.

It was Pandian who was in a tearing hurry. He appeared much more enthusiastic about going to the fair than Arumugam, laughed aloud frequently for no apparent reason, and could not seem to stand or sit still for a moment. Amused at his impatience and unable to put up with his pestering any longer, Kizhavar placed a bundle on his head, first. Arumugam and Dhanabhagyam lifted a bundle and placed it on Kizhavar's head. As the old man set off, Dhanabhagyam clutched Arumugam close to her. Taking hold of her son's hand, she followed Kizhavar. At the end of the street stood Pandian with his burden, amidst a group of people. Kizhavar joined them, and Arumugam left Dhanabhagyam for the group. As they all began to move forward, Dhanabhagyam asked Kizhavar:

"Appa?"

"Go if you think it's all right."

"I think it is."

"Make sure that you're back in a couple of strides," said Kizhavar. "Before my spit dries on the ground."

"Of course."

"Don't stay out alone, here."

"It's so dark that you can't see your own hand. Walk carefully."

Arumugam tore back to his mother, clutching her tightly; she had been hoping that he would. She held him close to her waist, kissing his oil smeared hair. Then she released him, pushing him onto the path. He ran and took the lantern from Kizhavar and began walking briskly ahead of everybody.

The group was visible for a little distance, up to the point where streetlights lit the way. After that, it entered the darkness. The light points of the lanterns bobbed one behind the other. At a bend in the road, these lights too winked out of sight.

Dhanabhagyam stayed there awhile. As she turned back on the path that led homewards, her thoughts lingered on Arumugam, walking, face lit up by the lantern he had been holding.

What'll this young one, who has now gone holding a lantern in his hand, be like when he returns tomorrow?

Tomorrow will appear, just as today did. And the next day. And the

next week. And the following weeks. And the months. And all the
festivals – Pongal, Dipaavali, Pathinettu, the temple festivals – all these
will pass too. Tanks, lakes and ponds will fill up, and dry out. He will
have become a man by then, and taken up a livelihood. He will marry
and have not just one or two, but ten children. They would bite their
mother's nose and ears just as Arumugam bit hers; all this would
happen in no time as though it were tomorrow. Tomorrow would
arrive, just as yesterday and today did.

Poor Raman, it was not given to him to see his son grow up. "Oh
god," she moaned, as she agonized at the way he had met his death.
Tears filled her eyes.

She didn't stop sobbing until daybreak.

D hanabhagyam stood up as she spotted Arumugam in the distance, smiling as though she had been waiting just for his return. He ran up to her and twined his hands around her waist, laughing aloud.

She held him close, and stroked his hair. "When did you leave school?" she asked, laughing like a child, herself.

Arumugam leaned against the thinnai, threw his bag inside, and began a recital of school happenings. This had been his routine for the past six months. Arumugam would arrive at Dhanabhagyam's place of work after school; she would always wait until he did, and together, they would walk home.

Jerry Albert came astride his bicycle as Dhanabhagyam and Arumugam crossed a grassy strip, and were walking past the Matru Mandir. He halted when he saw them.

"Hello," he offered his hand to Arumugam, seated on his bicycle.

Dhanabhagyam pushed Arumugam forward, and Jerry Albert shook the boy's hand. Then, with a cheery "All right, see you," he rode past, waving his hand for quite some distance along the avenue.

"You cat!" yelled Arumugam, intensely irritated.

Arms crossed over her chest, Dhanabhagyam, stood looking at the tree-lined avenue Albert had ridden through. Arumugam elbowed her, waking her from her reverie, and made her walk again. He kept darting looks at his right hand, disgusted, as though he had touched a cat. He did not want to look at it. He wished he could chop it off. He smelt his hand, and rubbed it again and again on his shorts.

He felt a sudden surge of irritation against Dhanabhagyam. Arumugam knew the kind of fellow Jerry Albert was only too well. During the past six months, he had seen him on the road or in Dhanabhagyam's company many times. Albert would wave his hand, laugh aloud and yell, "Hello Arumugam," for no reason whatsoever when he came across the boy, but however much Albert tried to engage Arumugam in conversation, the youngster never budged. For some reason, he had disliked Albert from the very beginning; he felt like throwing up whenever he saw the man with Dhanabhagyam.

Tearing his hand from Dhanabhagyam's grip, Arumugam said, "I don't like it."

"What don't you like?"

"This Poonayan."

"Why not?"

"He's a cat."

"Stop it. You mustn't say such things."

"Poonayan."

"Do you know that we're much better off now, because of him?"

"So, we'd die if he weren't here?"

"It's not his fault if his skin's different."

"That yellow-haired fellow. Cat."

"You shouldn't talk like that about your elders and betters. Is this how a student behaves?"

"That cat."

"Stop, or I'll thrash you."

"Poonayan."

"Leave him alone if you don't like him. He isn't one of us. What does it matter, anyway?"

"Poonayan."

Upon Kizhavar and Arumugam's departure to the fair to sell baskets, Dhanabhagyam had set off at dawn to Krishnapuram. Men and women who met her on the way criticized her, as did those in Krishnapuram.

"Doesn't know how to make a living. Imagine, a woman like her, in this day and age! Shouldn't she have some sense? Its enough if you bear a child, is it?"

They even reproached her for going to Pootthurai and staying there for four months. Some curled their lips with derision; others raised hands to their mouths in astonishment. "If only we'd had this chance. How will she survive here, if she's such an idiot?" Anjalai from the opposite house had been the one most concerned.

Dhanabhagyam proffered a variety of excuses to her neighbours, for not having gone to Auroville.

"I am ready to leave, Aachi. But my father isn't here today. How can I go alone?" "Whom do I know there?" "How can I park myself before them suddenly, and inform them that I'm so and so? Wouldn't I feel small?" She swept and cleaned the house, checking to see if everything remained in its place.

Chinnammal, an old woman living next door, came in and enquired about Kizhavar, Arumugam, and Pootthurai. "The little one's image still stays in my eyes. Has he put on some weight? Nothing wrong with his health, I hope?"

She too, urged Dhanabhagyam to go to Auroville. "Don't stop with asking for money. Make sure that they give you a job, too." She repeated this often, also volunteering information about Auroville.

These days, even women belonging to upper caste families such as Vanniars, Mudaliars, and Pillais worked in Auroville. People who owned a bare half or quarter kaani of land sold it to the Auroville management, and received, in turn, not just money, but also a job. Those who possessed lands in plenty too, sold them, and were using the proceeds to start some business or the other in Pondicherry.

Dhanabhagyam ought to go before the Women's Forum in Pondicherry, and explain how Raman had died, slipping down from the top of the meditation hall. She must ask for a job in the Adult Education Center or the hospital, or any of the companies of the Aurobindo Ashram.

"What's the use of mere money?" argued Chinnammal. "It'd be eaten up in no time and farted away. Haven't we seen people without a roof over their head or a piece of land, build bungalows? Haven't we seen them become rich enough to gobble three meals a day?"

Chinnammal's husband had been a bonded labourer in a Nayudu house. A snake had bitten him one night, when he had gone out to draw water for the paddy field, and he had died. The Nayudu family had paid a sum that barely covered burial expenses; they had not offered any for even the funeral ceremonies. One of the boys from the cheri had taken Chinnammal to Auroville, where, grief-stricken, she had sobbed about her plight. Taking pity on her, they had made her a sweeper in the hospital; her salary was five hundred rupees.

Chinnammal cited the cases of many others who had acquired jobs likewise, and how exactly they had got it. "I don't know what they're doing, and why they're doing it ... but what does it matter to us? They're doing us a good turn, and we're able to light our ovens. They're sure to help you out, so go over there soon." Chinnammal returned home, having advised her.

Dhanabhagyam had no idea about which of the many paths to take, the direction they took, or indeed, where each began and ended. Puzzled, she had to retrace her steps for a long distance, twice, after having started down one muddy track. She regretted that Kizhavar was not with her. Indeed, her first instinct had been to proceed the next day, along with Kizhavar, but the villagers had compelled her to leave that very day and she had started out to Auroville alone.

She walked again on a road that led at right angles to the one she had left. She walked back after a little distance; once, she lost her way. By now, she was at the end of her tether.

"I've lost all sense of direction. Which way do I go?" she asked, of everyone passing by. "Could you please come with me a while and show me the way? Do I take this path, or that?"

Her legs ached; the summer sun scorched the earth. White folks – men and women – were dashing by on bicycles, scooters and cars. She stared at the scantily clad white women with dislike. Didn't they have any shame? *Were* they women? Wearing pipes like men! Couldn't they drape a bit of cloth over their breasts? She spat at the sight. She had seen a few white women before, but had thought them the exceptions. Deep disgust filled her as she saw them all dressed the same way – especially the way women wore T-shirts, like men.

Dhanabhagyam went through one road after another, continuing her journey, searching for Tamil speakers. At long last, she met a boy from Idayan Chaavadi who told her what she needed to know, railing at her for not having stayed home. He took her inside a large building. Dhanabhagyam stood amazed, struck by the sight of so many people working in small cubicles, within. The boy asked her to stay, and went into a room. He came back after a long time and escorted her into another room.

Jerry Albert stood up, and joined his palms in greeting.

Dhanabhagyam shivered. A chill enveloped her. Her stomach churned, making her want to dash over to the toilet. She froze, unable to even lift her hands to return the greeting. She should not have come alone. She muttered curses against the villagers. She could not lift her head, nor look at him in the eye. She could not stand still; the floor was too cold.

Jerry Albert was speaking naturally, his manner free and easy. His gaze rested on Dhanabhagyam frequently. At times, he laughed softly. The only word she recognized in his speech was "Raman, Raman." The Idayan Chaavadi boy spoke to her when Albert had sat down, having finished his speech.

Cry, the boy told her with his eyes. She must weep and wail now, lamenting her pitiable condition. Don't say No, he gesticulated again.

"Do you agree?" He winked at her.

"Agree to what?"

"Just say Yes."

"You'd better tell me what for."

"Say Yes, first. I'll tell you the details later."

"I'll have to ask my father."

"You agree? Answer quickly. All right then, it's a yes. Matter's over."

The boy resumed his chatter with Jerry Albert, gesturing towards Dhanabhagyam off and on as he did so. She could only make out the words "Raman, Raman," and pricked up her ears whenever she heard that word in the conversation. Jerry Albert spoke to someone over the telephone; then he talked to the boy. Dhanabhagyam merely kept looking at them and the cubicle. It felt like a new world, to her. She looked at his hair, the rings he wore in his ears, his shorts and vest, and wondered if he were crackbrained. She did not like the boy at all.

She did not like Jerry Albert either. His complexion was far too white, his hair blond, like ears of maize, and his voice – it felt odd, to hear it. Why didn't he clear out his spit and talk?

The only thing she did like was the room itself. The bright walls reflected her face and she fell in love with their sheer, smooth beauty. Framed pictures of Aurobindo and the Mother hung on the walls, and piles of books and papers occupied one corner. A young girl entered and gave Jerry Albert an envelope containing currency notes. He did not count it, but gave it to Dhanabhagyam, who received it with the ends of her sari.

"Okay, mister," said Jerry Albert, and the boy signalled to Dhanabhagyam that they should leave. Dhanabhagyam joined her palms as she took leave of Jerry Albert and walked out of the building, hands still folded.

The cowherd came up behind her, shouting as though he were going to beat her up. "Why are you so frightened? Don't you have brains? Dumb folk. Why couldn't you tell him about your condition? I can't tell him everything – it's your husband who's dead, not mine, is it?" His words were jumbled with anger and he grit his teeth, flushed with fury.

He lit a cigarette. He looked like someone caught in a risky situation, struggling to save himself from it. She would be given a job, he said, as a compensation for Raman's death.

She must come to work. She mustn't reject such a stroke of good fortune. This was a good chance. She would live a life of comfort right until the end. She'd have money. But if she didn't work, they would take away the money she had received.

"You can go now," he finished. "Don't forget what I've told you. Come back saying, My father won't let me, or anything of that sort, and that's it," he warned. "When will you folk ever learn? You must give up the old ways – it isn't every day that luck comes your way. You should grab it when it does … go, go now."

Dhanabhagyam asked the boy why they had taken her thumb impression.

"You took the money, that's why," he screeched at her. "What else are they going to do with your precious thumb impression? Go. Nothing will happen, don't worry."

Ever since she received money at Auroville, Dhanabhagyam could not sit still.

"If there's one thing you mustn't ever do, it's going out to work," said Kizhavar, when she asked his opinion.

The Idayan Chaavadi boy came to Pootthurai twice, and abused not only Dhanabhagyam, but Kizhavar too. Off and on he ran fingers through his hair and ground out his teeth, muttering, "Stupid people, stupid people."

He talked a lot with Kizhavar, who gleaned details about the job not only from the cowherd but others too, in the village. When the cowherd came a third time, he plied him with further questions.

"Five hundred?"

"Yes."

"All through her life, until death?"

"Yes."

"No going back on it?"

"No."

"They won't find fault with her work?"

"Never. "

"This is all true?"

"Yes."

"Swear by god?"

"I do."

"All right."

Dhanabhagyam set up house in Krishnapuram the very next day after Kizhavar permitted her to work at Auroville. She admitted Arumugam in the Thiruchitrambalam Junction Road school. She replaced the roof of the house; she bought a veshti and bedsheet for Kizhavar, and plenty of clothes for Arumugam. She spent her money right and left, not really bothered about what she would do if she needed some in an emergency. Eventually, she spent all the money Jerry Albert had given her, without putting by even a little for contingencies at home.

She could not make head or tail of anything, on her first day at work in Auroville. It took her a month to understand and adjust to her surroundings, and even this was possible only because she had company in the workers from Idayan Chaavadi, Kuyilappalayam, Sanjeev Nagar, Accharampattu, and Krishnapuram. The place teemed with people, like crowds packing the grounds as though at a festival. Dhanabhagyam's main task was to water and prune the plants, potted shrubs and the lawn in front of the meditation hall.

She found this terribly amusing, on her first day at work. "How strange, Amma! It's something unheard of. I'm sure it couldn't be this way even in outlandish places like China!" She sniggered, at the diligent cultivation of plants that bore no grain.

In Krishnapuram, women generally engaged to weed groundnut, sesame, maize, bulrush millet, common millet and coriander fields were warned to be careful, lest they miss blades of grass while weeding. Young boys were not engaged, as they had a tendency to often miss weeds. Even if they were, grass missed out while weeding was thrown out, ending in the summary dismissal of those workers. Men would stand behind women weeding, examining each row closely, and railing at those who skipped weeds; the landlord himself would inspect their work. Women who went to the fields in the morning, returned only in the evening. Their wages were two maahaani of maize or paddy – scorched paddy and pest-ridden maize, at that. Even this was delayed, and given only after one or two weeks.

Dhanabhagyam laughed aloud when she heard the terms of her employment: a salary of five hundred rupees, and a Sunday holiday. "I know we're living in Kaliyuga and all sorts of strange things are supposed to happen, but can you imagine a miracle like this in any other land?" she shared her amusement with her neighbours. "I haven't seen anything like this ever since I was born!"

Never, in all her years at Krishnapuram and Pootthurai, had Dhanabhagyam ever hankered after any sort of hard work. Her condition, if ever she did agree to work, was that the work-place must be near home, and everything should be over by ten in the forenoon. She favoured drying paddy or millet, plucking coriander and transplanting crops, but if it involved threshing pigeon-peas, pounding tamarind, preparing herb and flour vadagams or paring onions, she worked even if she had not been asked to. She confined herself, like women with infants in arms, mostly to homes in her own street or very near the village. Raman had never compelled her to work and in Pootthurai, her only job had been to spread nocchi twigs to dry. She could not bear the heat of the sun, but if it were a question of picking or peeling groundnuts, she put up with the heat; no one could stop her then. Not a single twig, leaf, not a particle of mud or dust would there be, in the heap of nuts she picked. The landlord never could find a single nut among the discarded stalks, if he checked. Other women stealthily stashed away nuts in the folds of their sari or vessels, buried them in mud, or hid them in the village paths, while going out on the pretext of answering the call of nature – "How can a woman work for hours on end without getting up and walking about?" Such a way of shirking work had never once occurred to Dhanabhagyam.

When it came to her wages, however, she insisted on a one to ten ratio. She monitored the measuring process carefully, watching how the hand moved. If she thought that the measure lacked even a single palm-full of nuts, she screeched her protest so loudly that everybody in the neighbouring fields heard her.

"Look here, Ayya, haven't I picked so vigorously that my waist almost gave way under the strain?" she would argue. "Are you giving me alms? If you're paying wages, then pay them proper. If you can't, I'll take it that I did it for charity, and I'll leave you in peace. Did you think we'd starve without this tiny measure of nuts? You think you're the only one in this wide world with a field of groundnuts?" She amassed two sacks of nuts in a year by way of wages alone.

Equally matchless was Dhanabhagyam when it came to peeling nuts, and she was capable of cracking open three-fourths of a bag in a day. Others broke the shells with a stone or on the ground; she pared the whole lot with her fingers. Unlike young boys who peeled robust nuts at random and on whom no amount of scolding and threats had any effect, she never mixed quality nuts that were to be sold with the heap meant for domestic consumption. Old women often stashed away nuts in their betel bag and or within the folds of their sari and smuggled the loot home through their grandchildren, when no one was around. Dhanabhagyam never could consider stealing. Her protests rose only if she were cheated on her wages and then, she fought pitched battles with whoever it was who had cheated, man or woman.

"Look here, Amma, what do you think you're doing?" she would explode, making sure that the whole village heard her woes. "I've peeled so much that my fingers have nearly snapped. Hoard it all yourself – but next year, there won't be a single thriving plant in your field. Why are you cheating me and heaping sin on yourself?"

She pared steadily until she reached one maahaani of nuts; after this, she gathered the nuts home, roasted and ground them with chillies into a smooth, delicious chutney. The aroma of roasted nuts wafting through the house was appetizing; Kizhavar usually drank more than his usual quota of rice-water during the days Kadalai-karappaan was a side dish. As for Raman, he had been so fond of groundnut chutney that he would mesh cooked rice on the stone slab she had ground the chutney on, and snack on it. "Very tasty. You must try some too."

Reaping sugarcane was probably the only job Dhanabhagyam never liked. The highest wages could not tempt her, and if insisted, she found a thousand reasons to refuse it. "Who can work in that itchy thicket? Those stalks would gash me into strips. My skull would get dented, carrying load after load of canes. Can you even stand in all that tangled growth? I don't want that work, and I don't want scorched paddy from the Nayudu house as wages for that, either. Call me if there's any weeding to be done. Last night I boiled four marakkaal of paddy, and I've got to dry it now. Go yourself, I'm not coming."

There was something Dhanabhagyam would give her soul for, and that was fishing in the waters of the Osutteri Lake, in the vicinity of Pootthurai. Fishing was an enthusiastic ritual every year, during the season. No sooner the date was announced, than the entire fishing hamlet took out their nets and began repairing them. Crowds of people arrived from surrounding villages and thronged the banks of the lake, barely waiting until the white cloth waved, a signal to begin fishing. Dhanabhagyam caught fish with her bare hands much better than traditional fisherwomen; she caught many more, by fanning out the outer end of her sari.

Raman, an adept fisherman, travelled to many lakes, often taking Dhanabhagyam along with him. Other women let their menfolk get down into the lake and stayed on the banks themselves; Dhanabhagyam never did. She waded into the lake along with Raman, and did not stop fishing until she had netted enough for a month's worth of delicious kuzhambu. Only on the day of the catch did she make fresh fish kuzhambu; the rest was spread on the ground to dry, like chillies and tamarind. Dhanabhagyam covered it with cowthorn branches to protect it from kites and crows pecking the fish in their beak and flying away with them. And whenever she felt like it, she fried some fish or made kuzhambu, drawing on her stock of dried fish.

Having sent Arumugam to school at eight o'clock, Dhanabhagyam usually reached Auroville at nine and began watering the plants, sweeping the fallen leaves and flowers, working on the soft, downy lawn until four in the afternoon. She was rarely bored – watching the people working in the meditation hall was an interesting sight. Her day was generally spent planting new seedlings, and inspecting growing plants.

Dhanabhagyam had tried her best to persuade Kizhavar to come to Krishnapuram, crying, begging and pleading with him. Kizhavar, however, was equally firm in his resolve to remain in Pootthurai despite Dhanabhagyam's persistence, when she lay in her hut for two days, refusing to drink even fermented rice-water. Not even this moved Kizhavar – a fact that puzzled Dhanabhagyam greatly.

At last, however, Kizhavar came to a compromise. He agreed to visit Pootthurai on Saturdays and Sundays, arriving with Arumugam when he returned from school on Friday, and leaving on Monday along with Arumugam when he went to school. What was the bond that kept him yoked to Pootthurai? Try as she might, Dhanabhagyam could not fathom his reasons.

"Arumugam, never talk back to anyone – never provoke anybody," she was saying now, gently reprimanding him about the Poonayan episode. "If we were the sons of millionaires, we could behave anyway we please – but remember that we've been born to people who can't afford anything but a loincloth to cover themselves. We're folk who're not even used to covering up leftovers after any meal. We're the kind of people who say: Yei, I'm already late for work in the field; bring the plough along with the food. We can't pit ourselves against others. Our body's our only hope. We can survive anywhere if we're fit. Whatever others might take away from us, they can't take away our legs and hands. Until our thumbs and toes are tied together at death and we're carried with our legs facing south, our limbs alone are our wealth. Remember that." Dhanabhagyam rambled on as Arumugam walked with her.

She threw frequent looks at him. Suddenly, for some reason, she began to whimper. She walked silently for a while, wiping her tears with the edge of her sari.

Earlier, she had been talking to Arumugam mostly about Jerry Albert. "He's not quite like the other, ordinary foreigners, is he? Would he have quite so much influence, and get so much respect unless he was a specialist?"

There's so much more to tell this fellow, she thought. But how can I? What would he think?

She began speaking to Arumugam again. How he must behave towards others. Cultivate with people. Use their resources to make a living ...

It was only for his sake that she had taken up this job, watering lawns and pruning plants. Somehow, he would have to study well. Apart from regular school, he ought also to join the evening classes conducted in Auroville. If he went to work with Jerry Albert, part time, he could learn English as well.

"Will you, Thambi?" she asked.

Arumugam simply looked at her as he walked. In truth, he hadn't understood even half of what she had said. He did not argue with her, but padded along silently. By the time they reached home, darkness had draped itself onto the trees.

As soon as they came home, Dhanabhagyam told Arumugam to study, and went out to fetch water from the well. The street was steeped in darkness. Arumugam read aloud; a little later, he wrote in his notebook. Dhanabhagyam returned with the filled pitcher and lit the oven. Arumugam finished writing, and began reading. He drew one or two pictures. The smell of kuzhambu invaded his nose; he shut his books and went near the oven.

Dhanabhagyam was stirring the now boiling kuzhambu with one hand, holding the lantern with the other, her face glimmering in the firelight. Arumugam leaned on her back, took the lantern from her hand and held it high to show the light for her. He shook her to and fro, coiling his left hand around her neck which was damp with perspiration. Bending his head, he bit her ear.

She poured a drop of kuzhambu on her left palm, blew a little on it to cool it down and lifted her palm. "See if it has enough salt."

He bent his head without dislodging himself and tasted it. "Add a bit more."

Dhanabhagyam gathered her son's scattered books and notebooks, put them in the school bag and hung it on the nail on the wall. As soon as she spread the bed-sheets, Arumugam came running and Thop! – plummeted down onto it.

"Do you want your intestines in a twist?" she chided him. "Why don't you lie down slowly?"

She lowered the wick of the lamp and kept it in the corner, and lay down by Arumugam. She took his hand, placed it over her chest and caressed it.

Tears stung her eyes, and she closed them. She held her breath, suppressing the sobs that threatened to overwhelm her.

"Arumugam," she whispered.

"Yes, Amma?"

"I was trying to find out if you'd fallen asleep."

"I haven't."

"Will you go?"

"Go where?"

"To that white man."

"Poonayan."

"Don't say that. I've turned into a lump of burnt charcoal ... how can this charcoal glow again? I poured water on it as it burnt bright. There won't be any fire if this charcoal is lit again, just ashes. But you ... you won't be put out. Do you remember the kutthuvilakku — the lamp that looks like it's laughing? You ought always to be like that. Even if you are put out for some reason or other, you mustn't turn into the ash used to clean vessels, like me. Shine on forever. You see the shadows below and behind that kutthuvilakku? I'll be like that — always in your shade. Always, always, you'll be everything to me. There's shadow at the base only if the lamp is shining. You're not a lump of burnt charcoal like me. You must never be extinguished. I will breathe my last only in your shade. I could stop breathing this minute if I wanted to. I'm holding on only for your sake."

"Don't cry, Amma. Why're you crying? Stop worrying."

Jerry Albert's head had vanished under the black hood of the theodolite as he peered through its viewfinder, twisting and turning this way and that, trying to fix the alignment of proposed roads. The theodolite was mounted on the tripod, and he was standing under the black hood.

Arumugam stood twenty yards in front of him, holding a hammer, one-inch aluminium nails and a bag containing white flour. His job was to drive a nail in the spot pointed out by Albert, and spread flour around it. He shifted positions when Albert asked him to. Albert chose any moment to tell Arumugam to drive a nail at a particular spot, as he looked through the theodolite. Until he did, Arumugam had to stay where he was.

Arumugam's attention was centered on Jerry Albert. He did want to carry out Albert's directions without any opposition or resentment, and took great pains to make out Albert's words. But he never looked at Albert's eyes. His eyes were the same colour as his skin – in fact, Albert's hair, neck, eyes, nose, body and moustache were all the same colour.

He mumbled curses at Albert all the time, within himself. It didn't stop just with Albert, but included heaped reproaches on his mother, sisters and everyone else related to him, too. Sometimes, unwittingly, a few words escaped his lips, prompting Albert to ask what he was murmuring about. Arumugam generally shook his hands at him – Nothing. And then he began on Albert's sister.

Twilight was approaching swiftly. Arumugam was impatient. When would Jerry Albert call it a day? He didn't know why, but he felt he should go home early. Noticing Albert's hand pointing to another spot, he dragged the chain and measuring tape, walking backwards like a bullock drawing the enormous vessel of an irrigation well. He reached the pointed spot, drove the nail, spread the flour, and waited for the next signal.

Man, Boy – this was how Albert addressed Arumugam. Arumugam did not like this at all, and seethed with rage. When would Albert go back to the Netherlands? Was he the greatest engineer ever? Why couldn't he just die?

"Boy!"

Alerted by Albert's voice, Arumugam watched his arm move. He moved here and there, back and forth, according to Albert's arm. Albert retreated under the hood again to fix the alignment of more proposed roads, finalize how many curves there would be, how many bridges and culverts would have to be constructed, and where private lands came in the way of the alignment ... Arumugam wondered when he would shout directions again. His mind wandered to the tamarind tree's shade, where boys played Chillu, or marbles.

Nowadays, Arumugam could make out what Albert was saying. He was even able to say a few words in reply. Not that it stopped Albert from guffawing whenever Arumugam spoke in English. Arumugam had almost died with shame on his first day of work, because neither he not Albert could make out what the other was saying.

It was day, and there were people at a little distance, but he still felt as though he was trapped in a lonely place at night. He was alone, with no one but Albert for company; an Albert who couldn't talk the way Arumugam could. Albert's mouth hardly opened even when he did, and he didn't seem to use his lips and tongue properly. His voice irritated Arumugam – it translated into an odd kolak kolak, as though he were speaking with water in his mouth. Arumugam stomped angrily when he heard it, and felt like running away. He cursed Dhanabhagyam liberally at such times, for having brought him to work under Albert.

There were so many good places in Auroville where one could find work. There was a crèche for children. Children below eight were brought, fed, clothed, and made to study, and Arumugam liked this place the best. They played and sang for the better part of the day; if he had a job there, he could have played with them too. If only Dhanabhagyam had got him a job there ... he'd have been happy. But she'd thrown his lot with this bleating sheep.

He could easily quit and run away but if he did, Albert might dismiss Dhanabhagyam in a fury. Moreover, even if he did ask her to find another job for him, Arumugam doubted that anyone would hire him only for Saturdays and Sundays.

The sun had sunk quickly in the west, and a fresh breeze rippled through the foliage. Labourers, felling and burning trees and plants to the north, and stripping land acquired by the Auroville people were dispersing. Bulldozers brought in to level the land were being driven to the sheds. Two lorries unloaded pebbles brought in from somewhere, in front of the lawn. A few lorries unloaded red earth, dust rising in the air from them, and drove away.

People working in the meditation hall disbanded quickly. Men and women rushed home, their oily faces caked with red dust, chattering about the latest film released in Pondicherry's cinema hall. Workers erecting barbed wire fences around the land purchased on the side of the University bundled their tools, and broke up. White folk – men and women – were moving about in every direction, astride bicycles, scooters, cars and jeeps. Tomorrow was Sunday, and people were getting ready to celebrate it. Sunday, like the new moon day celebration in villages, had begun to be celebrated as a special occasion. Now, everyone was a Sunday person.

Jerry Albert yelled as though he had had a fit, and Arumugam sprang into alertness. He moved the chain and measuring tape, following Albert's hand. He halted at the spot Albert indicated, adjusted the chain, measured it with his tape, drove the nail in and spread flour around it. Albert came up to that spot, checking the nails driven in to see if they were measured out as he wished, and according to the plan he held. Then he moved the tripod. He shifted it again after five or six nails had been driven, and began looking through the theodolite. He was trying to fix an alignment for a four-way junction. Following Albert's signs, Arumugam stopped at various spots and drove in the nails. More than ten nails were driven; Albert inspected every nail that had been driven after midday, and Arumugam did the same.

Jerry Albert now stood leaning on the tri-cornered stand. He wanted to inspect the work completed that day, before winding up. Arumugam's attention was divided between Albert and the steadily sinking sun, yielding place to darkness. Trees and plants, tall and short, now stood wilted by the roadside, lashed with mud by rumbling vehicles. The land was bare of life as far as the eyes could see, shorn mercilessly of vegetation. New and exotic seedlings of trees and flowering plants were to be planted in neat rows, in a few places that had been leveled. A few rows had already been planted. People ambled in the paths laid out between the rows, tired out; only from their faces could one make out that they belonged to Idayan Chaavadi, Kuyilappalayam, Sanjeev Nagar and Krishnapuram.

Their walk was novel, indeed. Their expression, clothes, hairstyle, and speech were no different from those of white folk. They bobbed their heads when they spoke, like cattle swatting flies. The women could not give up their saris yet, but in everything else they took after white women, believing firmly that all their woes would end if they aped foreign ways. The white women, on the other hand, had begun to wear saris and bangles, plait their hair and wear flowers, and to wear kumkumam on their foreheads, like Tamil women.

Barring old men and women, most people from the surrounding villages worked in Auroville. Even students had found a place there, making money from part time jobs and going about with white girls. Homes in villages might not have vessels for rice or kuzhambu, but there was not a single house that did not have face powder, soaps and hand bags. The lower-caste cheri girls carried the vanguard in this respect, far more than those from the Vanniar and Nayudu families. These days, rearing cattle, goats, pigs, were being looked down upon in villages. Gone were the days when people lamented: Survive as long as you slog, god save you if you stop. Wasn't there any other way to make a living? These days, wasn't sowing seeds, planting seedlings or reaping crops beneath your dignity?

Young, good-looking girls working in Auroville moved freely with white folk, going about with them in bicycles, scooters, motorcycles and cars. Introverts, bashful or dark-complexioned people were given only inferior jobs, however much they were educated. Every girl, however, had a comb, mirror and face powder in her handbag. Now, all of them were rushing home with red dust smeared faces, like clouds blown away by the wind. In the fading light, they appeared like silhouettes in motion, to Arumugam.

Jerry Albert must have been shouting at him for a long time – his harsh voice grated on Arumugam's mind. It jolted him into awareness and he stood for a moment, confused, as though suddenly shaken awake from sleep. Then, he gathered his wits and went back to following Albert's directions.

Jerry Albert inspected the nails driven, one by one. He came over to Arumugam and smiled. Then he walked back, put away the theodolite in its case, folded the tripod and told Arumugam to carry the hood. Arumugam stuffed the nails, hammer, chain, flour and tape in the bag, and walked towards the Centre kitchen to deposit them. Jerry Albert accompanied him.

Avenue after avenue passed by, lined with numbered trees on the way. Light was already failing and in a few moments, everything would be swallowed up by darkness.

Arumugam ambled into the house, and flopped down onto the steel cot as though someone had shoved him.

He lay still, for a long time. He didn't know why, but he ached all over and there was a bitter taste in his mouth. His tongue felt dry and itchy as though he'd travelled a long way in hot, dry weather.

He sat up and stared at the walls and ceiling, analyzing every part of it. The whole house appeared neat and orderly. He pulled off shoes as heavy as horseshoes, shrugged off his shirt and baniyan, and arranged them in their place. He didn't quite know what else to do, and sat down to eat.

Arumugam usually came straight home from school. Each morning, he stuffed himself into his military uniform of shirt, tie, shorts and shoes and walked into his school's box-like classroom at eight – he didn't like the shift system at all – and left only at one in the afternoon, to an empty house; he was alone until Dhanabhagyam returned.

It'd be nice if it were an all-day school, he thought. He felt like going out, but he didn't know any of the boys here – in his street, or the neighbouring ones. His friends were all in Krishnapuram. There, Ramasamy from the opposite house had always been with him, and they would often play together. His street had the largest number of boys, and he spent all his time playing with them or Ramasamy.

Even in Pootthurai, he'd been left out from play only during the first week; after that, he'd become one of them. They had called him after his street. He was the Maadu Adicchaan Toppu boy, and they called him so whenever they wanted to tease him – "Dei, Maadu Adichaan Toppu!"

He wondered why he'd ever come to Pootthurai, when they did.

Five or six large tamarind trees shaded the place behind Kizhavar's home. Cows were slaughtered under them regularly, and this was the reason for the names given to the house and street nearby: Maadu adichaan Toppu Houses, and similarly, Maadu adichaan Toppu Street.

"Yei, Maadu Adicchaan Toppu!" – Arumugam felt like hacking down those wretched tamarind trees whenever the boys teased him so.

It was now two years since Arumugam had moved to Pondicherry, and so far, no boy had accepted him as his playmate. He shied away from going to them himself. He was often called a Pattikkaadu – a gawking village urchin, or a Gramatthaan, if he did.

He considered visiting the house opposite. Krishnamurthy would be at home. It was a habit of the man to launch into a long, enthusiastic speech about his stint in the army, fighting for the French in the Second World War – how he, a watchman in the Indian owned textile mill had been recruited, how Indians like him had been trained in camps in the war front, how in the first five or six months they had been scared to death, how, later, some of them had advanced with cannon and blasted the enemy troops, how they had fired, how many thousands of people had been killed, and so on. He would also tell Arumugam unfailingly about his pension – ten thousand rupees – his advertisement for marriage with any widow over forty, his morning and evening walks. Arumugam wasn't really keen on hearing it again, and so he fell back on the bed.

He wrote his homework briskly, filled with an urge to finish it before Dhanabhagyam came home. He studied the portions assigned as homework, and then repeated them to himself without looking at the book. He calculated the time left until Dhanabhagyam's return. She didn't walk down, or board two buses these days. The Auroville van brought her to her doorstep. And besides, she was not as tired as before, when she came home. Her skin glowed, and she had gained some weight.

What puzzled Arumugam in particular was the faint smell of camphor that wafted from her, when she came home from Auroville.

He'd noticed something else too: she didn't smile or laugh as much as she used to, after they came to Pondicherry. Now, she laughs and talks as if she's a machine.

Night had fallen by the time Dhanabhagyam returned. "Thambi, why haven't you lit the lamp? Why are you reading in the dark?"

She lit the lamp, hung her shoulder bag on a nail, and sat down by Arumugam. "When did you come? Had your lunch at noon? I had cooked your favourites – you should've eaten all of it. Why've you left some for me?" She got up and drank water. Then she changed her sari and washed her face. She lit the stove, hurrying to prepare the evening's meal. Arumugam sat near her, staring at the flame intensely.

Making small talk with him, Dhanabhagyam washed raw rice,

chopped vegetables, and stirred the rice cooking in the pot. She wiped her perspiring face and neck, listening to him repeating the lessons he had learnt. When he had finished reciting at breakneck speed, she twined her hands around him and held him in a tight embrace, laughing gently. Sometimes, she would smile when she held him like this; at others, she would cry.

Later, she washed Arumugam's face and made him sit down to study. Sitting at a little distance from him, she glanced through some of his books and notebooks. After a while, she tried to write her name in a notebook she had bought for herself, copying what Arumugam had written down for her. Sobs overwhelmed her suddenly, when she began her meal. She cursed Kizhavar, Raman and Auroville; she cursed herself. A good deal of her anger was concentrated on Kizhavar, for refusing to come and stay with her.

"Thambi, Arumugam," she pleaded. "You're the one who'll have to bring him here, somehow ..."

Arumugam was so distressed at her sorrow that he lost his appetite.

He tried to console her, crying himself. "Don't worry, Amma. Don't cry," he comforted her, much in the manner of a grown-up. "Leave it all to me. I'll bring him here."

He tried everything in his power to raise her spirits, but Dhanabhagyam remained inconsolable. She did not stop weeping; neither did she touch her food.

Kizhavar had advised Dhanabhagyam more than once, against selling the Krishnapuram house and shifting to Pondicherry. She had turned a deaf ear to his words, and Kizhavar was livid.

"Going against me, are you?" he snapped. "Talking back to me? Right. Go, then."

He never spoke a word to Dhanabhagyam, afterwards.

Dhanabhagyam put forth the same reason to the people of Krishnapuram, Pootthurai and to Kizhavar: "My son must have an education. His father couldn't even sign his own name – I don't want him to be the same. I don't want him to struggle along, like a labourer on his knees. Do you want me to give a shovel into his hands and see him dig earth all his life? I didn't bring him into the world for this! He's all I have. Must he sweat it out for two maahaanis of paddy in the Nayudu houses?"

Dhanabhagyam sold her house at Krishnapuram in defiance of advice offered, and paid advance for a rented house in Pondicherry. What money remained, she spent on various articles for the house, arguing, "What's a decent house without furniture and knick-knacks?"

She paid a donation and admitted Arumugam into school. She bought him expensive clothes – far more than he had ever had in Krishnapuram and Pootthurai, where a pair of shorts and a shirt with their buttons ripped out in washing, the stitches snapped, and the material torn at the seat, had been his only possessions. He usually dug in his heels for a new shirt only on Pongal or Dipaavali.

All that changed in Pondicherry.

She bought costly saris and blouses for herself too, the likes of which not even Kizhavar had obtained for her marriage. He had merely got her an ordinary cotton sari for her wedding, and had commented, proudly, "Ah, first class. Looks very well on you. Suits your complexion."

Raman had not bought clothes often either; neither had he purchased costly garments. "I'm not in Government service, am I?" he would retort. "This is all we can afford." He had favoured inexpensive saris and shirts, and that too only occasionally.

Dhanabhagyam spent as unstintingly on food as she did on clothes.

"My boy will grow up strong and healthy only if he's got good food in his belly," she reasoned. Despite good food to eat, clothes to wear and a comfortable house, Kizhavar's absence was a void that could not be filled. She made an emissary of everyone from Pootthurai that she met in Pondicherry or Auroville, asking him or her to persuade Kizhavar. "My father's memory haunts me ... put in a word when you see him next, do."

Some nights would be spent lost in anguished memories of Kizhavar and Raman. She would stay awake then, believing Arumugam to be asleep, sobbing until daybreak.

Arumugam had sided with Kizhavar, when it came to moving. "Why go to Pondicherry, Amma?" he had argued with Dhanabhagyam. "Let's stay here."

Dhanabhagyam had not listened to him. "There's no scope for a good education in the village, and what's on hand isn't any good," was her argument. There were good schools in Pondicherry; Arumugam could study well. He would be spoilt if he stayed in Krishnapuram, gadding about in the company of the village boys. I want him to get a good education, she said constantly. He must become an engineer.

She had not been pleased at selling the house in Krishnapuram either. True, it was a small house; four rafters. The crossbeams and roof had decayed. The walls were crumbling. More than half of the three hundred houses in Krishnapuram had been converted into tiled roof and double storeyed houses ... all with the money earned at Auroville. Those who still lived in thatched houses were mostly poor, or single women. Some families had shifted to Pondicherry for the sake of their children's education.

Dhanabhagyam had considered all this when she made her decision. Why must I hold on to all this, she asked herself. If I'm supposed to moan about my fate, I may as well give everything up and do it. You can't jump headfirst into a well just because your father dug it. Doesn't my son have a right to a good education? Thus, she reconciled herself to selling her home. She also sold away a couple of Poovarasu trees that stood in the backyard along with the poultry, for the price asked. She gave away without any compunction the full set of stone mortars, roller and pestle that Kizhavar had bought when she set up house.

The old man had spent a good deal in buying these kitchen implements. His daughter, he reasoned, must never set foot in other homes, begging for their use when she wished to thresh paddy or grind rice. No other house in the village possessed such a complete set, and the women had gaped when Kizhavar's purchases had been delivered at the newlywed Dhanabhagyam's home.

"Each of these would cost a small fortune ...!" they murmured, astonished. "The girl's father must certainly be well off."

On festive occasions, women of the village borrowed Dhanabhagyam's stone grinder to grind rice and pulses through days and nights. As for the pounding mortar, it was used constantly, sifting jowar, polishing rice, or pounding paddy. There were even times when, with no one to watch over Arumugam, a babe in arms at the time, she tucked him into the pit of the pounding mortar and went on errands to fetch water or purchase grocery.

She gave away this mortar too, for free.

Dhanabhagyam ate nothing. She washed the vessels and deposited them in the shelf like a dutiful servant as soon as the meal was over.

She never could rest content until she had emptied all the vessels and washed them up. She did not relish leftovers, and cooked only as much food as needed for Arumugam and herself. "Who can put up with old, rotting rice and stinking kuzhambu?" If, by any chance, any food was left over, she threw it away.

She had cooked a little more than what was required for Kizhavar, Raman, Arumugam and herself in Krishnapuram and Pootthurai, giving away the leftovers to dogs, cats, the washerman or the thomban, the low-caste street acrobat. "A cooking pot must have a few grains of rice in it," was one of her favourite maxims.

She spread a mat by Arumugam's own, lay down beside him, and told him to repeat the lessons he had learnt. She herself did not know enough to judge if he was correct; she had to ask him if it was.

Arumugam asked if he could put out the light. She replied that he could. She herself never asked him to put it out, and even when he did, she would reply with a, "Study a little more, why don't you?"

Today, however, she nodded "All right," and Arumugam was surprised.

Dhanabhagyam lay on her mat, silent for a long while. Finally, she asked: "Thambi, Arumugam ... are you asleep, yet?"

"Yes, Amma?"

"You're the one who'll have to bring your thatha from Pootthurai," she spoke softly. "I've been reduced to nothing – I'm living on night soil. You'll have to let me be with you, even if I've fallen to such rotten depths. You're the only reason I'm still alive. The body is one thing, but the mind is something else. Sunlight falls on shit too, and how can we blame it? I carried you within myself, with all the dirt and bone and flesh – don't you too leave me alone, like your father did. You're not like your father – you fly into rages at every chance that comes along. Don't let me die a worthless death. I might be stepping into shit, but remember that I'm doing it because you're perched on my waist. I never knew my mother – they only told me her name. You were the only reason I held onto life. My father doesn't care enough. You're not my son, you're my father – don't go away – don't leave me alone – you're my brother. That's how I think of you – I'm at your feet, now. You're my master, my lord, my god – you're everything to me. My body simply won't sleep anymore ... Thambi, are you asleep?"

Dhanabhagyam woke Arumugam at five in the morning, washed his face and set him down to study. She made him tea, and then bustled away to cook his lunch.

She fluttered about every morning as though she were the one leaving for school, not resting a moment until she saw Arumugam off. When the school bus arrived, she would clasp him to herself before letting the vehicle swallow him up. She would stand at the door, watching until the bus vanished from her view. And sometimes the bus would vanish sooner, blurred by her tears.

The bus had honked its arrival at the street corner by the time Dhanabhagyam dressed Arumugam. "The bus has come, the bus has come!" she yelled as she stuffed the boy into his knickers, shirts, tie and shoes. She hugged him tight, murmuring, "Be careful, now."

Arumugam waved a "Taa taa!" to her, and then scampered into the bus.

Dhanabhagyam stood at the door, watching a long time after the bus had gone. Her eyes swam with tears, as though she had sent someone beloved to her far, far away.

Abruptly, she slumped down on her doorstep, overwhelmed by exhaustion.

"Hello!" shouted Jerry Albert into her ears, rousing her from her reverie.

Dhanabhagyam jumped up. A trapped feeling stole over her. She shivered, and broke out into a sweat. Go away, she gestured, trying to get across her message. I'll come by the bus. Leave. Her arms and legs tingled with nervousness as she signed to him again and again, pointing towards the road.

"What?" asked Albert as he walked up the stairs, looking back as if he couldn't understand her. "What?"

"Go away, please," Dhanabhagyam repeated, quivering. She ran inside, snatched up her handbag, lock and key, came out and tried to lock the door.

Jerry Albert, however, stood in the way. "Nice, very nice house," he pushed her aside and went in, wanting to explore the interiors.

"Come out, it's getting late!" Dhanabhagyam almost screamed. "You know what'll happen if somebody sees you here! Do come out, Alberttu ..." Her tongue was parched, and refused to move. "Oh my god," she moaned, breath catching in her throat as she kneaded her hands, and shuffled her feet at the door.

Albert turned a deaf ear to her pleas and loitered inside the house, surveying it. Then, he beckoned to her.

Dhanabhagyam signalled furiously, trying to get him to come out. Which barbaric land taught you to behave like this? You mustn't stay here a minute. What if my son sees you here? A few vague rumours flying around were enough to make my father stop talking to me. You can't tempt me like this — crores of rupees won't make me do it — do you want to see me dead? What will the neighbours think? For heaven's sake, come out!

She wished to say all this aloud, but she doubted if he could understand her Tamil. She craned her neck from outside, and in spite of herself, shouted, "Get out!"

Jerry Albert reached out a hand, seized her neck nimbly with the dexterity of a snake charmer snatching a snake from its pit, and pulled her in.

Arumugam left school at eleven, that morning. The school bus wasn't running — one of the students had gone to buy sweets during the interval, and had been mangled by a passing car. School had closed for the day as soon as news of his death reached it. The boys had been allowed to see the body till it had been transferred into an ambulance, while the headmaster and teachers followed it as fast as they could, in the school bus. Arumugam decided that he would walk home and strolled along the road, taking in the sights.

The ebb and flow of vehicles and pedestrians had slowed to a trickle. The hustle and bustle typical of the road would start again in the evening.

Arumugam had little homework that day as school had closed so unexpectedly, and was in no hurry to reach home. In any case, Dhanabhagyam would return only by six; until then, he'd have to be alone in the house. He ambled along, looking at the buildings, hoardings and advertisements along the way, fascinated by the strange notices and unusual designs. There were cinema posters too. An obscene poster put up a daring display in front of the Naveena theatre.

Arumugam muttered a disgusted "Chi, karumam!" and turned his face away, walking past quickly.

Suddenly, Kizhavar came to mind.

Dhanabhagyam and Arumugam had gone to Pootthurai just the day before Kizhavar died, in another attempt to bring him to Pondicherry.

Kizhavar had spoken only to Arumugam, and a very little at that. "What is it?" he had asked, listless and sullen. "Are you well? How goes school? Does Krishnapurathare still remember me? Haven't forgotten our village?"

Dhanabhagyam forced herself on his attention. "What wrong have I done?" she argued. "I haven't let you down, have I. My boy was the reason I went – you must forgive me just this once. I won't go against your wishes, hereafter ..."

She fell at Kizhavar's feet and sobbed, clasping his legs. She knocked herself against the wall, thrashed about on the floor. She wailed, beating her chest, thighs and face. "Speak a word to me, won't you?" she lamented. "Just ask me: Enna pullay, how are things?"

Kizhavar spoke not a word to her. He took Arumugam with him, and walked towards the Vavva Canal outside the village. He did not speak a word to Arumugam either, on his own, and answered the boy's questions as shortly as he could.

"Maybe." "Is that so?" "I don't know. It's all right if you do."

Off and on he mumbled two three lines of a song. Hours later, he began a disjointed, "Krishnapurathare, Krishnapurathare ..." as they turned homewards, but did not continue. He walked, silent and withdrawn.

Dhanabhagyam awaited their return, having cooked for the night. Kizhavar sat down to his meal without a demur, clearly surprised, for it was obvious that he had not expected her to do so. He made Arumugam sit by his side too, and Dhanabhagyam served them both.

Kizhavar ate well, asking for a second and a third helping as never before. "Eat well," he insisted, to Arumugam. "Eat your fill. Don't nibble at your food like a rat. Krishnapurathare, do you hear me?"

Kizhavar asked them to leave early, that they might reach Pondicherry before darkness fell. Dhanabhagyam hadn't asked for his escort; yet he accompanied them until the Thiruchitrambalam Junction Road, holding Arumugam's hand. Dhanabhagyam wailed, as she walked a little behind them. "Yei murderess, my mother – why did you leave me?" she lamented. "Yei god, blind as you are – why did you bring me into this world?"

Kizhavar's grip on Arumugam's hand tightened, as he heard her agonized curses.

She boarded neither of the two buses that arrived as they walked into the Thiruchitrambalam bus stand, pleading with Kizhavar to come with her. He was adamant in his refusal. She bent down and clutched his legs.

"Appa, you can't do this to me, even if I have done wrong," she sobbed. "All right, fine. Bring up this young one yourself – and I'll be free to give up my life. This boy's the only reason I'm holding on. Why did mother have to die? She wouldn't have given up on me if she'd been alive, no matter what I did. Why did you raise me? You could've killed me when I was born, with a drop of yarcum juice. A woman who's borne children would've known what I suffer – she'd have been kinder to me. Did you raise me all these years only to see me shorn of everything? I've got no one in this world – no kith or kin worth the name. You're all I have. There's no point in living if you don't acknowledge me. I'll kill myself, that's for sure. It wouldn't be too difficult to get a yard of rope, would it? Or there're clumps of oleander in this canal. Better still, why don't you poison me yourself? Give me some, and if I don't swallow it, you'd have every right to call me, Why, you daughter of my concubine ...! Ah, what's the use of holding onto life any longer? Yei Amma ...!"

Kizhavar neither lifted her up; nor did he move away. But, for the first time, he said, "Go, now. I shall come the day after tomorrow. Don't make a scene. What'll everyone think? If I say that I'll come, then I'll come for sure." He consoled her, and made her board the next bus.

Dhanabhagyam sobbed throughout their journey, and all night at home in Pondicherry. "Oh my god, my father knows ... what can I do now? Yei Sengeniyamma, you've deserted me! I've no brothers, sisters, kith or kin to turn to ... what am I going to do?" she moaned in misery, until daybreak.

News reached them, a little after dawn, that Kizhavar had hung himself.

Arumugam was walking through Nehru Street. He passed through Rukmini Cinema Theatre Road, Jain Factory Road and the market, and turned into the street opposite Subbiah Marriage Hall.

Two more streets, and he'd be home. And when I get there, he planned enthusiastically, I'll go over to Krishnamurthy's home, and have a chat with him.

Trade was brisk in the streets – there was the vegetable vendor with his cart, the mobile laundry, people selling curd, fish, figs, stainless steel and aluminium vessels, blouse pieces, saris and what not.

Old women screeched their wares loudly, selling figs and buttermilk. Someone thrashed a young boy for whatever reason and dragged him away, growling, "You dog, you cur ..." Arumugam stared at them until they disappeared into a lane, feeling a surge of anger at the man. Why couldn't this man have gotten crushed underneath the bus, instead of that boy?

His thoughts wandered, leading him to memories of Raman.

Raman had never laid a finger on Arumugam. Even as a dutiful father wishing to discipline a child, Raman had never struck him; nor had he clouted his head. It was Dhanabhagyam who beat him black and blue, as though making up for Raman's lack of discipline in double measure.

"Get away!" she would yell at Raman, when he tried to stop her. "Interfering as the man of the house, are you? How dare this little one demand anything?" she would turn to Arumugam. "You want to gorge on food? Your appan has fields and fields growing anything you want. We'll go over there and stuff ourselves," she would thrash the boy, elbowing Raman away as she did. "Ask for what's not here, will you? Will you?" she would smack Arumugam again and again, glaring at him.

She would shriek at Raman if he were to buy Arumugam a tasty tidbit: "You'd turn the boy into a rascally urchin drooling at the shops, would you?" And she would pinch Raman's thighs and waist, punching him for good measure. Raman would ignore the abuse, laughing in great good humour ... for, was Arumugam the only one she subjected to such thrashing and pinches?

It was Raman who generally carried Arumugam atop his shoulders, and bought whatever the boy wished for at shops. It was he who ended up with an earful, if Dhanabhagyam caught Arumugam snacking.

"You chandala! He's the only one I've brought into this world and you're bent on killing him, feeding him trash ...!"

Raman would wait for a break as she raved and ranted, when he would jump up and squeeze her tight. She would manage to slip from within his grasp if Arumugam were around, but if he did manage to hold her in spite of her efforts to wriggle free, she would shriek, "Yei kolaikaaraa, chandala, paavi," trying to squirm out of his embrace. "Where on earth would you see such shamelessness – in broad daylight too? Amma, you'd never see a ruffian like this – let go, you brute. Plague take you ...!"

But if Raman had not returned from work at his usual time, she would worry, asking Arumugam to run up to the end of the street and see whether he had arrived yet. She would send the boy to look for him again and again; Raman, on his part, would not fail to bring some tidbit or other for Arumugam when he came home from work. He would often carry his son on his shoulders or his waist as he walked home from the street corner, the boy relishing such tidbits. One of Arumugam's greatest ambitions was to snack all the way home – perched somewhere on his father as he did so, and in full view of other boys, who stared after him, envying him with all their hearts. And so, Arumugam would flit away like a bird at Dhanabhagyam's slightest suggestion, to await Raman's arrival at the street corner.

Raman had chosen Arumugam's name. It had been his grandfather's name and Raman's favourite; Dhanabhagyam had not liked it at all. She had suggested a hundred other alternatives, none of which had moved Raman in the least. She complained about this to Kizhavar, who replied, "Arumugam? Excellent. The name of Lord Arumukha, the god with six faces. The name of Mailam Murugan. A first class name. No other name will do." And that was that.

Raman took him to the Mailam Murugan temple and had a ritual tonsuring done, on account of Arumugam's admission to school. He distributed betel leaves, nuts, sweets and five rupees each to the teachers, and sweets to the students as well, on Arumugam's first day there. The boys promptly voted Raman a Good Fellow.

Very few Krishnapuram boys had studied at the Thiruchitrambalam Road Junction School, during Arumugam's days there. This was an opportunity for him to gather his Krishnapuram mates, herd them to the tank bund after school, and tell them stories about the school, his teachers, the students, the building, et cetera. He gave a free rein to his imagination every day, enthusiastic with his audience's reception. Nothing could equal the joy of watching them listen to him, mouth agape, and their admiring looks were sheer bliss.

There were a few who declared, "He's just bluffing. There's nothing like that anywhere." Arumugam would feel a surge of anger and irritation at those who delivered such a skeptical verdict.

Here, in Pondicherry, he missed all this – the admiring crowd of boys who laughed with him and even the few who laughed at him. There was so much to tell about the Pondicherry school, but there was no one to listen to his tales; so much so, that he hated the school itself.

Arumugam had been playing in the street when Raman's corpse was brought in. He'd yelled a gleeful, "Dei, look! Someone's come home in a car!" when he saw the jeep parked in front of his house.

Wails greeted him as he ran back home. Many of those who had arrived to mourn the death tried to lift him up, hugged him and stroked his head. "He's gone and left this youngster fatherless. What kind of death is this – a bolt from the blue! He was full of life when he spoke to me this morning ... and now, he's dead! Great god ..."

It dawned on Arumugam, at last, that Raman would never, hereafter, stop Dhanabhagyam from thrashing him. He began to wail, distressed,

and those who had come to condole Raman's death looked at him
with pity, brushing away sympathetic tears.

His anguish grew, and he began to sob more than ever.

A bicycle hit his shoulder, and its rider screamed at him. "Can't you
see what's coming? Walking on a busy road with your head in the
clouds – ah, look at the fellow, half-asleep ..."

Arumugam shook his head, and regained his attention, slinging up
the school bag that hung on his shoulder. He had walked the whole
way, and hunger gnawed at his stomach. It was summer, and midday,
to boot. The sun burnt fiercely, high above a towering row of buildings,
and the strip of sky amidst them remained flat and empty. There was
not a speck of cloud to be seen.

Summer nights in Krishnapuram saw Raman and Dhanabhagyam lying
down in the open on mats, with Arumugam between them. Arumugam
would throw his arms and legs on them and look at the sky, trying to
count the stars. He would slip up at some point every time, and try
again. He would gaze at the moon travelling in the sky, while Raman
regaled him with stories about gods and goddesses. He would sing
drama songs too. Dhanabhagyam, on the other hand, would always
tell him only frightening ghost stories; this was her way of putting him
in his place.

The skies of Pondicherry seemed completely different from the
vast expanses of Pootthurai and Krishnapuram. Arumugam had never
seen a full sky in Pondicherry; here, he could see up to where the
road ended and nothing beyond, where it was snipped off by tall
buildings. It seemed to be a tiny stick-like strip, compared to the vast
skies of Pootthurai and Krishnapuram.

Arumugam never counted stars, here.

Arumugam felt a surge of elation as he thought about the very little homework he had to do. He planned on going to the cinema with Dhanabhagyam, as soon as he finished it. He walked fast, and began running homewards as he caught sight of it, in the street.

He was surprised to see that the door was closed, but not locked. Hasn't mother gone out to work, he wondered. Isn't she well? If she's all right, we could start for the cinema right now. He wanted to shout, "Amma!" even from the doorway.

On second thoughts, he decided that he would go in quietly, give her a surprise and clasp her from behind, murmuring a soft "Amma," and then bite her ears and nose for good measure. He hadn't bitten her once, ever since their arrival in Pondicherry.

He walked to the entrance silently; all appeared quiet. Was the door bolted from inside? He hoped that it wasn't, that he could push the door open slowly and enter without a sound.

"Mailam Muruga," he prayed. "Please don't let the door be bolted from inside ..."

He pushed the door gently. It was not bolted, and opened noiselessly. Elation filled him. He stepped inside, softly. His eyes spied the space where his bedding was usually rolled up, and there ...

There was Dhanabhagyam's well-shaped body, naked, intertwined with another, white one.

Darkness engulfed him the next moment.

He was blinded, as though abruptly thrown into a world of inky shadows.

"Amma!" he screamed.

A pair of cat's eyes fell in his line of vision, piercing the darkness.

Arumugam fled. Shock edged into pain as he ran from the house like one demented, not really caring where he ran, wanting only to put as much distance as he could from what he had just seen.

Street after street sprung up around him. He ran. Ran.

And ran.

Dei payya, drive on, drive on. When will brother dear die, when will the thinnai clear out? Your sister's girl is sweet on you only until her errand is carried out," sang Dharmamoorthy, nonstop. "Haha, get on with your job. You're paying for your sins, I'm reaping the reward for my devotion, my poosai. Go right royally, dei. Ah, I was born in a great land, sirs. Listen to my story. Go, go, go your way, boy. Don't stop for any dog that comes along. Don't stop, you!" he yelled, sunk in an alcoholic stupor.

He had been able to get two passengers on their way to the hospital that morning, and had promptly spent his fare on arrack. Now right royally drunk, he blabbered endlessly. His tongue would stop its senseless chatter only when he became sober, but he was entirely capable of getting stone drunk again when he did come to his senses — he was that kind of a fellow. He might look like a stick; for all that, his voice blared out like a trumpet.

He had folded down the hood of his rickshaw and lay resting his head on it, his legs dangling comfortably from the steel frame of the hood opposite. His lungi lay folded on his face, to ward off the sun, and he was yelling himself hoarse like a street-player, to boot. "Yei, yei!"

Arumugam did not have to exert himself too much to pedal. The road sloped downwards from Jipmer Hospital to the Jain Factory; all you had to do was give the rickshaw a slight push, and it would roll under its own force. Arumugam held the handlebar carefully, his fingers ready at the brake should any pedestrian, bus, lorry, scooter, tempo, or auto-rickshaw cross his path. He pulled the string and rang the bell off and on, steering the vehicle stylishly in traffic; he was in full control of the rickshaw. Occasionally, he looked back at the as-good-as-dead Dharmamoorthy. Shame and disgust washed over him at the man's condition.

"Yei you, careful! You shameless fellow," shrieked Dharmamoorthy. "Faster, you thoomappayya! "

Arumugam ignored the disjointed shrieks. He rang the bell, braked and drove expertly, adjusting his direction and speed in conjunction with oncoming vehicles, while Dharmamoorthy lolled about in the vehicle, his hands hanging outside. His outstretched limbs collided with an auto-rickshaw passing by and the irate driver vented his ire with, "Thooma, why don't you pick out a better place to die? Couldn't you find anything better than my rickshaw to get mangled? You'd better lie properly, if you want to live a few more years!"

Dharmamoorthy continued to stretch out as before, feigning a nonchalant air. Arumugam felt a brief urge to abandon the rickshaw then and there, and run away. Why's this fellow sprawled across the rickshaw this way, drunken idiot that he is? he asked himself, infuriated. Why can't he sit up?

Disgusted, he began to pedal furiously. When they reached the signal

beyond the Jain Factory, Arumugam turned to Dharmamoorthy.
"Where do you want to go?"

"Go where the wheels will roll," came the philosophic reply.

"Tell me."

"The lecherous husband fixed a rendezvous with his sister-in-law,"
sang Dharmamoorthy from beneath the lungi, "But whom did he see
when he went there, but his wife! That's exactly how you've ended
up in my net, too. Ah, look, the people on foot run faster than the
rickshaw ..."

"Which direction do you want me to take?"

"Go wherever you like. What does it matter? Who's going
to question us?"

Arumugam might have been staying with Dharmamoorthy for
almost a month, but he had started plying the rickshaw only a week
ago. The last month had changed him drastically; he had morphed
into a different being, almost. Those who had known him earlier
would not be able to recognize him now. No one would be able to say,
"Ah, this is our own Arumugam."

Arumugam had fled that day, a sparrow escaping the gunshot of a
gypsy. He ran past places he knew, places he did not, developing
settlements ... he ran past them all. He ran all day. He pushed back
sobs, gulping down his anguish. He wandered about for hours, caught
in a frenzy of agony and anger. He might not have cried, but tears
blurred his vision. Nothing appeared real; nothing seemed to be in its
true form.

"Amma, Amma," he wept, unable to control the cry that escaped
his lips. The next instant, he spat out a disgusted Chi chi!, feeling an
intense wave of mortification at having called her so.

He ran as though fleeing from a dreaded enemy, rushing past each house, each street, and every human being he came across. They were all the same, everywhere. He ran in a criss-cross fashion along main roads, crossroads and lines, trying to reach the end, but no matter how many times he tried, he always ended up in the midst of a four way junction.

It seemed to him that he had seen all the faces and places in the whole wide world in just one day, but only one image stood out in his tortured mind — two naked bodies intertwined. The veins on his forehead stood out. A splitting headache raged through him, and his skin burned, as though with a high fever. Perspiration poured down his body, giving off a revolting smell, and he felt as though his intestines were thrusting upwards from hunger.

A mass of darkness roiled within his eyelids. His head pounded with a relentless noise. He tottered, exhausted, and his legs entwined, colliding with each other. The thought of returning home occurred off and on, but he hesitated: What if Poonayan were there ...? The thought choked his brain, confounding him. He walked or ran hard whenever Jerry Albert's image came to his mind, but his path was hidden by tears.

"Amma," he sobbed, sometimes, wiping his eyes. Kizhavar's dead, or I could have gone to Pootthurai, he grieved. He tried to ease his hunger by gulping water again and again, but walking became difficult with so much liquid in his stomach, which made an odd kaluk, kaluk noise. This state of affairs existed only a little while, however; soon, his stomach shrunk, arching between and below his ribs. He had had to pass through many streets to get water or urinate, and he was tired out.

Homes twinkled with lamps, as evening crept in. After six, traffic reached colossal proportions. Even walking on the edges of the roads was a problem, and a cacophony of noise surrounded him on all sides. He retreated to the bus stand when night fell, and sat there a long time. Then, he walked up to the Raja Theatre. After a while, he returned to the bus stop. He walked in and around the bus stand. When he did sit, he shifted from one spot to another.

What do I do, he wondered. Where do I go?

He began walking on the Cuddalore Road again. It was not quite so crowded, now. The shops were closing, and only once in a while did a lorry, bus, a scooter or a tempo pass by. He could not walk anymore. His thick shoes pinched his toes. His head felt very heavy, and he was afraid he might slump down, dizzy with hunger. The deserted streets and dark houses struck a chill of fear in him. He decided to go home. He had formed a vague idea that he would sleep the night on the thinnai, and get away before dawn. He walked back along the road, quickly.

Walking became more and more difficult. His legs faltered, and his ears buzzed as though wasps had entered his brain. Someone seemed to keep shoving him down from behind. He could not take a single step, no matter the effort. Everything turned dark.

Pushed by the rush of air caused by a speeding lorry carrying road metal, he crumpled down as though he were a mote of dust caught in a wind, and lost consciousness.

When Arumugam came to, he found himself lying curled up like a bundle of cloth, in a rickshaw. Dharmamoorthy, who had woken him up, brought him a tumbler of tea. The man asked him again and again who he was. He got no reply, and began to scold him soundly.

Arumugam felt the bruises on his head, knees and right hand, the red welts and swelling in other parts of his body, and began to cry.

Fear gripped him when he saw Dharmamoorthy, and he tried to run away. Dharmamoorthy stopped him, sat him in the rickshaw and resumed his questions. Arumugam's shirt, shoes and tie had given him the impression that he must belong to a rich family, and he drove the rickshaw around four or five streets with Arumugam in it.

"Who are you? Who are your parents? Where do you come from? What's your caste? Upper caste? Mumble it in my ears if you don't want anyone else to hear. Who're your parents? Which great man's child are you? Who is that great soul whose prayers were answered with your birth? Tell me, Thambi. Tell me, you thooma, son of a harlot! Just tell me where you live, and I'll take you home safely," he insisted.

Clearly, in Dharmamoorthy's opinion, the boy belonged to a rich family, was lost in the city, and a handsome cash award awaited him if he took him back home. Arumugam, however, told him only his name and refused to volunteer any other information.

Dharmamoorthy railed at Arumugam whenever the boy cried, and consoled him in the same breath. "Don't cry, now. You mustn't lose heart, even if you lose your head."

Dharmamoorthy parked the rickshaw in front of the liquor shop and went in to guzzle down arrack, promising to escort Arumugam home. He got drunk swiftly, however, and soon, his attitude underwent a complete change. Old grievances had taken fresh hold, and plans to take Arumugam home were dispatched into oblivion, for he began to spew a spate of foul drunken abuse against womankind.

Dharmamoorthy's native place was a village near Jenji. He had four brothers and three sisters, and had married his eldest sister's daughter, Lakshmi. He had lived with her for four years, until a primary school had been started there, with two teachers.

News of Lakshmi's elopement with teacher George Stephen had reached Dharmamoorthy late in the evening, as he reaped the millet crop. He had left the village that very instant, throwing the sickle away in disgust, and had not stopped until he reached Pondicherry. Twenty years had passed since then, and it had been ten years since he had taken to pulling rickshaws.

"What did she see in him? What made him so special?" he asked in drunken melancholy, as he finished relating this history to Arumugam. "Two baby girls died at birth, and there was a miscarriage. I daren't show my face in the village after she'd run away with somebody. How could I look anyone in the eye? That's why I've been in hiding out, here. These wanton sluts need a new male every day, or their libido never will die down ...!"

Dharmamoorthy took Arumugam to a hospital, and bought him the medicines prescribed. He bought tea, steaming idlis, and fried vadais for the boy. Back at the rickshaw stand, he stationed Arumugam as a watchman for his vehicle.

As the boy began to cry again that night, he questioned him: "Well? What do you want, you son of a vagabond? Thoomappayya, do you want food? Tea? Money, do you want money? Why don't you ask me if you want something, you son of a rag-picker?" He dropped two rupees into Arumugam's pocket.

Dharmamoorthy pedalled through various streets with Arumugam perched in the rickshaw, hawking a raucous "Rickshaw, rickshaw ...!" at everyone he saw.

No one wanted to hire him.

He abused them all roundly and halted at the Newtone Theatre Junction, telling Arumugam to stay near the rickshaw.. He then walked to the western side of the road going to Chekkumedu, where women

vendors sold food, and bought rice and mutton curry for Arumugam
from his usual vendor. Having given the food to Arumugam, he sat
down near her and gobbled down some mutton and rice.

Arumugam felt like throwing up, as he looked at the rice and mutton
curry. His first instinct was to throw it away, but he started to eat a
little as he was very hungry, watching Dharmamoorthy chat with the
woman. The latter was calling other rickshaw drivers and passers-by
to eat food. Other women hawked food too, but her voice was
the loudest.

"You old man, yei rickshakkaaraa, don't you want food? Here's
some hot mutton curry, want some? The kuzhambu's sizzling, too.
Annae, some food? Do sit down here, Brother. Yei, get lost, you.
Look at him, the sissy. He's come around begging for credit before
the day's business has started. One punch with my fist and your balls
will split open. Get lost, you thooma!"

"Shall we go?" Dharmamoorthy asked Arumugam. Arumugam said
nothing. The man lit up a bidi, and pedalled towards the bus stand.

"Rickchaw? Want a rickchaw?" he asked two passers-by, one
after other.

"Where do you want to go?"

"Come, get in. Why're you walking? I'll take you up in the rickchaw."

"Annae, rickchaw?"

"The kind sir may give me any fare he wants. I'm not going to ask
anything more than the standard fare, am I?"

"Look at that thooma walk away."

Dharmamoorthy carried passengers once to the hospital, once to
Thattaan Chavadi, and once to Manikkoondu. Whenever anyone hired
the rickshaw, Arumugam walked behind the vehicle, and rode on the
rickshaw on the way back.

Finally, Dharmamoorthy pulled the rickshaw towards a few huts looking like pigsties, north of Lourde church, east of Thiruvalluvar Bus Stop and on the banks of the drains in the west. Passing seven or eight huts, he halted in front of one, and rang the bell. A man emerged from inside and ran towards the road. Chinnaponnu walked out after him, adjusting her sari. Dharmamoorthy took out a liquor bottle from the pocket in his shorts and gave it to her.

"He's our boy, now," he said. "Let him be. He might be of some help to you."

Chinnapponnu approached the rickshaw and scrutinized Arumugam. Clicking her tongue, she asked him his name and his village.

It was Dharmamoorthy who replied, "His name's Arumugam. He wouldn't say anything more. I've asked him many times, but he won't tell me anything else."

Chinnapponnu went inside, saying nothing, and Dharmamoorthy followed her.

Maybe I could go home, thought Arumugam and stepped down from the rickshaw. The place was dark as ink. He could not figure out what was where, and stood still, perplexed and confused.

Chinnapponnu came out, took Arumugam inside and made him sit down. Gulping down the liquor Dharmamoorthy had given her at one go, she pulled out a piece of meat from the bundle kept in front and crunched it up. She offered some to Arumugam, who refused it. She did not compel him, and after a little while, Dharmamoorthy told him to bed down for the night in the rickshaw. Chinnapponnu offered him a sari to wrap around, and the boy lay down within the vehicle.

In a little while, the light in Chinnapponnu's hut flickered out. People milled about the huts in plenty; the voices of women were predominant. Someone, somewhere was beating a woman for whatever reason.

The woman was screaming. The more she screamed, the more the man thrashed her. He left after a while.

"Yei, you thrashed me, didn't you? Just you wait and see, I'll deal with you in my own way," she shrieked after him obscenely. "You're questioning me, yei? Yes, my mother lifted her skirts, I lift my skirts, and my daughter will too, for anyone who comes along. We're not meant for shame and honour. Are your people going to feed us if we're hungry? Chi, my fluids on your damned kith and clan! The shameless fellow beats me up because he doesn't have money for wretched liquor ... thoomappayya! Ah, just let him get back here, and I'll deal with him well and good. Why does a woman need caste, clan and pedigree? Yei, every idiot, caste high or low, has his Thing only for the hole in between a woman's thighs, doesn't he ...!"

So many fences surround a woman,
The wretch heeds none, she jumps over a dozen,
A coward, disgraced, he lives and dons saffron,
But how can I live a life so brazen?

Arumugam repeated this limerick to himself often, but he could not make head or tail of it. Kizhavar had crooned it many times as he took Arumugam along to the Vavva Canal, the evening before the day he had hung himself, his voice low, as though he was completely oblivious to his surroundings.

Dhanabhagyam had questioned Arumugam repeatedly that night, on their return to Pondicherry.

"What did Thatha say? Did he say something – anything – wrong about me? Didn't he say anything else? True? You aren't lying, are you?" she asked, worried. "Thambi, are you sure he'll come here tomorrow? How did the old man get to know? How can I face him now, with this body of mine? Did Thatha say anything else?"

Arumugam assured her that Kizhavar had hummed only a limerick and nothing else, but she did not believe him. In fact, it was only after Dhanabhagyam had asked whether Kizhavar had said anything, did Arumugam even recollect the little four-lined verse. Why had she trembled, shrinking within herself, he wondered. Why had her eyes shifted so restlessly? Why was she huddled in a corner, so tortured that she couldn't even speak? The questions puzzled him even more than Kizhavar's limerick.

Days after Kizhavar had hung himself, Dhanabhagyam continued to ply Arumugam with questions about the evening before his death. Had Kizhavar said anything? Arumugam had replied in the negative, each time.

She had wept then, sobbing hysterically, screaming abuses at the old man.

"You've cut me off from your heart – you've gone without speaking a word to me! Was yours a heart of stone? You didn't even feel that I was your own daughter ...!"

Arumugam was walking towards home; he wanted to see Dhanabhagyam. He stopped at the entrance to the street, determined to wait until darkness set in, before he went in. Shame crept over him when he considered going into the house and he cowered, overcome. Suddenly, it seemed to him that he was being followed, and that a coarse voice was calling out to him. He looked back. There was no one around, except the usual passers-by. No one seemed to have followed him, or called out to him in particular. Why would a stranger do so, after all? Only those who knew him would, and there were none behind him.

Fifty days had swept by since he last walked the street. He adjusted his hair and shirt in the streetlight and then considered turning tail as he surveyed himself with disdain and disgust. He wiped his face however, and proceeded forward. He could not contain his tears. He walked with head bent lest anybody should see him, like a cow tied down by the neck to a log of wood. Nevertheless, he threw stealthy glances at the houses on both sides and the passers-by.

His body began to tremble as he approached his house; his throat was parched, as though he had run a long while. His legs sagged when he tried to cross the door. He choked back tears, wiped his face with a palm, and stood near the door.

It crashed open suddenly, and two boys ran out, laughing. They went up to the end of the street and ran back into the house, pushing Arumugam aside. A man's coarse voice rasped out from inside. A young woman, walking from the main road, saw Arumugam by the doorstep as she shrugged off her handbag, and asked him hesitantly, "Who are you?"

Arumugam said nothing.

Irritated, she repeated her questions. "Who're you? What do you want?"

Arumugam merely told her his name. The woman drew closer, and peered at him. Her first thoughts, at the sight of him, had run along contemptuous lines. What business had this fellow in a decent locality, with his crumpled and dirty shirt, unwashed, stinking body and unkempt dirty hair? Why must he come up to the door to beg for alms and at night, to boot?

The moment she heard his name, however, her tone changed completely. She began inquiring about him. She switched on the electric light in the verandah and looked intently at Arumugam.

"Is it ... it is you!" she murmured, astonished.

She plied him with questions, and said that it had only been a month since her people had moved in here, and that the woman who had been living there previously had come a week ago, asking if anybody had come in search of her. She had left, sobbing, when they replied that nobody had. She hadn't returned last week. If the woman did come again, the young woman promised that she would tell her about Arumugam, and asked for his address.

"Lata ...!" somebody called for her from inside. She bade Arumugam wait, and stepped in.

Arumugam waited no more. He stepped down into the street, and ran.

He ran until Subbiah Kalyana Mandapam and had almost reached the Jain Factory, when he finally slowed down to a walk. He could not lift his legs and put them forward without great difficulty; he felt as though he were pulling them out from slush. People walking around him looked like figures moving in a cinema screen. Though mercury lamps burnt bright, the road appeared dim to his eyes.

"Amma, Amma," he whimpered, sobs overwhelming him. It was only as he was passing the Jain Factory did he realize that he was not really asleep, but walking. His body shuddered and his throat felt parched. He could drink a whole pot of water if he could get one, he thought.

Suddenly, intense anger overwhelmed him about everything and everyone. He walked like someone stumbling through a forest in pitch darkness, head bent. He wanted to see no one.

Where could Dhanabhagyam have gone, he wondered. Where could she possibly ask for shelter? She had very few relatives. Pandian's mother Malar was her aunt – her nearest relation, and Malar's daughter Mangalakshmi lived in Aanpaakkam. There weren't any others who could be called kith and kin. Besides, she'd never been to Aanpaakkam – Kizhavar had never sent her to any of their relations. She'd never visited any other village in Raman's company either. Was she ... was she dead?

The thought struck him with the agony of a thunderbolt. "Amma ..." he moaned, praying to Mailam Murugan fervently. "Muruga, my mother's everything to me. Bring her back safe, alive and well, and I'll break ten coconuts in your temple. I'll even shave my head on the day of the festival. Please, please lead me to where my mother is ..."

He could not walk anymore. Heaviness enveloped him as though he carried a great load. He closed his eyes, frightened. The bodies of people who had died in Krishnapuram and Pootthurai passed through his mind in a procession – people who had died of fevers, who had hung themselves, who had jumped into wells, knocked down by cars, in childbirth, stillborn children, and so on – so vividly that it seemed all the dead bodies lay right in front of his eyes.

Could my mother have really died? Why, oh *why* did I run away from home, that day? Why did that boy have to be mangled by a car? I should have returned home that night. Why did my mother go away from that house? And she came in search of me after that ...! How she must have wept, *how* she must have searched for me!

"Amma!" Arumugam wailed aloud, oblivious of the fact that he was not alone with his thoughts, but stood in the middle of a busy road. He stomped on the ground in frustration and sniffled woefully, swallowing his tears. He thrashed his arms in the air. He raised his head and looked at the road that was noisy with traffic, as usual ... but did not feel himself a part of the scene at all. No particular image or event imprinted himself onto him. He had a splitting headache, and the entire road vanished from his vision frequently, blurred by his tears.

Why did Thatha have to die, he lamented. How much better would it have been, if he had been alive? What's become of my mother? Why did all this have to happen, he thought, as he stumbled along. Whose fault was it all?

Ah, what a beauty Dhanabhagyam had been! Her eyes had been her most beautiful feature. They had radiated a shimmering aura of pride, as though she were challenging everything and everyone,·capable of bringing them all to her feet. The lure of her eyes would enslave anybody. Pootthurai womenfolk were wont to comment, "She should have been born in a Seth family."

Her voice was clear, resonant and could rival a radio announcer's; when she laughed, she was more entrancing than ever. How could she die? Could death possibly touch someone like her?

Arumugam prayed again to Mailam Murugan, as his thoughts ran along such unpleasant lines. "Muruga, if I survive this, I'll come to your temple and shave my head ..."

Dhanabhagyam had never raised her hand against him, after Raman's death. "All that I do is for your sake, Thambi," she would say. "You are the reason I live."

Will I ever see her again, he brooded. What had happened had happened ... what of it? Weren't there other women like Dhanabhagyam in Krishnapuram and Pootthurai? There had been no end to such happenings, especially after Auroville had been established, and companies had been started in Chetharappati and Mettuppalayam. Hadn't many women eloped? Weren't there many women in Krishnapuram and Pootthurai, who had left their husbands and were now living in sin with other men? Had any man or boy run away from their homes on account of these affairs, Arumugam asked himself. Why, then, did I run away from home?

Arumugam walked past the staff-quarters, the new bus stand and crossed the Thiruvalluvar Bus Stand. If he found Dhanabhagyam, he decided that he would bite her nose and ears more than ever before. But *would* he find her? He wouldn't really mind it, now, even if she was with Jerry Albert. It would be enough if he could just glimpse her face, he thought, and prayed again that he should.

"Mailam Muruga, take me to my mother, wherever she is. I'll drop a handful of coins in the offering-box in your temple, if I'm reunited with her ..."

No flickering light welcomed Arumugam when he returned to Chinnapponnu's hut, except for the kerosene lamps in the twenty or thirty huts nearby. He saw a drunken Dharmamoorthy lying like a bundle of clothes, dishevelled, outside Chinnapponnu's hut, just as he had seen him earlier in the evening. Two dogs hovered around him. Chinnapponnu, at the door, did not notice Arumugam coming and ran ahead, stopping a man who was on the point of going into a hut nearby, to another woman.

"Come over here," she called out to him.

"How much?"

"Thirty."

"Not for twenty?"

"No one here's willing to go for that rate. You want me to do anything you please, you'll have to give as much as you like as tips. The room rent's two rupees ... you've got a condom? That's a rupee extra, if you haven't."

"All right."

"The money."

"I'll hand it over when I'm done."

"None of that. Cash down."

"If you're going to shriek that time's up even before lying down, I won't give you anything."

"You want me to take off my blouse? You'll have to shell out ten more rupees."

"No. If *you* say No, *I'll* say No too. Forget it, I'll find another party."

"Oh, all right. Quick. Fork out the cash."

Arumugam did not enter Chinnapponnu's hut, choosing, instead, to walk towards the road. He heard Chinnapponnu tell him, "Go inside and wait. I'll be there in a minute," after which she dragged the man standing in the dark and went behind the hut. Arumugam tarried awhile near the rickshaw, and then entered the hut briskly.

Inside, the lamp flickered dimly. He raised the wick, brightening it, and sat nearby, looking at the flame.

Sobs choked him. He wished he could pound Dharmamoorthy and Chinnapponnu into a pulpy mess. "Muruga, Muruga," he moaned. It seemed he could not control his tears, no matter how he tried. "Amma ...!" he wailed aloud, agonized.

Chinnapponnu entered at that moment, adjusting her sari and abusing someone. She wiped away the dust that stuck to her hair and forearms. Perspiration drenched her, and she was gasping for breath.

Arumugam wiped his tears surreptitiously lest she notice his state, and fetched her a jug full of water. She drank it in one gulp, noticing only then, and with some embarrassment that her blouse hung open, unbuttoned at two places. She buttoned it up.

"Tea?" cajoled Arumugam.

She said nothing in reply, dead to the world.

He repeated his question. "You'd better have some tea if you're tired. Or shall I get you something else? Curry? Arrack? Call it a day. Rest now, and get some sleep."

Chinnapponnu looked at Arumugam a long time. She brought the lamp to his face, and stared at him intently. She started to say something, but could not proceed beyond a broken "Arumugam." She began to cry.

This was not the person who had fought with a party, a while ago. Now, she sat like a bed-ridden, sick child.

Arumugam clasped her hands. "Why're you crying?"

Chinnapponnu said nothing, but bent her head. Sorrow gripped him as he took in her pitiable condition. Why not bite her nose and ears just as I bit Dhanabhagyam's, he wondered.

Out loud, he said, "I don't like it here. I'd like to return to Pootthurai. All my relations are there, after all. I'll leave in the morning."

Abruptly, Chinnapponnu pulled Arumugam into an embrace. He wriggled out of her hold with some difficulty.

"Who'll call *me* a relative? Who'll own this prostitute as kin? Whom do I have to feed me as I go about from one place to another? I'm cursed. I've got to put up with such words, just for a cup of rice-water. You're not to leave me as long as I'm alive. Think of me as your mother. Bury me when I die, and then go where you will."

Ah, the whims of a woman's heart ...! Her life crumbles into dust because she trusts blindly, and then adores him whom she trusts. That's the real cause of her ruin, I tell you. You desire a yacht, but your fortune leads you to a vessel in a well! If you stuck your hand into a hole, be it a rat or a snake, you can't escape. Who bears the most burdens — a vagabond without a trade, or the one who feeds others for no gain? Ah, what could your mother do, poor woman ...? She trusted him. All that is white is milk; all that is dark is a cloud, she thought, and she was taken in completely. Our lives are nothing but long, painful experiences in a wilderness, until our thumbs and toes are tied together for our last journey. Not all that ripens is a fruit, and all that unfurls isn't a flower, either ..."

Vasantha talked on and on while Arumugam sat dumb, as though her speech had nothing to do with him. Every noon saw her begin such a discourse, her manner radiating utter frankness. She would blurt out every thought that occurred to her and at the end of it all, her eyes would glisten with a sheen of tears. Arumugam generally said nothing, choosing, instead, to gaze keenly at every part of her body.

Vasantha usually whisked Arumugam away to the dining shed as soon as the whistle blew, for noon meal. She began talking as soon as their meal was done, beginning with Dhanabhagyam and then proceeding in a gradual fashion to her own family, the honour of Nayudu women and the wrongdoing prevalent in the companies. Nevertheless, all her meandering grievances seemed to be centered on one principal complaint: her brothers had not taken care of her.

Working in a company was a dishonour to the whole Nayudu clan in her opinion, and in the six days that had passed since Arumugam joined the company, Vasantha's conversation had revolved almost exclusively around these topics.

Vasantha had first caught sight of Arumugam last Sunday morning, as he was taking up a passenger to the Korimedu Jipmer Hospital. A passenger had stepped down that moment, and Arumugam was hawking "Rickshaw, rickshaw!" when Vasantha had spotted him, and at once, pulled him swiftly into the shade of a peepal tree nearby.

"Have you seen Dhanabhagyam? Where's she? I didn't even recognize you, at first. How could anyone change so much?"

Not all her questions could get a word out of him in reply. Arumugam was regretting ever having come across Vasantha. He kept his head lowered from the beginning; not once did he raise it to look at her face. Sobs rose in his throat. Had Vasantha not been present, he would have wept aloud.

Dhanabhagyam had gone in search of Arumugam the instant he had fled from home, hunting in every place she could think of. That night, she came down with a fever that raged all week. She lay in a corner, insensible, and did not rise even to cook her food. Her search led her to Krishnapuram, Pootthurai and even Aanpaakkam, and passers-by on the streets labeled her insane as they glimpsed her roaming the streets, with just one name on her lips.

She stumbled upon Jerry Albert when she arrived at Auroville, searching for a clue about Arumugam's whereabouts. He tried to console her; she abused him using the filthiest words imaginable. A crowd gathered swiftly, drawn by her shrieks and soon, everything was out in the open.

Auroville quivered at Dhanabhagyam's screams as she slapped herself mercilessly on her head, stomach and thighs. She delivered a few well-placed knocks on Albert with a thick stick when he tried to stop her; his left shoulder ball and socket joint slipped. She tried to bar those who gathered to rush him to the hospital, but they pushed her aside and carried Albert away.

Anger at not having punished Albert enough tormented her, coupled with the agony of losing Arumugam. The tirade went on and on, as she continued to shower abuses on Auroville and Jerry Albert.

"Dei, do you add salt to your food at all?" she shrieked. "You brute, may your family be laid to waste – may your home turn into a burial ground – your clan ground into the earth! There shan't be a name to keep it alive – your people will be wiped out without a trace and disappear into dust. Just as I've lost my son, just as I stand here, heart-broken – so shall you stand in the streets too, miserable and wretched! I've been reduced to standing alone, a temple chariot abandoned in a street corner after the festival because of you. Did *I* ask you ...? God knows where my son is and what he's suffering! You chandaala, I warned you so many times – but did you listen? My son's gone – who'll accept me as rice, or discard me as chaff? I've sat under a palm tree for shade, and I'm being accused of drinking toddy!

The barber knows where one started life, and the washerman knows how one leads it – ah, god, how true that is! I've become the laughing stock of the village, the whole world mocks me. I've chosen thorns, when others wear shoes ..."

"No one will mourn my death," she grieved. "No kith and kin will carry me to the burial ground. Just you wait: my son has disappeared, and so will these buildings, crumbling into a heap of dust. Wait and watch, you scoundrel. You'll turn into a rubbish heap. Your home will be ruined. God above, you're my witness! Punish those who've brought me to this! Yei Thambi, Arumugam, Arumugam ...!"

Dhanabhagyam wailed aloud, rolling about the earth unabashedly. She flung handfuls of mud in the air. She slapped herself. She heaped dirt on her own head, insane with grief. A large crowd gathered around her, drinking in her performance. She rolled on the ground like one demented, her sari slipping and trailing on the ground, blouse buttons ripped off and hair dishevelled. A white man clicked photographs of her from several angles.

"Arumugam, Arumugam ...!" Dhanabhagyam fled, flinging dust all around her, screaming in anguish.

None stopped her.

The Auroville administration repatriated Jerry Albert as soon as he was discharged from the hospital. It also dismissed those he had recruited, that year. Vasantha, looking for a job then, had been one of those recruited by him, recommended by Dhanabhagyam who had introduced her to Jerry Albert as, "My master's daughter."

In consequence, Vasantha lost her job when Jerry Albert left. She remained at home for a month; after which time, taking a friend's suggestion, she applied for a job in a cardboard manufacturing company at Mettuppalayam.

Vasantha related one episode after another to Arumugam, her eyes filling with tears on occasion. She inquired about him some more, and insisted that he take up a job at Mettuppalayam. Dhanabhagyam's words, when she had recommended Vasantha to Jerry Albert, came to her mind.

"She's our master's daughter," Dhanabhagyam had announced. "You must give her a decent job. And the salary must be First Class too."

She could not contain her tears as she mentioned this to Arumugam. Then, she turned to Dharmamoorthy.

"Look after him well," she spoke in a warning tone, referring to Arumugam. "Don't let him get a bad name; people mustn't whisper this and that about him."

She pressed a ten rupee note into Arumugam's hand, instructed him to, "be here, tomorrow, at eight in the morning," and then ran and boarded the bus.

Dharmamoorthy did not break his silence towards Arumugam all day. He clanged the bell of the rickshaw unnecessarily and went in twice to the arrack shop, as against his usual routine. He pedalled his rickshaw himself when passengers hired him. He spoke not a word to Arumugam until they reached Chinnapponnu's home at ten that night. As they stepped in, however, he was the first to tell Chinnapponnu about Vasantha and her conversation.

Arumugam saw Chinnapponnu in the dim light of the flickering lamp as she lay exhausted, cigarette stubs littering the floor around her. She could not talk, but gesticulated.

"What's the matter?" Arumugam asked, as he lifted her and sat her against the wall. An overpowering fragrance of flowers arose from her; crushed flowers stuck all over her body. She brushed away the faded flowers from her hair and limbs. Her unbuttoned blouse exposed sagging breasts, and her petticoat hung unknotted. Arumugam covered her with the sari she had thrown aside lest it get rumpled, and brought her water.

No longer was Chinnapponnu the woman who could manage any number of Parties. She could barely accommodate two or three in a day and often sat still, clutching her underbelly. Today, somehow, she had managed to get hold of five or six boys. They had finished one after another in quick succession and left speedily, afraid of being caught in the act.

Dharmamoorthy smoked his bidi, merely intent on flicking away ash that fell. "I couldn't find any party today," he mumbled as Chinnapponnu began to breathe freely, and placed the liquor bottle and mutton curry he had purchased, before her. She drank the liquor in one gulp and began to chew a piece of mutton slowly, not bothering to adjust the sari slipping from her shoulders.

Arumugam walked out and sat in the rickshaw. Darkness had enveloped all but a few huts in that area. Mini-kerosene lamps flickered in one or two; there were kerosene lanterns in others. Two men walked by, their loud conversation liberally sprinkled with obscene language. The noisy bargain between a man and woman in a hut nearby was fast deteriorating into a quarrel; the woman began screaming abuses at him.

"Get lost, you shameless thooma, you! Even a bitch won't show its genitals to you."

Chinnapponnu herself was apt to be pleasant only until she got some cash into her hands. She would act coy until then, and flaunt her curves. She would pull away the edge of her sari, pretending to fan herself because of the heat, flashing tantalizing glimpses of her breasts. Once she got hold of the money, however, god knows how, but she turned into a different person altogether. She spat fire; sometimes, she simply ran away from her customers midway, punching and shoving those who tried to drag her back. She threatened them with the Police, vowing that she would complain of rape.

It might be a quarrel between Chinnapponnu and Dharmamoorthy, between other women and Dharmamoorthy, or even between one woman and another, but if Dharmamoorthy were the reason, he would slink away silently if he was sober.

If he was drunk on arrack, however, he would tell Arumugam, "Ah, see how they sparkle like fireworks during Dipaavali," he would mutter. "They throw their words about like corn sizzling in a pan, don't they? No fellow can get the better of them."

Chinnapponnu asked Arumugam, sitting in the rickshaw, to sit with her. "Have you had your food?"

She inquired about Vasantha, the job he was going to start on at Mettuppalayam, and wanted to find out if he were willing to work there. Arumugam did not reply.

"You may take up this job if you want, but you *must* stay with me," she insisted. "Or you can go if your mother comes for you. I won't stand in your way if she does. Nobody's been around to care for you in the past four years ... why this sudden burst of affection, now?"

Arumugam rose early the next morning, went to the public tap at the Cuddalore road corner and had a bath. He washed his clothes and fetched tea for Chinnapponnu and Dharmamoorthy. Chinnapponnu handed him a ten-rupee note. "You're to return here this evening, whatever happens."

Arumugam bade her goodbye and left, ignoring Dharmamoorthy. The latter, who was smoking a bidi, threw him a look of great disdain as Arumugam walked down the road.

Vasantha was waiting for Arumugam at the Jipmer Hospital gate. As soon as he arrived, both of them proceeded towards Mettuppalayam swiftly.

"I was afraid you mightn't come," confided Vasantha as they strode along a path of rich, red earth. A canal cut across it; Vasantha informed him that it was the Pootthurai Canal.

They entered the Mettuppalayam Industrial Estate, and Arumugam was struck dumb as he looked at one big building after another. It was a strange new world to him. Men, women and boys walked into the buildings in a great hurry. They crossed many more buildings and lanes, to finally reach Ram Industries.

"Stay here, I'll come back in a minute," Vasantha told Arumugam and went inside.

Nervousness and amazement alternated in Arumugam's mind. He felt confused, having lost all sense of direction, coming through the maze of buildings in the Estate as he did. He tried to calculate the direction in which Korimedu might lie.

The manager arrived at the gates a few minutes after Vasantha came back. He looked at Arumugam intently, as though examining a goat brought to the fair for sale. Vasantha placed a hand on Arumugam's shoulder and smiled at the manager, and intervened when the manager tried to say something.

"Sir, please say yes. I know there's no appeal, if *you* agree. I'll take complete responsibility for him – he's our boy. He'll be correct in everything. His name's Arumugam, sir. Sir, there's no one who can overrule you, is there?" She did not give the manager a chance to say anything.

When the manager began to smile a little, she hastened to clinch the issue. "You agree? Sir, don't you?" and took Arumugam to a cubicle inside.

She signed against her name in the notebook that lay on the table. She positioned the notebook in front of the manager who had followed them inside, and now stood behind them. "Arumugam, sir," she said.

The manager looked at her intently, as though he wished to enter the very core of her being through her eyes. Then, he wrote a name where Vasantha indicated – Arumugam.

Vasantha washed and powdered her face. She asked Arumugam to powder his face too, but he refused with a firm No, preferring to watch Lakshmi, Thaiyalnayaki, Tamilarasi, Porkodi, Kumar, Velan and Selvam chat under the shade of a eucalyptus tree near the building, after lunch. He stared at them as though seeing them for the first time. The shrill whistle sounded.

Their meal at an end, the boys worked with renewed energy. They worked in two teams; one team loaded the dried cardboards on a pushcart and unloaded them at the godown, while the other team brought the cardboards moulded by the machine to the road, and spread them out to dry. The latter had to be more careful. The cardboards, slimy as cow dung, stuck to one another if they were even slightly careless. The cardboards had to be discarded when this happened, or if they were torn in the attempt to detach them. The manager usually turned into a brute if the word Damage was uttered, and raised hell.

The boys worked tirelessly, yet Vasantha kept prodding them, "Quick, quick!" Occasionally, the manager came out and did a routine check.

There were four or five factories specializing in cardboard production, aside from Ram Industries. A large factory, producing face powder was situated to the south of these, with more than a thousand workers. Adjacent to this were factories manufacturing manure bags, paper, needles, pharmaceuticals, and chemicals. On the western side was a factory that made glass; it was the biggest in Mettuppalayam and was housed in a big building. Smoke rose from its chimney in such copious amounts that the whole sky was smeared with an acrid gray.

Boys worked briskly in all companies; the cardboard making factories had the largest concentration of youngsters. Cardboards had been spread out to dry in the open spaces outside the buildings, and from a distance, it looked as though wet sacks had been rolled out to air. The boys had to check that not a single cardboard was split, clipped, or warped during the process of spreading out cardboards to dry, or collecting them and stacking them when they were dry. Vasantha was always with the boys to ensure this, supervising their work.

Were there to be any damage, the pockmark-faced manager would fly into a rage and abuse them, his face livid. "This is your father's property, is it? What do you care? You'll walk away as soon as the whistle blows. I'm the one who'll have to face the music!"

And he would go on and on, his body beginning to shudder as his anger grew. The boys generally ceased talking when he came out, not even daring to look at each other. The manager was very keen on not having a single cardboard damaged. He would inspect the pieces spread out and the dried ones being loaded every time he came out. Each of the cardboards ought to be completely dry and stiff. If anyone were to load them before they were completely dry, he would rage at them.

"Why have you fellows come to work? Do you think you can walk away with a sheaf of notes, come Saturday? Who's forcing you to come here? Leave if you can't work. I can get any number of boys to do the job."

Vasantha's face was a sight to see, when the manager screamed at them. She shuddered and perspired like someone caught stealing and was tongue-tied, gathering the courage to speak only a long time after the manager went back.

"I've warned you so many times," she would implore the boys, half-crying. "Do we have to be careful only after someone tells us? You're not working at this the first time, are you?"

Arumugam was dear to her, and she did not work him too much. Often, she sent him to drink water, or gave him a break to visit the toilet. He understood why she was doing this only one or two days later, when he saw other boys pleading with her.

"Akka, I need to go to the toilet."

"I want a drink of water."

Vasantha would laugh at them. "How many times in a day do you people have to visit the toilet?"

Sometimes they went with her permission; at others, without. Arumugam, however, never did leave his work unfinished, even when Vasantha asked him to rest. He never wasted time like the others either, neglecting work and gaping at the ice, buttermilk and fig vendors.

"What should I do next?" he asked, always. Nor did he tell tales to Vasantha or the manager that the others are not doing their work properly. The manager himself had noticed Arumugam's work, and had remarked once that he was a good boy.

"He's educated, sir. He studied in an English School," Vasantha informed the manager, and from this time on, even if the manager did scold him, his words were mild. Once in a while, he would even pat him on the back and murmur, Good.

When Vasantha announced, "The whistle's going to blow now," the carts rattled faster and faster, out of sheer happiness in going home. At other times, they would stand around, complaining.

"Akka, look at Lakshmi, she's doing nothing!"

"Am I bound to this place or something, to work without rest?"

Now, cart after cart sped towards the godown. Everyone was keen on going home before the workers from other factories did so, and they hastened to finish the work.

The whistle blew.

A few minutes passed before anyone could make out anything amidst the din of the factory. The moment the whistle blew, buildings began to empty. It was Saturday: payday for the workers. Labourers received their wages and went out, following on the heels of the others. Crowds of men, women and boys emerged from buildings, rushing to go home, matching a festival procession. The crowd was moving forward in mixed patterns: in groups, alone, or one after the other.

Vasantha gave Arumugam one hundred and fifty rupees, his wages for the first week.

"Why are you giving this to me? Keep it yourself," he said.

"What am I to do with this? You could give it to that Chinnapponnu, if you'd like to," Vasantha suggested.

Arumugam bought some tiffin for Vasantha and Porkodi from Nehru Street while Vasantha bought flowers, fruits and snacks for Chinnapponnu, and gave them to Arumugam. He saw Vasantha and Porkodi off in the bus and walked towards Chinnapponnu's hut.

He gave the flowers, fruits and snacks to Chinnapponnu, who gazed at them as though seeing such things for the first time.

"Must you waste whatever you've earned? Haven't I seen such things before?" she chided him. "Who are you to buy such things for me?" She could not control her tears even as she admonished him — she did not know if they were tears of joy or sorrow.

She must have had a bath, combed her hair and made herself ready just a little while ago; there were fresh flowers in her hair, and her powdered face was unmarred. The folds of her sari were pristine and unruffled, too. Barring what little had been spent on snacks in Nehru Street, Arumugam gave all that remained of his wages to Chinnapponnu, not even counting the money. Chinnapponnu would normally stuff any money she received underneath her blouse or tuck into her waist, but this, she deposited between the folds of a sari inside her steel trunk.

She made Arumugam sit beside her and gazed at him fondly, raising the wick and brightening the lamp. Arumugam tried to get up and leave, but she pressed him down.

"Where are you going? Just sit by me, won't you?" she pleaded, dragging him beside her as he tried to move away. She did not know why, but tears streamed down her cheeks. "I'm just a lowly prostitute. Ah, why couldn't I have had someone like this ...?"

She took Arumugam's hands and slapped her face with them. She hugged him twice or thrice, pressing fond kisses on him. She wanted to talk to him a great deal, but could not say anything ... a barrage of sobs prevented her.

Dharmamoorthy came in and placed a liquor bottle and mutton curry in front of Chinnapponnu. She pushed them back towards him.

"You trying to be snooty, di?" sneered Dharmamoorthy. He pushed them towards her again; she pushed them back sharply towards him.

"What can I do if no one came today?" Dharmamoorthy barked at her. "Get out into the street, you street-grazer!"

She spat on his face, frenzied. "Get out yourself, da. I curse and abuse you right and left and you still haunt this place! Haven't you any self-respect? How dare you talk to me like that? Yei, am I your wife? Who're you to me, and who am I to you, da? Who're you to come in here and lay down rules? Look at this fellow's face, just like a vulgar konkaani ... get lost, da!"

Dharmamoorthy smoked a bidi nonchalantly, her foul words falling off him like rain on a buffalo.

Chinnapponnu turned to Arumugam. "Arumugam, go outside and stand guard. Thrash any cur that walks in with your chappals, and chase him away. Their mothers also have what they want. Tell them to get It there."

I t had been raining day and night, for the past two months.

When is it going to stop? was the general, sickened refrain. People were drenched during the day; at night, they could not sleep.

Booth, booth, mourned a ceaseless breeze, ululating without a pause. The sea, nearby, meant that the wind and rain lashed out with increased ferocity. Even if people could put up with the cold and rain, mosquitoes effectively kept sleep away. Insects bred happily in ponds and puddles. An open drain near the huts teemed with mosquitoes even in summer and now, there was not a moment when the huts did not reverberate with their loud buzzing.

Chinnapponnu did not sleep a wink day or night ever since the rains began, instead, swatting mosquitoes away with the edge of her sari. Sometimes she sat still, waiting for the hovering mosquitoes to settle down and bite her; then she slapped at them sharply.

"Only a speck in size," she cursed. "But they wrench your life out." Then she began to swat at them again.

The past two months had seen Chinnapponnu's income dwindle a good deal. Customers were few and far in between on account of the rain and cold. One or two men arrived between bouts of rain; a knockdown, drag-out competition generally commenced to get their custom. Each woman tried her best to drag a man into her hut, and violent quarrels erupted practically every day. The normal rate would be quoted first, and then one or two women would plunge in, lowering the rate by five or ten rupees. The party would try to beat them down further. "I'll come in if you're willing. Otherwise, I'll leave."

One of the women would agree and drag him to her hut while the others joined force, shrieking abuses at her. "I'll split your Thing open like a prised mango, di. I'll tear your sagging breasts apart. Chi, get lost! They'll ask your sisters free, and you'll offer them too, shameless wretch. Why're you starting a new practice? Why do you want to sell your honour and make a living? What's so special about you? Do you have two of them? Di, what did you say? Yes, I'm a low-caste paracchi. Do the upper caste women have It cast in gold? Get lost, you! Wait till we get hold of you, we'll tear up your Thing into pieces. Ah, look at her go, that two-penny whore. Look at how she stands – like a bride waiting for her groom ...!"

As far as make-up was concerned, Chinnapponnu lacked nothing either. She caked her face with powder and strung flowers in her hair as usual, but none of it suited her, these days. Whoremongers weren't too choosy when they were in large numbers, competing for women; they didn't flash torchlights in the faces of women, one after another, to gauge their looks. But now, they scrutinized the women a lot. They tried to scout for fresh girls, young and fair.

"These are all old – there's nothing new. When will I see a new item here? ... No, I don't like this. That's no good either. Nothing's good enough."

They pursed their lips; they found as many faults as they could, to lower the rate. Having no other option open to her, Chinnapponnu went to Chekkumedu where there were more customers, as were prostitutes. There, however, one had to stand about in slush and Chinnapponnu fell ill, drenched in the rain. Many other women suffered her fate, went down with fevers, and had to go to hospital.

Dharmamoorthy very seldom plied the rickshaw when it poured; only if it was a clear day, did he do so. His legs led him to the liquor shop as soon as he got some money and he spent it on drink, after which he came to Chinnapponnu without fail, demanding money for more liquor. The cold had reduced the effects of drink on him, he said, and he shivered and shook.

"Get lost!" Chinnapponnu would screech. "Look at him come, that excuse for a man. The cur can't even get me a tumbler of tea, but he's asking for money. Yei, your mother's probably lain for a man somewhere and he would have thrown some money on her breasts. Scrounge that for your drink. Get lost, you son of a whore ...!" She would land him blow after blow, abusing him roundly. Not a day passed without the two of them in some heated quarrel or the other.

He in turn, would retaliate, yelling at her foully. "It's true enough when they say: The man who tills – his eyes are on the sun, and the whore who rolls out the mat – her eyes are on the money. You, the worst slut, with your foul mouth – bedding a different man every day! Your fate's going to be like The shameless wretch, who lay dead and still, none to cremate her, none to foot the bill." Dharmamoorthy raged on and on. "A man looks at the breasts, while the woman has her eye on his purse ... ah, how true that saying is. Let the rains stop, woman. I'll show you what I'll do to you. You may bare yourself, but who's going to come up and fling a coin on your breasts? Yei, who?"

The factory was worse than home. The cardboards would not dry easily because of the rains; they stuck to the floor, and about one in ten was invariably wasted. Even if they did lay out the cardboards to dry on the uppermost gradient of tarred roads they could find, they remained stubbornly stuck to the floor when the workers tried to remove them. And if there happened to be a cloudburst, a good many of the cardboards simply dissolved into nothing, on the roads.

The manager raged at them as though his very life had been lost, when this happened. "Has it gone? All of it? Whose property do you think it is, da ...? Who'll answer for this with hands folded? Not a single fellow will be given wages. There's no place here for people who say, It's someone else's property, let it go to the dogs!"

The rainy season meant that workers were employed for only two or three days in a week; even this would not be uninterrupted. No work could be done if it poured continuously and the workers had to go home, drenched. Boys who endured more than one such soaking in a single day fell ill, and had to stay either at home or in the hospital. Eventually, when the sky did clear for a day, there was a shortage of labour in the cardboard factories and they were operational only for a small part of the working hours.

Come rain, managers of all cardboard companies spent numerous sleepless nights. They considered quitting; they thought it "the worst job in the whole world." It was at times like this that they went to extremes, abusing the workers; if the latter happened to be boys, they were beaten up. They could not afford to close the factory, nor could they discharge the regular employees. Where could they dry the cardboards? How could the company afford to pay wages when no work was done for two months? The company could do without the weekly paid staff, but it could not do without the daily wage boys.

The workers often waited under the awning until the skies cleared, but sometimes, there were sudden downpours that drenched them, and they fell ill if this happened too often. They did squeeze their clothes from time to time, but how long could they work with wet clothes on? It was not so much the rain or the wind as the wet clothes, that made them shiver with cold beyond endurance. Sometimes, the damp wind was enough to soak their clothes; it was cold so often that they could not stand straight. Their legs trembled, and they shivered as though with fever.

Arumugam alone tried his best to withstand the rain and cold among all the other boys, but even he could not do it for long. Amidst the vagaries of the weather, Vasantha's supervision, the manager's visit and adjusting with other boys, the day was stressful enough, and to add to it, he did not rest well at night either. He could not stretch himself out for a good night's sleep, since, despite everything, the roof of Chinnapponnu's hut was riddled with holes leaking in the rain. The hut was barely big enough for just two to lie down and yet it leaked in twenty different spots; they had to place tumblers, plates and bowls in strategic positions, to hold the water dripping from leaks. Gunny bags were spread out in the room to sit down. Those bags soon became damp in turn, and Arumugam often spent whole nights sitting up. He had to leave for the factory in the morning, regardless of rain, sleet or storm.

Arumugam rubbed the sleep from his eyes at dawn, and rushed at once to the hospital to see Chinnapponnu, who had been taken ill and had been in the hospital for the past fifteen days. She grew furious – he could not understand why – when he gave her the ten rupees he had received from Vasantha the day before. He said nothing about

Dharmamoorthy when asked, and so she abused Dharmamoorthy the most.

Bidding goodbye to her, Arumugam left for Mettuppalayam swiftly. It was ten days since the rains had stopped, and work had resumed in full swing in the factory. He slept well these nights, exhausted after work, despite lying in the rickshaw itself, and the raging mosquitoes.

Arumugam was late when he reached the factory. The manager said nothing. Arumugam was surprised, but wasted no more time in starting work. He began pulling the cart, asking another boy to push it from behind. They brought coated cardboards and spread them out to dry. Vasantha was separating cardboards that were stuck, adjusting those spread on the ground. All were of different sizes: some three into five feet, others four into three, and still others, five into five. Some were thin, while others were thick.

The lunch hour whistle had not blown yet, while dried cardboards were yet to be collected and carried to the godown. If the sun was scorching hot, the cardboards would dry in an hour. "Quick, quick," the workers goaded each other, looking forward to lunch and the one-hour break.

Glancing at the manager who had come out to see how work was progressing, a few boys whispered amongst themselves.

"Yei look, Rotten Face's arrived."

"Why's his face like a pitted grinding stone?"

"Forget that, da ... but why does Rotten Face fly into such rages?"

"If this fellow continues here, I swear I'll leave for some other company."

"Oh? Which one?"

"Come on, is there a shortage of companies around here? A new one sprouts practically every day. Were there as many companies when

I first joined work, as there are now? So many have come up even in Chetharappattu."

"I'd smash that rotten face if I were a grown up."

"Yei, Rotten Face!"

The whistle blew and workers dispersed swiftly, each hastening to join his or her relative or acquaintance of the same caste, or girls of his liking. Some loitered about aimlessly. Most hovered in the vicinity of the powder making factories, for it was here that a large number of girls worked. Some girls wandered from one company to another, exchanging lunch boxes either directly, through young boys, or friends who could keep a secret. Groups of people chatted over lunch, under each eucalyptus tree. Somebody from a group would call over the ice or fig vendor, grinning when the vendor approached, "I didn't call you, he did," pointing out to someone else.

Lunch at an end, a few girls asked their friends to pick lice from their hair. "God knows where this army of lice comes from ..."

Vasantha placed some of her curry and rice on the lid of her lunch box, and offered it to Arumugam. He declined, but she insisted on his taking it. It was she who had given him lunch for the past nine months, ever since he joined the company. She ate her lunch only on some days and even then, she was a poor eater. Arumugam ate the whole lot mostly, for he almost never had any breakfast at all. Sometimes, if he had time, he would stuff three or four idlis into his mouth at Korimedu, and rush to the factory.

After lunch, Vasantha asked Porkodi to pick her lice-infested hair. Porkodi glanced at Arumugam often as she did so, and smiled. Arumugam smiled back at her.

In a little while, Vasantha asked her to stop. "Enough, I've got a crick in my neck." She ruffled her hair twice or thrice and massaged her neck, then took out a comb from her handbag and ran it through her hair. Porkodi combed her hair too, and both of them washed and powdered their faces, all the while looking at the hand-mirror that they pulled out of their bag. Arumugam watched them intently. Then, gathering his courage, he asked Vasantha something he had wanted to for a long time.

"Why don't you ever smile?"

She stared at him for a long moment.

"What's to do if I don't?" she spoke, finally, in a broken voice. "Did god really intend me to smile at all? What good will it be if I do smile? What's there for me to smile?" She began to cry, then, and Arumugam felt sorrow grip him. He could not bear to look at her.

He apologized, regretting that he had ever asked her anything. "I'm sorry. I didn't know it would affect you so much."

That aggravated her misery, and she sobbed as though someone dear to her had died.

"Akka, don't cry. Just ... forget everything, sister," Porkodi began to sob herself, even as she tried to console Vasantha.

Arumugam was overwhelmed. Vasantha ought not have come to work in the company, he thought. He could not understand why she had; her father was a virtual chieftain of the Nayudus in Krishnapuram, and held a position of great respect. No one dared question him, even if he did commit a grievous sin: "How could you do such-and-such a thing?" or "Is it right that you said this?"

Arumugam had seen Vasantha go to school or fetch water, her thick tresses neatly braided, and had admired her good looks as had much of Krishnapuram. She was a gentle, well-behaved girl. Once she came of age, however, she was seldom seen outside her home. Arumugam's family considered her household their masters; he himself had visited it often, with Dhanabhagyam and Raman. He had spoken to Vasantha before this, but he had never so much as touched her. It was Vasantha's mother, he had been told, who had given them ten rupees and a bottle of castor oil at Arumugam's birth, expressing happiness that "Our parayan has a son."

Today's Vasantha was not the Vasantha he had seen then. She has lost her figure, and her complexion lacks the old brilliance. Her eyes are sunk like an old woman's, and when she speaks, her voice sounds like that of an asthma patient.

Arumugam felt a great deal of pity for her. Were it Krishnapuram now, for instance, he would not have been able even to talk to her. The whole of the Vaanur Taluka was a fiefdom of the Nayudu clan, and each Nayudu house often had four or five families from the cheri, bonded to it in labour. Raman had been a bonded parayan himself, working in Vasantha's house from his youth, and Raman's father had been the same.

When Auroville's development and reputation grew, creating employment for the people of surrounding villages, the colony people had gradually ceased to work for the Nayudu families, preferring to work in Auroville, instead. When the Nayudus had tried to prevent them, some of them had railed at them, standing in the streets, dead-drunk, while others had tried to reason with them: "We've worked for you so long, why won't you release us from bondage and let us move on to better jobs in Auroville?"

When Raman too opted for a job in Auroville, Vasantha's father had not tried to stop him, or ask for a refund of the money he had given, upon Raman's bondage. "Let him go if that's what he wants," he had said, dismissively. "He'll return to us when his stomach's churning with hunger."

Raman and Dhanabhagyam had visited his master's house often,
when the former had been a bonded labourer, carrying Arumugam
along on for a special meal on festivals. If it were the harvest festival,
Pongal, husband and wife would bow respectfully, murmuring
"Master, give us some Pongal kaasu," and they would also petition,
" ... for the little parayan too, Saami," and receive Pongal money for
Arumugam as well.

As soon as the forenoon whistle blew, workers entered the buildings
promptly. Arumugam stood on the cart, receiving cardboards from
other boys and stacking them. "Quick, quick," he goaded them often.
"Come on, throw them up quickly. Don't dawdle about like an old
man, already!"

Vasantha hastened them too, and went inside to see whether
cardboards that had to be dried were ready. The manager came out
and tested the cardboards loaded on the cart, pinching and patting
them fondly. Pursing his lips, he looked at Vasantha, whose face was
bent, her attention on the cardboards. The manager went back to his
room swiftly.

The boys worked feverishly, loading the cardboards to be dried on
the cart, and carrying them to the godown to be unloaded. As they
worked, they chatted.

Sasirekha turned to Velan. "Tomorrow's Sunday, no? Will you be
going to the cinema?"

"Of course," Velan replied promptly. "Is there anything more
important than that?" and he turned to Arumugam, asking whether
he would come too.

"No," replied Arumugam, in a quiet tone.

Velan turned to Sasirekha. "Which actor's film do you like? MGR
or Sivaji?"

"I love Sivaji films!" laughed Sasirekha.

Velan countered this with, "Chee, there's a lot of crying in them. I like films with fights!"

Gopal stopped his work, chiming in with, "I like fight pictures too," and Vasantha, returning from the rear after having inspected lorries in which cardboards were being loaded, scolded them soundly.

"Why're you people wasting your time, chit-chatting? Don't stop working."

The boys cursed her within the secret confines of their mind, but acquiesced aloud, with a respectful, "All right, Akka. Anything you say, Akka."

Three batches of cardboards had been dried, and four cartloads had been transported to the godown after the lunch recess. The sky was absolutely clear, and they had to work at a brisk pace. The workers in the machine department cursed the sun, and prayed for a downpour.

"May all the cardboards get soaked, and may Rotten Face get it in the neck."

The whistle ceased. It was as though thunder had stilled abruptly, yielding place to dead silence. It was Saturday – payday for workers engaged on a weekly basis. The boys went ahead of the girls to receive wages, and found, unexpectedly, that Porkodi's and Arumugam's wages had gone up by fifty rupees.

"Why haven't we got a raise?" fumed Velan, and the others joined forces, raging at the injustice. "Were we idle? How is it that you've raised the wages for just those two? We'll leave for another company from tomorrow. You'd better get a raise for us too, next week, or else ..." They walked away swiftly, raging at Vasantha as they went, eager to catch up with those of their own caste and living on the same streets.

How did this happen, wondered Vasantha as she went in to receive her own wages, and was as surprised as any of them – her pay had been raised by a hundred rupees, too.

Arumugam and Porkodi were standing outside the exit. The watchman was closing the doors and windows.

"How long do we have to wait?" Arumugam asked Porkodi. "Get Vasantha. Everyone else's left."

He himself tried to push the main door to go in and see why Vasantha had not appeared yet, but though he applied force, it didn't budge. He went round the corner of the building, and tried to peer through the office room window. The window, however, was higher than eye level. He jumped, then, and tried to see whether Vasantha was still there, calling out, "Vasantha! Vasantha!" five or six times.

Vasantha opened the glass door of the window. "Wait a moment, I'll be there soon," she promised.

Arumugam jumped up again, trying to see what she was doing, but he slipped and fell down. As he rose and brushed the dust off himself, he heard Vasantha's voice, raised against someone.

He walked back swiftly to the main road, whereupon Porkodi asked him about Vasantha. He gave her no reply, but began walking fast towards Korimedu.

Porkodi overtook him swiftly, and barred his way. "Why're you running away? Stop running away from everything. It's this running that's turned you this way."

She grabbed his hands and made him sit down on the ground, easing herself as close to him as she could. When he tried to get up, she clutched him tight. Her body felt cool to the touch; Arumugam felt hot all over. He wriggled out of her hold and looked to the west. The sky was darkening over the buildings in Mettuppalayam.

They saw Vasantha coming at a little distance, in a pitiable state. When she joined them, Arumugam began to walk ahead without a word.

He felt like screaming at her. Why must she stay in the manager's room, pleading with him? There were so many in the village, who would help her at the mere mention of her father's name ... he wondered what had happened at home, that they must send her to work here.

"Let's find work in another company from tomorrow," he suggested to her.

"How many companies can I change?"

"What did he want?"

"Just ... something, that dog."

"He should be thrashed. "

"That's the fate of a woman, anywhere."

"If that's so, I'm not coming back tomorrow."

"Where will you go, then?"

When they reached Korimedu, Arumugam forced Vasantha and Porkodi to drink some tea. He offered the extra fifty rupees to Vasantha who turned it down, despite his insistence that she accept it. He then offered it to Porkodi who also refused it, but he pushed it into her handbag anyway.

"Tell me if you'll come back tomorrow," pleaded Vasantha. "Is this how you protect your master's daughter?"

Arumugam said nothing. He saw them off, staring at the receding bus for a long time with vacant eyes, as though he had lost his mind.

R ickchaw ..."
   "Rickchaw!"
"Rickchaw?"

"Come, Amma."

"Where would you like to go, sir?"

"Sir, sir!"

"Amma ..."

"Want a rickchaw? Would you like to go to the Raja Theatre? Take a seat, sir ..."

"Come on."

"Get in, I'll take you wherever you want."

"Rickchaw ...!"

Arumugam accosted people going in and out of the hospital, calling out to them to hitch a ride in his rickshaw, his tongue giving the word an un-urban inflection. Other rickshaw pullers were similarly bent on getting passengers. Dharmamoorthy squatted in the park opposite the hospital, smoking a bidi as though on a picnic, his gaze straying only occasionally towards the rickshaw; he avoided looking at Arumugam, even then.

He had spoken very little to Arumugam, in the six days since the boy had left the company.

"Get out, you've no place here. Do you think this house was earned by your parents?" Dharmamoorthy had scolded him severely all day, when Arumugam informed him of his decision to give up his job at the factory.

Chinnapponnu, however, had been inclined to sympathy. "What's the matter? Steal something, did you? Did you fight with the other boys there? Anyone scold you? Beat you up?"

"Don't like that place," had been Arumugam's disgusted reply.

Chinnapponnu had not argued further. Instead, she went out to pass the time with her friends. The fever she had caught during the rains had never really left her, and she had had to visit the hospital for treatment, twice a week.

"Rickchaw, rickchaw ...!" Arumugam hawked for fares, dogging the steps of a few people, in an attempt to get a ride. Some abused him in filthy language, while others were more courteous and merely shook their heads, No. Women and girls smiled bashfully and walked on. Many curled their lips as though they had stepped on shit.

Undaunted, Arumugam continued to bellow. "Rickchaw, rickchaw ..."

Every other rickshaw puller did the same. Some grabbed the hands of passers-by, trying to make them sit in their rickshaw – an effort at getting passengers that often led to violent altercations and fist-fights. A scuffle had broken out between Arumugam and another rickshaw-kaaran the previous day, on the beach road. Two white women had been about to get in Arumugam's rickshaw, when the other rickshaw-kaaran waylaid them, and led them away to his own rickshaw. When Arumugam took objection to this, he had not only abused the boy, but had dealt him a few slaps too. The quarrel had reached the ears of Dharmamoorthy who had sauntered away to purchase bidis, and he went looking for the errant rickshaw-kaaran despite all of Arumugam's attempts to stop him; Dharmamoorthy had ended up searching the length of the beach road.

A spark of irritation rose within Arumugam, as he watched the progress of a similar quarrel in front of the hospital.

"You son of a harlot, who fixed up the party first? Not you. Go away, you dog. Chee, get lost, thooma!"

As the two began hurling abuses at each other, the man seated in the rickshaw stepped down adroitly, and proceeded on foot.

Arumugam, who had walked some distance, and was hawking, "Rickshaw ...!, stopped suddenly, catching sight of Chinnapponnu who was walking back from the hospital, a packet of medicines in her hand. She clambered into the vehicle, throwing a disdainful look at Dharmamoorthy, who had returned and was now sitting by the side of the rickshaw. Dharmamoorthy leered at her. Chinnapponnu was heaping curses on someone. She was invariably irritable whenever she had to go to the hospital, and ended up abusing somebody or other.

Doctors and nurses usually treated women like Chinnapponnu with a condescension laced with heavy contempt. They flared up, venting their ire on them, and medicines were usually flung into their faces; rarely handed over. Injections were administered with merciless, hard pricks, causing a good deal of deliberate pain.

Lady doctors and nurses were the worst of the lot. "Why've you come here? Come searching for a groom to suit you? Why don't you people just die? So many die every day in this country. What's so special about you people that you must live? You wouldn't leave well alone even if your Thing is stitched up. Oh, look at her, the slut."

Male doctors, particularly the older ones, often eyed them lasciviously and made lewd jokes, brushing against them suggestively. Bold women teased the doctors, "Well Mama, want to come home with me? Oh, don't like me, do you? I won't charge a thing if you're my customer. Come over for a day and see how it suits you. Yei, Maama doesn't like me, di ...!" they would cackle, at the expense of lecherous male doctors. Doctors of the standoffish variety they shrugged off. "Ah, let him go, that sissy. He's thrashed by his wife everyday, I expect. That's why he's the way he is. Not man enough, is he?" They whispered to each other. Some doctors, on the other hand, were jubilant at the very sight of these women.

Chinnapponnu was abusing a lady doctor at the moment. "Thevideya munde, that widow prostitute. Thinks she's a saint. Talks like she's never gone to bed with a man."

Dharmamoorthy got up, approached the rickshaw, and grinned. Chinnapponnu neither smiled, nor spoke a word to him. She called Arumugam and asked him to drive. Dharmamoorthy tried to clamber into the rickshaw, but she pushed him out with a clipped, "Walk." Then she instructed Arumugam, loudly, "Move on!"

Arumugam looked at Dharmamoorthy for a second, pulled the rickshaw for a little distance, hopped onto it, and began to pedal.

Dharmamoorthy began to follow the rickshaw on foot.

Chinnapponnu reclined comfortably, crossing one leg over the other, and enjoying the passing scenery – the Governor's mansion and the four streets behind it, adjacent to the beach.

This area was the most beautiful in Pondicherry. Not a speck of dust could be seen anywhere, and not many people passed through the streets. The compound walls of the cement coloured residences were more than ten feet high, along with the wooden gates that were the entrances. Each compound contained a great many trees and bushes within, only the foliage of which could be seen from outside. They formed an effective screen; none from outside would be able to find out what happened inside. French residences and offices maintained a uniformly rectangular pattern, like closed boxes.

Arumugam had passed through these streets often on foot or while pulling the rickshaw but in all those times, he had never seen children playing about, or heard the voices of children at play or fight, from within the houses. The gates were never open. No kolam decorated the front of any house. One had to wonder if these houses had entrances. No matter how beautiful the buildings, they held no appeal to Arumugam. In fact, he felt a kind of repugnance.

But even if the compound walls did remind one of prison, the streets were good to look at. Every main street ended at the beach. The streets always led straight, whether one walked east to west or north to south; no lanes existed in between. The new settlements, on the other hand, invariably looked like pots arranged in a haphazard fashion by the potter.

A monkey-entertainer squatted in the vicinity of the Court, making his monkey perform tricks. Two foreigners touched the monkey curiously, and then arranged for the monkey to sit on the shoulders of the entertainer's son in different poses, and photographed it.

The foreigners reminded Arumugam of something unpleasant; he clutched the handlebars tightly, and looked behind him.

Chinnapponnu was absorbed in the scenery, the sights around her reflected in her eyes. She looked at herself often, for some reason, and twisted her face, as though her make-up was disgusting even to herself. She wore the sari she usually wore at night – it was faded in some places, frayed in others. It did not suit her at all, and the eye-liner smudged in her eyes made her look too old and hideous. Her pose suggested a hint of arrogance: Who's to stop me? All of this is mine; why should I get down? I'll step down only after I've sight-seen to my heart's content.

Passing the signal, the Children's home, Kamban Kalaiarangam and Newtone Theatre, they reached Lourdes Mary Church, when Arumugam turned to Chinnapponnu. "Home, then?"

"No, ride on. What's waiting for us at home? Want me to loll about on the bed in my ten-storey mansion, do you?" She looked around, and resumed her enjoyment of the scenery. Arumugam flexed his legs and pedalled vigorously, raising himself from the seat. He brought the rickshaw to a stop at the Nellitthoppu corner, beyond the bus stand. Chinnapponnu did not ask why he had stopped, but guessed that he was thirsty.

"My throat's parched," she announced, and entered the hotel nearby, dragging Arumugam along.

"Chi, why d'you refuse every dish that's served? You won't have any stamina in you unless you eat well. And if you don't have stamina, how can you pedal a rickshaw? You're young, you can digest even stones. Eat well," she instructed Arumugam. She dealt him a fond knock. "Serve him well," she directed the server. "Pile up stuff on his plate. What're you looking at? One more helping of poriyal," she ordered. She herself, however, bought only mutton curry.

They returned. Chinnapponnu climbed onto the rickshaw and asked Arumugam to ride on.

Enthroned like a queen, she pointed out something or the other to Arumugam all along. "Look over there," she remarked, on occasion. "What's this, Arumugam?" Arumugam found it difficult to pedal on a full stomach; still, he exerted himself, clutching the handlebars tight, pushing his feet hard on the pedals, and drove the rickshaw fairly fast.

After a little while, he turned back to Chinnapponnu. "What would you like me to call you?"

"What's it matter what you call me? What's to do about sounds from a throat?"

"It isn't that. Everybody keeps asking me how I'm related to you."

"Must there be a relationship? What's lost if one doesn't call the other by a relationship? Why must there be any relationship between people who meet at a resthouse and part company at a three-way junction, the next day?"

"Tell me, anyway."

"Everything's just words."

"Should I call you amma?"

"If I'd been lucky enough to get married, I'd have had a son your age, by now. Ah, Thambi, the trials and tribulations I've gone through ... what good will any relationship be, to me? I'm heartbroken, Thambi."

Arumugam felt distinctly uncomfortable. He had never before seen Chinnapponnu so happy and carefree as today, and now, suddenly, his question had destroyed it all. Chinnapponnu turned her eyes away from the road and looked at Arumugam. He kept pedalling without looking back, and deliberately avoided her eyes. His muscles bunched and his spine was rigid as a metal rod. Perspiration drenched his shirt.

Chinnapponnu stared at the sight. Tears overwhelmed her. The road, buildings, pedestrians and vehicles blurred in an instant; she wept aloud, not caring in the least that they were out in the streets.

"Why're you crying?" asked Arumugam.

"Who's related to whom, anyway?" was her anguished answer. She forgot that they were in the street, and that people might be watching them. She slapped herself, and wailed aloud. Arumugam regretted having asked her the question.

Passing Kuyavarpalayam, he stopped the rickshaw under a Thoongumoonji tree, and tried to console her. "There, there, now. Don't cry." He went to the tea-stall nearby and ordered tea for two, glancing through the newspaper lying on the bench as he waited.

A man stood chatting by the tea vendor. "Why only a second term? Our ministers are going to be cinema people, man or woman, from now on. Why talk of Tamil Nadu? This is how it's going to be, all over the world. When's our party going to pick itself up, again? When have people ever been willing to accept what's good for them? All that they'll believe is what's said in the cinema." He continued to talk politics, and Arumugam looked at him keenly. He wanted to go and stand near him; he sympathized with this man whose party had failed to become even the opposition. Dharmamoorthy belonged to this party too. He had painted the party's flag on the rear of his rickshaw, and whenever Dharmamoorthy cleaned the rickshaw, he would rub reverently over the spot where the flag was painted. Arumugam himself had become a supporter of the same party ever since his acquaintance with Dharmamoorthy.

"Tea!" He heard the yell and fetched the beverage in two cups, giving one to Chinnapponnu. He looked at her as he drank his tea. Her eyes were filmed with tears. She spoke nothing, sitting as though stricken dumb.

Not waiting for her commands, Arumugam pedalled the rickshaw.
Neither spoke a word until the corner of Nellitthoppu appeared.
Chinnapponnu looked as though she was returning from the funeral
of a loved one.

Arumugam pulled the brake when he saw Dharmamoorthy at the
corner of Nellitthoppu. The latter approached the rickshaw, and asked
money for liquor.

"Nothing doing," refused Chinnapponnu. "Where's the money,
anyway? Have you deposited any with me?" she asked.

He begged again, but Chinnapponnu did not relent. "I've got to go
somewhere nearby," she told him. "I'll come back later." She gestured
to Arumugam to drive the rickshaw.

As Arumugam started, Dharmamoorthy began to scream abuses at
her. "You harlot, lifting up your skirts for every man that comes along!
Who's the maaplai you're going to meet? Di, shameless slut, you've
disgraced your clan and caste, going about from place to place ... how
many more maaplais will you go to bed with?" He began to rain
blows on her, punching her in the face.

It was too much for her; she aimed a kick at him, and
Dharmamoorthy fell flat on his back, sprawling on the ground.

"You pimp, you son of a harlot! Why're you asking me for money,
da?" Chinnapponnu shrieked at him. "Have your mother and sisters
bared themselves to Parties? Yei, do you think I've been guarding
their flesh-traded money?"

Dharmamoorthy got up and abruptly, began to beat Arumugam, who
was taken by surprise. The boy tightened his grip on the handle bar as
blow after blow fell on him. He kept his feet firmly on the ground,
raising his face so that Dharmamoorthy might beat him, offering neither
protests, nor resistance. Not a single sigh or moan escaped his lips.

Chinnapponnu stepped down from the rickshaw, and kicked Dharmamoorthy from behind. Before he could turn around and gather his wits, she kicked him between his legs. Dharmamoorthy collapsed wordlessly, clutching his groin. Pushing him down flat on the ground, Chinnapponnu sat on his chest and pummelled his face relentlessly; only when her hands began to throb with pain did she stop. Gasping for breath, she spat a "Chi, thooma," in his face, and then looked up.

A large crowd had gathered around the rickshaw.

For a moment she was unnerved, but nobody from the crowd attempted to stop her – they were watching the scene intently, brows knit with concentration. People milled about, negotiating between auto-rickshaws, tempos, rickshaws, bicycles, scooters, lorries, vans and buses, peeping and asking, "What's happened? What's gone wrong?" There was no elbowroom. Vehicle horns were deafening. Heads poked out of every vehicle to see what was happening.

Arumugam dodged the crowd and walked fast, feeling a desperate urge to run away from it all. His roving eyes searched for a latrine. It would be a great consolation if he could find one. It had become a habit of his to go inside a latrine whenever frustration and anger overwhelmed him, and stay there. He would tarry even an hour if nobody knocked at the door. And sob quietly, during these minutes.

He walked at a fast pace, followed by a frantic Chinnapponnu. "Stop, stop, where're you going? Listen to me!" She waylaid passers-by, pleading with them. "Yaanga, sir, please stop him ..."

Eventually, she caught up with him and barred his way. "Where're you going without a word to me, da? Don't you worry, I'll deal with him. Wait until this evening, and I'll put an end to his sabre-rattling antics. You idiot, he was beating you black and blue – why didn't you hit back? What's the good of sprouting a moustache and claiming to be a man? You mustn't go anywhere as long as I live. You mustn't be quite so meek, all the time. I'm here for you, aren't I? Must you run away because that fellow thrashed you?"

Chinnapponnu caught him in a hug, and led him to the tea-stall. Traffic had resumed its normal pace when they returned after having some tea, and was moving without any hold up. Dharmamoorthy lounged in the rickshaw, nonchalant, smoking a bidi. Chinnapponnu commanded him to get down, and he obeyed as though he had been waiting for it. She stepped into it and made Arumugam, who was hesitating, sit by her side, and ordered Dharmamoorthy to take them home. Unperturbed, Dharmamoorthy pedalled.

Sobs rose in Arumugam's throat. He wanted to wail out loud. He gulped down the cries that threatened to rise from the pit of his stomach, breath catching with small sighs and sobs, instead. Abruptly, Dhanabhagyam came to his mind. If there wasn't anyone around, he thought, he could let go and cry aloud. He closed his eyes tight.

It was around three o'clock, and the sun burned so fiercely that he could see mirages shimmer ahead. A man waiting under the shade of the banyan tree, near the gate of the Anglo French Textile Company, waved his towel towards the rickshaw. Chinnapponnu noticed this, and asked Dharmamoorthy to halt. Dharmamoorthy did not ask the reason and applied the brakes obediently.

Chinnapponnu stepped down and walked to the shade. Cook Kuppusaami began to talk to her, laughing with an easy air of great familiarity.

Chinnapponnu had known Kuppusaami through Bhagyam, who ran a mutton shop in Chekkumedu. Bhagyam and Kuppusaami had known each other for the past ten years; Bhagyam had often told Chinnapponnu that he was a good man. Chinnapponnu had seen

Bhagyam and Kuppusaami conversing many times; she herself had spoken to him on those occasions.

The first thing she asked, as she approached Kuppusaami was, "Did Bhagyam give me a message?" Then, she enquired how he was getting on with his cooking contracts.

Kuppusaami stopped her when Chinnapponnu tried to return to the rickshaw, and talked to her about various things. He pressed a few betel leaves and areca nuts into her hands.

Dharmamoorthy came up to Chinnapponnu. "I want some tea. Give me some money." Kuppusaami took out a ten rupee note at once and gave it to him and he made a beeline, at once, towards the tea-stall.

Two others had seemingly agreed to accompany Kuppusaami, and assist him on a certain cooking assignment. But a death had occurred unexpectedly in the assistant's family, and Kuppusaami said that he was short of three hands. He reiterated this often.

"No one's going to volunteer from our place for that kind of job," Chinnapponnu said crisply, wishing to put an end to that topic. It was usually Bhagyam who arranged workers and helpers for funeral dances, pasting cinema posters on walls, displaying political party flags in roads. "Why don't you ask Bhagyam to arrange for help?"

This presented a problem, however, as the marriage was the very next morning. The persons he had engaged and sent to the marriage hall fell short of his requirement. Kuppusaami could manage very well, indeed, if he could get hold of at least two more persons. He had been in this profession for thirty years; he was anxious that his reputation should suffer no harm, for if there were to be a mishap, nobody would engage him again. He asked Chinnapponnu herself to help him out.

She began to laugh. "I'm not used to this kind of job and in any case, it won't suit me," she said, amused. "Get someone else, and don't waste your time."

Kuppusaami looked as though he would burst into tears. "Tomorrow's marriage is only a small function," he began, and meandered through various other marriages, the hassle of the cooking profession and the problem of last minute defaulters.

By this time, Dharmamoorthy had returned from the tea-stall. He railed at him as he listened to Kuppusaami's pleas, "You remind me of the chap who said, Come alone, my girl, my darling Tankacchi, I'll quench your thirst, and carry your water-pot for free – you think we'll be taken in by this sweet talk?"

Chinnapponnu threw a look at Dharmamoorthy. He turned away swiftly and lit a bidi.

Chinnapponnu insisted repeatedly that she could not assist Kuppusaami, but he did not cease pleading. "I think of you as my own sister, and I'm asking you to help me. Save me just this once. I won't forget your help as long as I live," finished Kuppusaami and wiped his face hard, twice or thrice. His eyes were blood-shot.

Chinnapponnu had spent a good deal of thought, secretly wondering what she would do if Dharmamoorthy began a quarrel that night, in retaliation for what had happened earlier in the day. "All right, I'll do what I can. But you must relieve us early, and pay all three of us the correct wages." She woke up Arumugam, asleep in the rickshaw, and as soon as he stepped down, Kuppusaami promptly climbed in.

Dharmamoorthy began to push the rickshaw towards the marriage hall in Muthialpettai.

"Go on ahead, we'll follow on foot," informed Chinnapponnu, upon which Dharmamoorthy swung himself onto the rickshaw, and began to pedal vigorously.

C ome on, come on ... finish the job quickly, you people. It's almost dawn, there's no time for idle talk. Your tongues may wag, but your hands should work," Kuppusaami was yelling himself hoarse. "Yei Kasturi, don't doze off. Why're you so slow? You people realize that there's work to be done only when the sun actually scorches your buttocks ...!"

Kasturi was resentful. "Doesn't this reject have anyone else to drive? I'd give my life to get away from him, but I don't have a choice," she snapped her shoulder at her chin defiantly.

Kuppusaami's voice resembled a goat's pathetic bleating as he shouted at Mallika, Chitra, Mariamma, Arumugam, Subramani and Bhoovarahan. "Get to work, don't waste time. You're getting paid, no? Or do you think you're doing it all for free? Anyone would think you are, to look at you dawdling away. Only with me, Kuppusaami, would you people get away with such a third rate performance. No fool but me would even dream of employing people like you."

Kuppusaami turned the idli vessel upside down, transferred the steaming idlis to another vessel, and then ordered Chitra to pour fresh idli batter for a fresh batch. He went over to the vegetable cutting section, threw down a bundle of plantain leaves in front of Arumugam to trim into appropriate sizes; he cut a sample, and Arumugam followed suit. Then, he sat by Kasturi, who was grating carrots, and began to peel radishes. Mallika settled down with a resentful expression and began to shred a cabbage, having swept aside beetroot peels and shavings. In a corner sat Bhoovarahan, kneading Bengal gram flour dough with salt.

Suddenly, Kuppusaami rose and walked away swiftly to meet the gentleman conducting the marriage, and Kasturi began to abuse him as soon as his back was turned. "When will this dog die? So many get crushed to death by cars and buses, don't they? Ugh, may cholera plague his life out. He seems to be immune to all diseases. It's only us people who fall ill at the slightest excuse – as if we'd drunk poison just by gulping down ordinary water. Look at him now, romping about like a temple bull ..."

Mallika grinned. "Softly, he might hear you," she warned. "You can't be sure. He might still be eavesdropping. He might romp all over the place, but his attention's always here. Careful."

Loudspeakers blared out music. The ear-shattering noise did not, however, disturb the endlessly chattering women in the audience, the men walking about here and there importantly, or the children playing.

As in all marriage halls, the kitchen, with its distinctive, unpleasant smells, was in a secluded area; who would want to visit a kitchen that had a damp, unclean floor, soot-blackened roof and heaps of garbage lying about?

Kuppusaami prodded them into work as soon as he returned from the ceremonial dais. "Quick. Finish the job. Take the stuff out now, don't let it fry too long. Yei, Kasturi!" he called out.

"What've you got for Kasturi, I wonder," Kasturi grinned at Mallika.

Taking along Arumugam, who had been grating coconuts, Kuppusaami went to the hall.

"The milk hasn't been delivered yet," he informed them, and reeled off a list of items he still required. "There mustn't be a single lapse in the marriage ceremonies. The food should be superb, and our guests should have nothing but praise for it. We must see to it that there's nothing's wanting. This is our function after all," he laughed, and returned to the kitchen. He poured oil into a large, stainless steel vessel he had brought from home, concealed it with a square of cloth and handed it to Arumugam, with instructions to make a stealthy exit homewards. The oil would spill if Arumugam walked too fast; he had to move slowly, holding the oil filled vessel gingerly. His duty would be something of this nature until eleven o'clock the next morning, at any rate.

Kuppusaami had used Arumugam to smuggle home materials from the marriage halls right from the time Arumugam had begun work in the cooking department. If Arumugam were to be caught red-handed, Kuppusaami would shift the blame onto him swiftly. "Someone's given it to him when I wasn't there," and he would thrash Arumugam soundly, yelling, "How dare you? Do this again, and I'll ...!" This had already happened twice or thrice. Kuppusaami would trounce Arumugam and push him about in front of his audience, apparently insane with rage; he would cringe and try to appease the boy when they were alone. Arumugam, on his part, took advantage of Kuppusaami's vulnerability in his own way. Whenever he was sent on these secret errands, he would take time off after delivering the material, and would return only after a long time; Kuppusaami would never berate or beat him.

Ever since Arumugam began work as a cooking assistant, he spent most of his time in the marriage hall, or with Kuppusaami. Chinnapponnu had come too, in the beginning, to assist Kuppusaami at work. Her visits began to dwindle into occasional events as time went by; these days, she never came at all. On the rare days that she did, Dharmamoorthy accompanied her, guarding the rickshaw throughout the night. Kuppusaami generally packed the surplus food into large hampers at the end of the morning feast. Dharmamoorthy was allowed to drive away the rickshaw only after Arumugam had dumped the hampers into it and Chinnapponnu arrived: "Let's go."

She and Dharmamoorthy would snarl at each other like wildcats on the days Chinnapponnu did accept a cooking assignment, since the man was against the whole idea. She usually retorted with a, "Mind your business. Who're you to object – my kith and kin?"

She would distribute the food packets brought from the wedding to the children of the neighbouring houses. Often, Kuppusaami would supplement these offerings with stealthily acquired rice, pulses and vegetables, and these too, she gave away to her neighbours. There was not a woman in the huts by the side of the drain or at Chekkumedu who did not taunt her relentlessly for having taken up cooking, but this did not affect her. She usually answered them by arguing, "I'm not paid much, but I'm free of tension," and that was that.

These days, not many whoremongers wanted to rub against her the wrong way, either. "She's old stuff, nothing attractive. Who'd go to her?" they walked away. Four new girls from Thuvarankurichi added to her woes, for, after their arrival, not only Chinnapponnu, but other women of Chekkumedu too ceased to have any income.

Once in a while, she forced a man and dragged him to her hut, but she never could claim the rates she demanded; she was forced to accept what little they gave. Two or three men arrived together, sometimes, and when the job was done, not only did they leave without paying her, but dealt her a few blows into the bargain. Only fledglings came to her, these days.

When Dharmamoorthy objected, she usually came back with, "Who're you to tell me what I should do, or shouldn't?" Despite her disregard of him, however, she stopped undertaking cooking jobs as she could not bear his nagging.

Arumugam walked very slowly, carrying the vessel to Kuppusaami's house, and called out twice and thrice as he reached his destination. Out came Sivaraman leisurely, and took the vessel inside. He came out again, after a little while. He and Arumugam then began walking, side by side.

As always, Sivaraman had shrouded the left side of his body with a towel. He had been injured in a bus accident while in the tenth standard, and his left arm had been amputated. He talked a lot whenever he happened to be with Arumugam; he repeated the same things over and over again. It was the same, this time too.

"Arumugam, what do you think has happened to your mother? Did you search for her? You must find her, somehow. She wouldn't have died. She must be alive somewhere."

Only to Arumugam did Sivaraman talk quite so much. He spoke but rarely, to Kuppusaami, or even his own mother. Sivaraman waited nights for Arumugam whenever Kuppusaami went out on cooking assignments, and when Arumugam came, began talking. He talked incessantly; it almost seemed that if he did not seize the opportunity offered, he would not have another chance to do so.

"Listen Arumugam. I can't get it right, whichever way I try to figure it out. Something's very wrong, somewhere. Even as I lie down on the thinnai outside, my mother and my uncle are in bed together, inside. It's that way even now, this moment. How my uncle comes to know the exact day my father goes out to cook, I'll never know. All my mother has to do is smile, and my father's struck dumb," Sivaraman lamented.

"Don't worry," Arumugam tried to console him. "Let go of it all."

"Tell me just this much," Sivaraman asked him. "Do I look like my father or my uncle?"

Arumugam said nothing, and remained silent until they reached the marriage hall.

Arumugam made three trips between the marriage hall and Kuppusaami's house. On the last trip, Sivaraman went home alone, while Arumugam stayed back.

Kuppusaami was in a flutter of impatience. "Ready?" he bustled about here and there restlessly, asking his assistants. "Is it ready yet?" His eye was on the clock constantly, counting the hours left till daybreak. As the hour of breakfast approached, Kuppusaami's anxiety increased. "Is everything ready? Have we missed anything? Make sure," he yelled. He tasted each and every item, and ordered that a little salt be added to some.

He ushered in important members of the marriage party into the kitchen. "Could you taste a bit of the food?" he urged them. "Please tell me if everything's to your satisfaction, and set my mind at rest."

He made them savour every item, bragging about his reputation as a head cook; the thirty years that had passed without a blot on his reputation; the strict standards he still insisted on maintaining. Even as he talked to others, his eyes shifted towards the knives, tumblers, buckets and vessels, checking to see that nothing was missing. He flitted in between the marriage dais and the kitchen often, checking on his assistants, ensuring that they were all doing their jobs; he was vigilant lest they should go out for half an hour or an hour on some excuse or other, and waste time.

Arumugam was feeling feverish that day, but he persisted in working. As the hours went by, however, he could not keep up with his pace. Kuppusaami noticed this, and in spite of Arumugam's refusal, led him to the storeroom, and made him lie down. Never did Kuppusaami allow any worker to rest or lie down even if they were genuinely ill and if they did, he threatened that their wages would be slashed, and had even been known to kick them out or beat them, if they happened to be weaklings. His contrary attitude towards Arumugam surprised the young man; nevertheless, he lay down, and soon, went to sleep.

He woke up very soon, having slept only for a little while. He shifted his position, feeling an odd sensation of ants creeping under the skin. His feet felt cold, as though a block of ice were being pressed to them, and he felt a distinct tickling as though someone was dragging his legs and rolling him over. There was a pressure between his groins.

He tried to turn himself to the other side. He couldn't. He stretched out his arms, trying to push away the bundles he thought had been stacked there, and encountered hair. Startled, he shot up, and saw Kuppusaami sitting by his side.

"Chee, you pig ...!" He threw a curse at Kuppusaami and rose, ignoring the man as he tried to stop him. Arumugam pushed him away, and rushed out as if he was possessed, dragging up his veshti that had unwound itself. He wiped away the spit that clung to his thighs and stomach and stood just for a minute, thinking. The next minute, he walked out of the hall at a frantic pace.

Bhoovarahan and Subramani ran after and stopped him, asking why he was running away. Arumugam gave no answer.

"Fine," snapped Bhoovarahan. "If you do want to leave, leave after telling us why you're going. You were all right until a minute ago. What's come up, suddenly? Someone yell at you?"

Arumugam maintained his silence. Bhoovarahan grew angry and dragged Arumugam inside, where Kuppusaami asked Subramani to keep an eye on him, lest he run away again.

Plantain leaves were spread out as early as five o'clock, and tumblers were filled with water. Food was brought in vessels from the kitchen, and placed in readiness in the dining hall. Contrary to his wont, Kuppusaami's manner was listless as he counted the invitees, walked to and from the marriage dais and kitchen, uttering not a single word.

Mallika cursed him despite his surprising silence. "That vagabond is driving us like slaves."

"Does he allow anybody even a moment's rest?" cut in Kasturi. "So many people get knocked down fatally by cars, every day ... isn't there a single driver to crush this fellow to death?"

"I can't help wondering, though ... would this fellow be the same way even when he's with his wife?"

"Oh, come on, now. Do you think his kneecaps are blunted because he bedded his wife? All that he's had from her are kicks. Let him to go hell, that good-for-nothing wretch."

"Quiet. The dog's coming."

"Let him, then. I'm not a tiny bug, am I, to be caught and crushed under his heels?"

Arumugam's task, in the beginning, had only been that of removing the leaves after people had eaten. Later, he was told to pour water in tumblers, and still later, the task of serving vadais. It was only in the

past two years that he had been entrusted with the responsibility of
serving the hot stew, sambar. However much one tried, you could
never serve sambar without spilling some on your veshti, unless you
were an expert. Apart from anything else, you had to be fleet footed.
After the first serving, when people asked for a second or even a third
helping, calling out "Sambar, sambar!" you had to rush to the caller
in a split-second, running over damp and sticky floors. No matter
how much you scrubbed away at your body after the feast, the
unpleasant odour of food never could be washed clean.

The feast began; food was served briskly. Subramani served the
idlis, while Bhoovarahan took over pongal. It was Kuppusaami who
invited the guests, in a tone even sweeter than that of the hosts
themselves, calling out, "Please step in, the feast's begun."

He saw to it that one batch after another went in to eat without
interruption, and shouted, standing in front of one row of guests or
the other: "Yei, serve those idlis!" or "Yei, get the pongal over here!"

If there were a delay, he would abuse his assistants mercilessly. "You
want to fatten yourselves up at your age, do you? Do you honestly feel
that you're doing the right thing? The man who pays will not shell out
currency notes to you, without getting some kind of a return for it.
Remember that."

Kasturi served the chutney, while Mallika doled out as small helpings
of sweet kesari as she could. Kuppusaami's voice held forth above
all the other voices, goading everyone, and keeping them all on
their feet.

Two rounds of breakfast were over; most of the guests had eaten.
Not much of a crowd remained, and there was no need to work quite
so feverishly any longer. Latecomers and stragglers ate now, dotting
the hall. The marriage hall emptied swiftly, within an hour of the

main ceremony of the taali adornment, much like a cinema theatre clearing out as soon as the film was over.

Kuppusaami called Bhoovarahan and Subramani to him, and assigned them to pack away the surplus food. Earlier, this job used to be assigned to Bhoovarahan and Arumugam. Today, however, Arumugam was sulking. He did one or two odd chores and that, only after Mallika and Kasturi took him to task. Kuppusaami did not ask him the reason for his un-cooperative mood; in fact, he went nowhere near him.

Calling "Yei, kutti Kasturi," he ordered her, Chitra and Mariamma to scour the vessels clean.

"We're barely free of the dinner serving and only just beginning to rest our hands and feet a little, but does this dog allow us some rest?" Kasturi cursed Kuppusaami, as she grabbed and banged down vessels violently – Damaal! Poter! – carrying them away to be scrubbed clean. Kuppusaami was particular that each and every job must be done well before the stipulated time. Once work was done, he wanted to leave the marriage hall as swiftly as he had entered it.

By ten, everything was done. It was a simple marriage, arranged on a small scale; Kuppusaami always got contracts only for such middle class marriages.

He now urged the manager of the marriage hall. "Come and check for yourself, or the vessels might be misplaced. Who's going to be responsible if something's missing ? Come on, we can finish the work in no time. We'll have to sort out the tumblers, buckets, chembus, et cetera, and count." Dragging him along, he asked his assistants to sort out and place vessels, counting the different categories in front of him, that he may check it all up.

It was Raja who counted the utensils and then told the manager, "Please check the items and verify that everything's in its place. Later, you mustn't complain that a vessel's gone missing." After the manager nodded concurrence, other assistants took the vessels and deposited them in the storeroom. Kasturi and Chitra began to sweep the floor; Mariamma went in favour of a bath.

Kuppusaami was arguing with the people belonging to the marriage party. "Ah, come now, you mustn't say that. You've come here for an auspicious ceremony after all, and on such an occasion, you mustn't use these kinds of words. Is something wrong with my work? Tell me if you felt that there were any deficiencies, and I won't argue against that. I'll forego the entire remuneration, and leave. You're honourable people, after all. What do I ask from you but a handful of cooked rice!" he pleaded, bargained, cajoled. "Believe me, I predict that the first child will be a son. Just send word to this Kuppusaami if there's any other function, and he'll be here the next instant," he finished arguing his case.

This done, he received and distributed the customary quota of rice and vegetables due to every employee, along with their wages. Subramani and Bhoovarahan went out, taking with them the packets of surplus idli, vadai, kesari, pongal and uppuma distributed to them, along with other articles each had managed to secret for himself, without the others' knowledge .

Arumugam walked out, disgusted, carrying his packets as though doing someone a favour, lugging them about for their sake. Kuppusaami came running, forced a twenty rupee note into Arumugam's shirt pocket and went back. Arumugam pulled it out, looked at it with loathing, threw it out on the road and began walking fast. But for the bundles he carried, he would have run where his legs took him. But what could he do about the packets he carried?

What had happened to Dharmamoorthy? He usually arrived

promptly to escort him from the marriage hall, Arumugam mused. Was he lying about somewhere, stone drunk? Or had he quarrelled violently with Chinnapponnu? Had the police, perhaps, arrested him and taken him to the station?

A posse of policemen surrounded Chinnapponnu's hut; a crowd of passers-by and vagrants had gathered too, watching the scene in great excitement.

Arumugam could make out the women inside the house even at a distance, as they wailed aloud, beating their breasts.

It was Bhagyam's voice that rose distinctly, soaring above all the others who had come to mourn the death.

"Aren't there any number of harlots in this world who deserve a worse fate?" she wept loudly, her cries rending the air. "Oh god, why must this poor girl be condemned to such an end? Such a timid girl she was too, and never a one to hanker after another's possessions. Ah, even if I were to get a thousand others, would I have another like my little bird, my annakkili? My daughter's turned into dust ... how can I bear this loss?"

The policemen drove away crowds of onlookers who had gathered, drinking in the scene. They measured the place where the dead body lay, the wall of the drain, and the length and breadth of the hut; they interrogated a few women. Later, they dispersed the women who had gathered there with a harsh, "Get lost, you whores. Look at them come, displaying their Things. Why don't you people hang yourselves? Lock them up for six months. Let's see if these brazen harlots know their place at least then."

The dead body was transferred to the hospital as soon as the ambulance arrived, for a post mortem.

At the sight of Arumugam, Bhagyam cried louder than ever, as though she had been waiting for him. Arumugam felt somebody pull at the bundle on his head from behind him and turned, to see Vasantha standing there.

He looked around him, startled. What's happening, he wondered, nonplussed. Who were all the people clustered here?

He turned back again, and saw Vasantha standing in the same spot; a woman in the crowd was chattering away to her without a pause.

How had Vasantha landed up here? Had she stumbled upon this crowd, and stayed back to watch what went on? he wondered. All the women of Chekkumedu, it seemed, were assembled; there were not less than fifty of them. Most clutched at Arumugam in their distress or pointed at him, sobbing. Try as he might, he could not understand the reason for such behaviour.

All the women wept for Chinnapponnu; they found numerous faults with her, railing at her that she had not known how to make good of her life. In between, they made isolated remarks about Arumugam and Dharmamoorthy. There was so much noise and hullabaloo that it took some time for Arumugam to get the hang of it. By the time he began to understand what went on, he had a splitting headache. The women sobbing their condolences were the main cause of his headache, as they dragged him about from one place to another.

He wanted to lie down. I shouldn't have left the marriage hall quite so soon, he thought. A sleepless night, walking over to Kuppusaami's home that morning, and the hard work afterwards had left him dead tired. Kuppusaami's indecent behaviour had infuriated him the most. He wanted to see Vasantha. He searched for her, but she was not to be found; others milled about where she had been standing, earlier. He craned his neck, turning this way and that, looking for her in the crowd.

Abruptly, he found himself clasped by a sobbing woman. By his side sat Bhagyam on the ground, wailing. "Ah, my daughter's gone ... how could she leave me alone and die? Who's there for me, now? Ah, she's lucky, she's gone, she's rid of all her troubles. God above, when will my time come?"

Holding onto Arumugam's hand, Bhagyam boarded the Korimedu bus. He wished to ask her what had happened to Chinnapponnu, and gazed at her face. Her eyes were closed and he too sat still, silent. His head ached unbearably; he tried to divert his attention onto other matters, but could not take his mind off the disgust and irritation that had welled up in him at Kuppusaami's defiling touch. He closed his eyes and tried to sleep in order to forget it, but failed. Why, after all this time, would Kuppusaami suddenly indulge in something like this today?

It was four o'clock when they reached Korimedu. Bhagyam had grasped his hand so tightly that it looked as though she was afraid of losing him, if she did not hold on as much as she could. Arumugam allowed himself to be led by her like a blind man.

They entered the Jipmer Hospital, and went to the postmortem room. Thangamani, Lakshmi, Valli and Prema were waiting under the shade of a Neem tree. Dharmamoorthy lay crumpled within the rickshaw.

Thangamani clasped Arumugam when she saw him, and sobbed. "The poor woman's gone – god knows how she met her end. Which thooma, which son of a harlot is the culprit, I wonder. Did she have to die falling in the drain? Was it for this that she went through so much trouble, the chandali?" Freeing himself from her, Arumugam moved away and sat leaning on a tree. In a little while, he dozed off.

It was Vasantha who woke him up. He opened his eyes, irritated and angry. Had it been anyone other than Vasantha who had woken him up, he would have yelled at them without compunction. His eyes were burning; he could not keep them open. He wanted to look at Vasantha, to talk to her and ask her about Chinnapponnu, but could not. Sleep overwhelmed him. Vasantha dragged him along with her and went into the postmortem room.

All the women who had been waiting under the tree had gathered there. The marble floor was cold and damp. Chinnapponnu's body was laid on a granite slab at waist level; there were no clothes on it. On another slab nearby, five feet away, had been laid the body of a woman who had committed suicide by burning herself. Blocks of ice had been placed in two corners in the room. A human brain had been drawn in coloured chalk on the blackboard on the wall, and arrows marked the parts. Everyone except Arumugam had covered his or her mouth and nose with a piece of cloth.

"Yei, my daughter, you've met your end, Amma," wailed Bhagyam, and the morgue attendant signed to Bhagyam to be silent.

He then shooed everyone out, saying, "I let you people see the body when the doctors were not there. Give me something, why don't you?"

Thangamani thrust a ten rupee note in his hand. When he insisted on "ten more," she went at him, prepared to fight it out.

They came out and sat under the neem tree, and Bhagyam began lamenting, again. "I've seen so many girls in my lifetime, but no one like her. Why must death take her, of all the people? She was such a simple girl. So naive that she never tried to hide herself during police raids ..."

Other women now began reminiscing about Chinnapponnu too. Vasantha dragged Arumugam out of the hospital and took him to where he had been dozing before. She also volunteered him information about Chinnapponnu.

Apparently, Chinnapponnu had readied herself as usual the previous day, and had stood about in the street at seven, that evening. An unusually large number of people were moving about in the area. Chinnapponnu had been walking from her home to the end of the street, trying to grab Parties. Since every other woman had also been bent on snatching up Parties, sending away those that were done and grabbing others, no one paid her any attention.

The crowd had swelled at about ten o'clock, when the first show had ended. The harsh voice of a man and Chinnapponnu's voice had been heard, from behind her hut near the drain for quite some time.

"Why're you covering It with your hand right now?"

"Try anything, and I'll scream. Want me to remove my blouse? That'll be another ten rupees."

"Hell, nothing doing."

"Yei, what do you mean?"

"Di, quiet."

"Why, you thooma, get lost."

"Yei, yei."

The other women had been preoccupied with grabbing men; no one had paid attention to the voices they heard. Each had been keen on making as much money as she could – and moreover, altercations of this kind were common in the locality. Not a day passed by without a fight there or in Chekkumedu.

Eventually, the dead body had been discovered by a few small boys the next morning, when they had gone to the banks of the drain to answer the call of nature.

News spread like wildfire, and the whole locality had gathered in no time. Passers-by had collected too, eager to watch the proceedings. The police were intimated, and a posse arrived on the scene. They removed the body from the drain, and dispersed the crowd. The press descended on them, and took photographs.

Vasantha walked, relating all this as told by Thangamani, in a voice drained of emotion. She dragged Arumugam with her into the tea-stall, and ordered tea for both.

"Not very strong, make it medium. Give me a glass of warm water, first."

Arumugam had not said a word, all this time. Vasantha looked at him intently, as though raking through his mind. Arumugam badly wanted to talk to her, but did not know what he should say. How had Chinnapponnu died, he wondered. Had she slipped and fallen into the drain, or had she been shoved? Had she been so drunk that she could not shout or push the fellow back and beat him? Or, having slipped or having been pushed, hadn't she been able to get up? Vasantha says that, according to the Chekkumedu women from whom she had gleaned the information, the marks caused by fingernails around her neck resembled a wound inflicted by a sharp instrument.

The man must have strangled her and thrown her into the sewer. She must have asked for five or ten rupees more, and that, only if the man had insisted that she unbutton her blouse, and that he would not use a condom. Would a man go to the extent of strangling a woman just for that?

Or, could it have happened this way? Perhaps the fellow promised her money after the job was done, and later, refused to give anything, and tried to get away. Maybe she stopped him and demanded money. He choked her just to hurt her a little, but the pressure turned out to be fatal. He might have dumped the body in the drain, stunned by the unexpected turn of events.

And where had Dharmamoorthy been all this time? wondered Arumugam. Why did I have to leave for a cooking assignment, yesterday? He cursed himself, and anger rose in him against Kuppusaami, like a raging fire.

Vasantha noticed his flushed face and clenched fists. "What's the matter?"

Volunteering no answer, he finished drinking his tea, rose, and began to walk. He was confused. What was going to happen next? What must he do, now?

"Why're are you so silent, like a dumb fellow?" Vasantha asked.

He gave no answer, and they walked towards the hospital. He found that he liked walking beside her. Meeting her after so many years was a definite surprise. The feeling was so strong that it persisted a long time.

Once inside the hospital compound, Arumugam washed his face. He took a pill but the headache did not abate. His eyes burned and his vision played tricks on him, as though everything were under a disturbed pool of water. He felt depressed and angry.

Noting his silence, Vasantha took hold of his hand. As though waiting for it, he accepted it and began walking in step with her.

He let recent events recede from his mind, and stepping light-heartedly, like a carefree child, eventually asked her, "How did you happen to come to this place?"

He repeated his question twice or thrice. Vasantha did not answer. She continued to walk with her head bent.

"Are you crying?" he asked.

She did not raise her head and look at him then, either.

"My daughter's gone. Why must she, of all people, meet with an end like this? Aren't there so many fellows about who live on urine and deserve a worse fate? Why couldn't death have taken them away instead of her? Ah, she's gone and left me an orphaned corpse ..."

Screaming with grief, Bhagyam ran out to the road to hire a public transport van. The dead body had been wrapped in white cloth, with only the face showing. Turmeric paste had been applied lavishly on the face, and kumkumam had been daubed on the forehead.

The body was carried out just as Bhagyam arrived with a hired van. The driver was in a hurry; his face was as blood-shot as someone caught in the throes of fury. The mortuary attendants began to quarrel, unknown to the doctors. "We don't want anything less than fifty." The policemen demanded tips too, and the women pleaded with them: "It's an orphan's dead body, sir. If it weren't for us, the hospital would have disposed of it without informing a soul. We're the ones who've paid money out of our pockets and arranged a van. And you ask us money for this? Sir, we're arranging a funeral only because we were friends, when she was alive. Sir, she's no sister or daughter of ours, but we believe that even if a person's not related, their body shouldn't lie about, unattended. We were in such a hurry to get here that we didn't bring money with us. Everything happened so suddenly, that we weren't prepared for it, sir. Would you ask for money if death occurred to someone in your family?" Bhagyam tried to put them off, sobbing piteously.

The two policemen who were present gave no sign of relenting, however. Whatever Vasantha and Arumugam had with them was given to the policemen; only then did they allow the van to move.

Bhagyam and a few other women got into the van. The cleaner shut the door. The van rattled on its way, belching smoke. The other women dispersed. Dharmamoorthy pedalled his rickshaw.

Bhagyam cursed the man as she looked at the dead body. "He's the one who sent her to her death. He won't live a good life. He's sure to be ruined, that wimp — that scoundrel who wouldn't feed his own mother. Why did my girl even trust this fellow?"

The body had been laid on the bench, face upwards. The van rattled as it moved, and the bench, in turn, rocked this way and that. Three people on each side bolstered it with their knees, to keep it from rocking too much. A hospital van would have been fitted with a steel bench designed especially for transporting bodies, and there would have been a belt to fasten the body to the bench, so that it did not move, or fall off. Normally, however, the hospital van was not made available to carry a dead body from the hospital to the house or burial ground; it could be used only to bring the corpses of orphans for postmortem purposes.

Thus, any dead body had to be transported to the house or burial ground only in privately owned vans and cars parked outside, by the side of the road. The rate was generally dictated by the owners. If it was an urgent business, the rate would shoot up. The cars were worse than vans, for the body would then have to be bent, twisted, squeezed and stuffed into the dickey. This was why Bhagyam had avoided the cars and brought a van, instead.

Arumugam was staring at the body. Valli and Prema were seated beside him. The aroma of joss sticks lit by the body's head pervaded the van. The faces of those inside the van had frozen into a cheerless, stiff expression, with no trace of laughter or speech. Everyone avoided looking at each other; their thoughts were far away. The smoke from joss sticks curled in the air, twisting itself around their faces.

Arumugam placed his hand on the body, as though wanting to wipe away the thick layers of turmeric paste. The body was cold as ice. He felt the cheeks, nose, lips, forehead and so on, with his fingers. Years had gone by since he first met Chinnapponnu, but never before had he looked at her face at such close quarters, and with a mind empty of thoughts. What he saw even now was a lifeless face, slathered with turmeric paste. Arumugam closed his eyes, seeing Chinnapponnu's face in his mind's eye. The image appeared fractured and vague, like a coloured kolam distorted by a sprinkling of water.

He ran his fingers over the mouth, neck, chest and stomach of the dead body, as though touching a log of wood. He tried to lift the head and place it on his lap, but Vasantha put her finger over her lips in a gesture of disapproval; perhaps she was apprehensive about breaking the prevailing silence. The driver and cleaner, sitting side by side, spoke not a word to each other either. They were smoking, and sat as though observing silence as a penance.

Suddenly, when everyone least expected it, Bhagyam began to wail aloud. "Will death come to you like this without warning? Did she die because she'd suffered so much, and she couldn't suffer anymore? Why do women like her come into this world? Daughter of mine, you've become dust. Didn't you take mutton curry and dosai from me and eat, only last night? Will death ever come to me too? Oh god, what form will it take?" Bhagyam did not stop wailing until they reached the burial ground. She had the build of two women fused into one, so obese was she; but when she cried the way she did now, beating her breasts, she did not appear quite so fat.

It was eight o'clock that night, when the burial and connected rites were completed and they finally returned home. The other women left for Chekkumedu as soon as the body was buried, as though consumed by urgent business; Dharmamoorthy hastened away to the arrack stall. Arumugam and Vasantha alone stayed with Bhagyam until the end.

Arumugam was silent throughout. Bhagyam bathed at the roadside tap as soon they approached their home. "Let me pour water on by head. God knows who'll pour water on to their heads, when I die ..."

Vasantha bathed too, and washed her clothes. She also forced a half-dozing Arumugam to bathe, saying, "You mustn't sleep, polluted this way. You must pour at least a chembu of water on your head. Only then will death's pollution be removed." She gave him one of her own saris to cover himself.

Bhagyam stood at the door, calling out for somebody "Yei kutti, yei kutti!" five or six times.

A girl, seven or eight years old, answered her stiffly. "Why did you call me?"

Bhagyam gave her an empty bottle and asked her to fetch arrack. The girl returned with liquor in a little while and gave it to Bhagyam.

Sitting in front of the lamp, Bhagyam drank down the arrack in one gulp. "Chinnapponnu, Chinnapponnu ..." she moaned, often.

She sat still for a long time, staring at the ceiling vacantly. Then, she looked at the lamp. She placed her hands on the floor, and gazed at them, palms upturned, a long while. She stared at Vasantha and Arumugam.

She stared at the darkness enclosed by the gabled thatched ceiling again, and then broke down and began to sob. "How can I live without you, my thangam? I've become on orphan. Ah, she's left me, and her story has ended ...

A King was he crowned;
a mansion he lorded over,
Ruled the land did he;
With health and wealth showered,
For years he held sway;

Of long life, no dearth,

But disappear he did,

Under six feet of earth," she lamented. "She threaded together a garland of flowers, but fell under the earth, forgotten by others ..."

"Don't wail so," Vasantha tried to restrain Bhagyam. "People who're passing by may think that there's been another death."

"What would you know, you cunt? Oh god, what'll be my fate if everyone turns into dust like this, one after the other?" Bhagyam continued to lament in her characteristic fashion as she cursed first one and then the other, calling them up by name.

The lamp remained lit until the small hours of dawn.

C ome over here."

"Welcome, Annachi. "

"Would you like some mutton curry?"

"Or fish, maybe?"

"Don't you want some kodal?"

"Have a dosai?"

"Here's some ratthapporiyal. "

"Want an omelette? Two plates?"

"Get a lobster, then."

"Want some prawns?"

"Hot parotta, maybe?"

"What will you have?"

"And for you, sir?"

"Everything we've got is fresh and hot."

"Come over here ..."

Arumugam hawked, on and on. He thrust firewood in the oven and tapped the steel dosai pan with his flat steel spatula often, producing a tak tak noise. Fish, mutton curry, prawns, kodal, ratthapporiyal, lobsters et cetera, had been stacked neatly in separate compartments on a broad aluminium plate, divided by leaves and placed on the mud shelf three feet high.

Bhagyam sat on a small stool beside Arumugam. The dosai batter rested near the firewood with the parotta plate beside it, while the egg-holder stood behind, all arranged conveniently as though the mud shelf had been constructed with all these in mind. The oven burnt bright; Arumugam fed firewood at regular intervals. He stood directly in front of the bright oven, and his body was bathed in yellow light. Few customers straggled in; it was only five o'clock. By seven, there would be a huge crowd, jostling about.

The ceiling was a thatched roof twenty to thirty feet long, stretching from north to south. A short mud wall a foot thick supported the sloping thatched roof on the western side. Seven feet away towards the east was a waist-high mud wall, two feet thick. Space was allowed between these walls for people to move around, and to stack arrack, soft drink, as well as empty bottles. The eastern wall served as the counter for selling arrack bottles and receiving cash for them. The place reserved for customers lay further to the east of this wall, and farther away, was Bhagyam's stall. Her stall was the only one within the thatched building; other, smaller stalls, numbering around a hundred were situated outside, selling mutton curry, chundal, varuval, fish, et cetera. A little to the west and north of the thatched roof stall were not less than fifty huts, clustered around a depression that resembled a dry pond. Further to the west was the Naveena Theatre and to the east, Kuber Bazaar.

"Mutton curry? Wait a little, I'll heat it up. You don't want a dosai or parotta along with it?" Arumugam asked as he placed the mutton curry on the steel pan, and sautéed it efficiently. He ladled it on a plantain leaf when it was sizzling hot and handed it to the customer; Bhagyam had already received the money for it.

Another customer came up and ordered, "One omelette. Get it ready, I'll be back in a minute," and sprinted away to the arrack shop. A third customer ordered dosai. Arumugam sprinkled water on the steel pan, brushed it briskly with a short broom and poured the batter into round dosais. He then took out three parottas and reheated them.

He had a good idea of his customers' tastes, and could anticipate their orders quite well. Boiled eggs, fish and others were always kept in readiness depending on the customer's preferences, and he served them even before they asked him for it, Bhagyam having been paid in advance. Bhagyam was all smiles only till the money came into her hands, after all.

The customers gathered into quite a crowd. People were waiting in line, one behind the other in the arrack and toddy shops, as though standing in queue in front of the ticket counter in cinema halls, and they were all shouting at the same time. Their words and behaviour would indicate that they had urgent business to attend to and could not afford to wait at all – many were shrieking like urchins flocking around ice and balloon vendors. The people in front of the arrack shop held tumblers of different shades, while the people in front of the toddy counter held out smelly jugs, flies hovering over them. All were impatient and pining for their drinks, like beggars waiting for alms.

"A hundred."

"Pour me a fifty."

"Annae, over here ..."

"Pour a hundred for me."

"Give it to me, first."

"Where's the balance?"

"How long have I got to wait? Give my shot quick. Here, take the note first."

"Hand over the tumbler."

"Mudalaali, pour one here."

"You've already taken cash ..."

"Brother!"

"Mudalaali."

Arumugam called out loudly to those drinking at the arrack and toddy shops, smoking a cigarette or bidi, as did Bhagyam to the people loitering in front of stalls and the passers-by. She invited people in tirelessly, and gave ceaseless directions to Arumugam.

"Step in, step in, everything's fresh and hot."

"Thambi, Arumugam, see to sir's needs, first."

"Sir, if the food isn't up to the mark, you may thrash me with your chappals and get your money back."

"Heat it up, pour some oil, and give it to Annan. What we serve him today must tempt him to come to our stall tomorrow, to taste the delicious items we prepare."

"Omelettes? Two? Arumugam, spice them up with extra pepper and hand it to sir."

"Ah, come in, Annachi."

The arrack and toddy shops rang with a babel of voices as though in the middle of a riot. Bedlam reigned all over the area, with people spitting harshly, vomiting noisily, forcing drink on their companions, resisting drink, asking for a loan, or compelling a companion to buy a drink. Others got dead drunk; some threw empty tumblers where they stood; some more hunted for jugs or tumblers with which to buy drinks.

Large groups of flies buzzed eagerly where people had vomited, poured down arrack they could not gulp down, let spit dribble to the ground with tongues lolling out of the mouth, thrown down bones of the mutton or fish they had munched down, spat to get rid of the bitter taste of drinks, or blown their noses and left behind the mucus. Waste paper wrappings of eaten-up chundal, emptied pickle packets and cigarette packets were heaped in one place, and it was here that most people stood about and chatted.

Heavily made-up women began to arrive from various localities. Most came from the Mutthamizh Nagar area where Bhagyam lived. Those who had engaged women for the flesh trade and the owners of the huts, both men and women, made the women wait inside or stand outside the huts to grab Parties, and were themselves hovering around the arrack and toddy shops, gesturing people into their huts.

Electric lights twinkled only in the arrack and toddy shops. The others were lit with kerosene lamps. All the lamps shone dimly, as though covered by a cloth, smudged by soot or deprived of fuel, and the area was in semi darkness despite all the illumination.

A swirling pattern of noise, hustle and bustle, quarrels, fights, fracas, fun, laughter, altercations, pushing and shoving built up gradually, the air sizzling with the frenzy of a temple festival. Only up to midnight would this whirling drama continue; later, the place would be deserted, like a circus tent after a show.

"Give me three plates with two dosais each, and some mutton curry, too," a woman ordered, and took the plates to two sickly looking women who sat near a small shop, clutching their lower stomachs. They must have come there straight after finishing work as labourers in a building site. Their hands were smeared with lime, such as those white washing.

Near Bhagyam lay an old woman, unconscious. Her clothes had slid away from her body, and ants crawled all over her. Flies buzzed around her mouth and head. She had vomited; her hair, left hand and the top end of her sari lay crumpled on the vomit. A dog licked her hand. Another dog, trotted in from somewhere else, barked at the dog licking away at the old woman, and the two began to roar at each other, beginning a full-fledged fight. Bhagyam told Arumugam to chase away the dogs, drag the old woman and leave her far away. As Arumugam obeyed Bhagyam's command, a young girl came running and pushed him aside as she rained blows on him.

"Why're you dragging her da?" she shrieked at him. "Leave her alone, you kammanaatti. Thevideya Mavane, you dog. Thooma!"

Bhagyam came running as she heard her shrieks, pushed at the girl and abused her in turn. "Shut up, you cunt. What do I care if it's your mother? If you think I fit the saying, She brings together the woman and the party and if that isn't enough, she'll lie down herself, you'll have another think coming. You naadheri, don't you flaunt your superiority at me, with your morals. Chee, get lost, you reject! Get lost, you who bedded down my uncles, and probably all my brothers too. Do you think I hawk my body in the Kootthadikkudi fair, as you do? Get away, you shameless slut ...!"

The girl shouted and abused in return, raising her voice to a high pitch. Soon, they were at each other's throats without any let up, oblivious to the crowd that had gathered. Arumugam finally came up and dragged Bhagyam away to the stall. The girl took two or three steps forward, and yelled at Bhagyam.

"Adi, why're you running away? Look at the shameless, thick-skinned wretch. Podi, thevidiya munda."

The girl dragged the old woman away. Bhagyam continued to scream at her: "Just wait until the shops close down. Ha, we'll see what shape she's in when day dawns, won't we? How dare she talk to me that way, that stinking lice picker?"

The noise in the place was deafening, increasing with every minute; pandemonium ensued, created by those who were lounging about in front of the liquor, toddy, mutton curry shops, and stalls. Pimps – men, women, small boys and girls were running hither and thither, shouting to get parties. When they did catch hold of a willing party, they spun colourful accounts of the women waiting, seized his hand and rushed with him to their hut, lest somebody else should snatch him away.

"Absolutely fresh, and arrived just today," they would tempt, if a party appeared hesitant. "With skin glowing like the bright fire of the oven. Very young." They forcibly dragged away those who were reluctant. The owners of those shops selling various foods invited people in, too, adding to the uproar.

As usual, only quite some time after night fell did Vasantha arrive from Bhagyam's home, with chundal. Bhagyam and Arumugam bundled it in small packets; the former asked Vasantha to take Arumugam's place in the oven department. Arumugam borrowed some cash from Bhagyam, bought some cigarettes and smoked two of them in quick succession. Walking between the huts, he searched about for a spot to urinate.

Men, women and young boys moved past him at a frantic speed, jostling against him in the narrow path. Quite a crowd of men stood about in front of a few huts, smoking cigarettes and bidis. Voices rose from some huts as women shouted and abused someone or the other, while laughter rang out from others. A woman kicked out a man from one.

"Poda, you pimp, you fraud ...!" she yelled. "Oh look at him, coming here to lick my cunt. Get lost, you. If you don't, I'll rub your face with my ..."

Arumugam returned to the stall. A crowd of customers had already gathered and he attended to work, standing between Bhagyam and Vasantha.

Vasantha was an added attraction to the customers. She pandered to their lasciviousness, chitchatting and laughing along with them. Bhagyam often reprimanded her swiftly if she did not chat or simper enough. "We're going to have to fill our stomachs only if we work day in and day out. If we don't, we'll have to lead a beggar's life. No one's going to say, Throw the worker's plate into the dustbin, and heap the idler's plate with food, hot and filling. Are they?"

Vasantha's skin dazzled in the light of the oven fire, and crowds would gather just to enjoy the sight of her body glowing in the firelight. Vasantha, on her part, would take her time in adjusting her sari if it slipped from her breasts. She draped her sari well below the waistline, making sure that her navel and a good deal of skin lay exposed. She would call out loudly to those standing at a distance, to step in and eat a little something, and would ply them with hot curry placed on a piece of plantain leaf even before they gave an order. She would adopt, in fact, any tactic necessary to ensure that the food brought from home was sold out, for she was keen on leaving Chekkumedu as soon as possible.

The customers, on the other hand, would engage her in idle conversation and laugh along with her, making eyes at her all the time. They would wipe their faces often; take the arrack in one gulp without once throwing up, and would chew mutton curry and pickles in an elegant fashion. They would smoke cigarettes with style; they would order mutton curry and omelettes again and again, throwing cash away nonchalantly, dismissing the change offered with a suggestive laugh.

Bhagyam's income soared to hitherto unattained heights only after Vasantha's arrival at her shop; she now began to offer loans to other women at Chekkumedu.

Arumugam never could bear to see Vasantha as long as she stood in front of the oven, in charge of customers. He simmered with anger and irritation, and went out frequently to have a smoke, in an effort to suppress his emotions. This was not the Vasantha he had known in Krishnapuram, Mettuppalayam and Auroville.

On her part, Vasantha did not have the moral courage either, to look at Arumugam as long as she went about her work. She would behave as though he was a stranger and would stand, clothed in a distant air, as long as she stayed in the shop.

Arumugam had stayed with Bhagyam ever since Chinnapponnu's death, over a year and half ago, now. He would quiver with suppressed anger if anybody smiled at Vasantha. Why did Chinnapponnu have to die, he would mourn. Why was it fated that I must see Vasantha with Bhagyam?

A man came to buy mutton curry from Bhagyam's stall; three boys and a woman tried to force him into their huts. He yelled, pushed away the boys and woman, and went and stood a distance, not even taking the mutton curry. Bhagyam screeched at the boys, and chased them away. "Get lost, you idiots! I mustn't see you anywhere near this place. Is this where you grab a party? Ah look at the dogs, running over here. Show your damned faces anywhere near this place again, and I'll trounce you to death. Why're you standing here, yet?"

Sales were brisk as soon as Vasantha began attending to the oven;

more than half the food was sold. Heavily made-up women came in, and having purchased arrack, yelled "Mutton!" "Fish!" or "Give me an egg!," either exuberant at having earned a goodly amount, or depressed at not having earned anything, and rushed back to their huts.

Valli came up to Bhagyam and related, with tears in her eyes, about how she had conceived in spite of all precautions, how the doctors had refused to carry out an abortion, and how this was the first time in ten years she had had to retain the foetus. Her woes seemed centred around the fact that no man would approach her once he took a look at her swollen belly, and that she could not earn enough even in the Procurement business.

Bhagyam criticized her roundly. "How could you let this get beyond your control? You let them graze on you, and then closed your eyes and dozed away, didn't you, kutti? The doctor didn't say that you'd die, did he? Try again, anyway. He might take pity on you. You must get rid of it, somehow. How many months is it now?"

"Even if the doctor does agree, how do I pay for it? They'll charge a hefty fee since it's been so many months." Valli sobbed as she purchased mutton curry and dosai for the women in the huts.

The hour was advancing, and large numbers of women loitered about the street. It was nine o'clock, and the crowd of men and boys had also built up steadily. The place heaved tumultuously, like waves at high tide. Many swayed or staggered about, dead drunk, barely aware of what they were doing. Others wandered about like tree branches buffeted by the wind. Some had come alone, drunk heavily and were now squatting on the ground, unable to proceed further. Others had collapsed, face flat on the ground, lying unattended. Young boys took advantage of this state of affairs, pilfering their wristwatches, rings, and purses.

"Sir, want a party?"

"Sir ..."

"Come over here, sir."

Five or six boys were running from shop to shop, trying to get Parties. Prema went behind three or four men too, in a vain bid to nab them, walking from stall to stall. Pestering and pleading came to naught; she gave up, came to Bhagyam's shop and ordered two dosais, promising to pay when she snapped up some party or other. In a little while, a young girl came looking for her.

"Come quick, Akka, the party might slip away if you don't. He's asking for the whole night. Better settle the terms yourself. Come quickly!"

She dragged at Prema, and the woman rushed with the girl to her hut, without even eating the dosai she had ordered.

The crowd swelled at the end of the first cinema show, and it seemed as though Chekkumedu had been waiting for that hour. People wandered about like ghosts in the dim light. Their carnal desires had turned them into animals.

After an hour, the crowd began to thin.

Abidha came in a hurry, bought some mutton curry and hastened away towards a hut. Arumugam looked at her departing form avidly, feeling an urge to talk with her. Suddenly, for no apparent reason, he felt a surge of irritation at Chekkumedu.

Curry shop Karim Bhai arrived, a little later. Bhagyam talked to him in an intimate tone, as though he was a close relative, addressing him Thambi, and Bhai. Even as he spoke to Bhagyam, Karim Bhai made eyes at Vasantha; he caressed his cheek and moustache, and smacked his lips often. Bhagyam, who owed him money, gave it to Vasantha and asked her to hand it over to him. Vasantha handed over the money to Karim Bhai, not even counting it, and Karim Bhai stuffed it in his pocket without checking the amount.

"Why don't you taste some of our mutton curry," Bhagyam asked Karim Bhai, noticing Vasantha's drawn face. She turned to Karim Bhai again. "Don't you have to go to other shops? If you'd come early, we could have spent some time talking."

Karim Bhai moved to the next shop, while Bhagyam scolded Vasantha for not talking enough, or being full of cheer, to suit Karim Bhai's tastes.

"Be pliant and pleasant, Vasantha," she admonished. "Don't talk back to anyone. Don't show your resentment or anger when you're dealing with customers. The docile cattle always ends up getting the most advantages, and everyone knows this. But, remember: only if we are pleasant and friendly will people flock to our stall. Don't nurse your anger. Our resentment will only spell our ruin. I've seen enough of all this in my own life, no? You don't have to use poison to kill someone. You can kill him even with jaggery, if you choose."

Vasantha said nothing. After a little while, she said, sotto voce, "If all you have is a donkey, what's the fun in riding it or getting down?"

"It's getting late. Shall we leave?" asked Bhagyam. "Get everything ready. Don't dilly-dally now, and finish quickly." The crowds had begun thinning. No longer did people have to jostle others; they walked comfortably. One could have a clear view of what was happening all over the area.

Lakshmi came running, took two dosais drenched in the chaalna side-dish and stuffed them into her mouth, hardly taking the time to sit down. Her glance fell on a man standing a little apart, with a hesitant expression on his face. She accosted him, holding the dosai plate all the while.

"Come on, its absolutely new. You can spend as much time as you
like – there'll be no problem. Are you new to this? Why would a man
be afraid? What's the use of sporting a huge moustache, then?" she
laughed. Then, she caught hold of him, left the dosai plate in
Arumugam's hand and hurried away.

Prema and Valli arrived, and talked a little to Bhagyam. Then, they
began roaming around the toddy shops and the bunks.

"Vasantha, why're you dawdling?" snapped Bhagyam, and Vasantha
began to wash the empty vessels quickly, setting apart the leftovers.
She shut down the oven; Arumugam assisted her. Two customers
came, asking for dosai and curry; Arumugam said that they had closed
shop and nothing leftover was hot enough.

"Cold food will do," they answered, and Arumugam served them
some cold mutton curry and dosai.

They chatted and drank, as they stood in front of the shop:

"I won't have any more."

"I won't sleep well tonight, if you won't drink this. Drink at least
a fifty."

"Later."

"Later? Later, when?"

"When I've had some mutton curry."

"Don't you worry about money. Order it to come, and it'll come.
Tell it to go, and it'll go. But you, I want always."

"All right then, pour a little."

"Drink as much as you like. Shall I buy two hundred more?

"You know, a woman betrayed me."

"Really?"

"I swear on your name. I'd been courting her for three years.
One day, a letter that I'd written to her fell into her husband's

hands. That did it. After that, she said that she'd clobber me with
her chappals."

"Ah. Women."

Bhagyam went in front, carrying a few articles, while Arumugam
went to buy Bhagyam's night-cap. When he returned, Vasantha picked
up whatever remained, and they began to walk together.

P rema, Malar and Valli arrived a little after Thangamani and Lakshmi came in. Arumugam tried to get up as though nothing extraordinary had happened, but Vasantha pushed him back onto his bed.

Thangamani wept a little. The rest spent a while with Bhagyam, as usual.

Vasantha announced that it was getting late, and the others informed Bhagyam that they would come by later. Thangamani, Lakshmi and Prema left, with a brief, "Take care." Valli and Malar tarried, yet. Valli sobbed, giving no reason for her tears. Her belly was more rounded now, and she was finding it difficult to walk.

"I can't understand what happened that day. The police are still there," complained Valli, who was feeling very sorry about her penniless state.

"I think I'll move to Ulunthoorpettai," announced Malar.

"Why would you want to go there?"

Malar grinned. "Won't we have a few men waiting for us there?" she gurgled, barely controlling her laughter, which rang out for a long time. "I don't know why, but I've had bouts of shivering for the past two days. I must go to the hospital. Akka, give me a hundred rupees," she wheedled.

Bhagyam refused at first, but relented later and gave her fifty.

"I don't know when the police will leave Chekkumedu," said Malar. "I think I'll leave for Ulunthoorpettai tomorrow." She left, Valli in tow.

Dharmamoorthy entered in a little while; Bhagyam elbowed him out roughly almost at once. "Get out. Whose urine have you come to drink here? This boy your kith and kin? You've already killed her – do you want to kill him too? Get lost. You'll invite trouble if you stay – I'll kick your balls in. Look at him come, that pimp ...!"

Vasantha tried to soothe her, but Bhagyam's ravings continued unabated. She began to wail now, dwelling on her friendship with Chinnapponnu ... while Dharmamoorthy stood outside the door, not batting an eyelid.

Bhagyam had known Chinnapponnu for eight years. Indeed, hers was the hut Chinnapponnu had lived in.

Bhagyam had run away to Pondicherry, having quarreled with her parents-in-law, and had spent the whole of the day in the bus stand. By nightfall she was at her wits' end, consumed by anger, tears and irritation, walking to and fro on the road.

It was at this moment that Karim Bhai's father had accosted her. "Coming? What's the rate? How much do you charge for the whole night? Only one man, though."

She'd grabbed him by the neck, clutched his hair, and spat in his face. She hadn't felt an iota of fear as she yelled at him in the middle of a public road, using the foulest language possible.

Karim Bhai's father, Kaja Bhai, had been taken aback. He had trembled as her voice rose in a crescendo, regretting ever having stopped by her. Humiliated, he began to walk fast in a bid to escape, and looked back once or twice.

What does it matter to me if she's still there, he wondered. He wrung his hands as he walked twenty feet, and then turned to look back again.

She still stood there.

He was startled. Doubt rose in his mind.

If she's a Chekkumedu woman, he mused, she wouldn't have spurned my advances. She wouldn't have slapped me, and cried out aloud. She'd have bargained her rates as soon as I made insinuating suggestions. Maybe she's a woman from a good family, who's lost her money on a journey. Maybe she's stranded and is in a fix about how she can take a bus to her destination. Why not find out?

He retraced two steps, and then hesitated. What if she thinks I'm returning to her with the same intention?

Gathering courage, he approached her. "Don't be angry, Amma. I asked you what I did, since you were standing alone. I'm sorry," he babbled. He looked at her anxiously, wondering what her reply might be.

Uncombed hair gathered and tied indifferently, a sari that came only a little above the ankles, a dirt smudged neck, the large, winnow-like nose ring, eyes sunken in hunger — how could he have thought this simple rustic woman, a Chekkumedu whore?

He felt some remorse. "What's your village?" he asked. "Where were you going? Did you miss a bus? Don't have money for a ticket? Are you looking for someone? Did you come with a group and get separated from them? Have you lost your way?"

His questions provoked her. "What's it matter to you where I come from?" she snapped. "What're you going to do about it? Mind your own business. No one's doing a striptease here. Why are you still hanging around?"

Kaja Bhai, however, persisted in trying to pacify her and enquiring about her. She sulked, looking for all the world like a child that had been slapped. Kaja didn't give up. He ignored her tongue-lashings, and plied her with questions. His persistence, altered attitude and the gentleness in his tone had their effect; eventually, she related her present situation and all that had happened to her.

"What are you going to do now?" asked Kaja Bhai.

"What can I do? Jump into a river or pond and die."

"For someone who talks with so much spirit, it doesn't make sense that you should kill yourself."

"What's the alternative?"

"There are so many other solutions to a problem. Killing yourself isn't the only way out."

"In that case, can you get me a job in someone's home?"

"Fine. Stay with my mother, tonight. We'll see if morning shows us a way."

She looked at Kaja Bhai intently, as though probing his intentions.

"There's no need to think anymore," he insisted. "I jumped to the wrong conclusions when I saw you standing alone in the street. This town has such a reputation. You wouldn't know anything about it. I'd have gone my way if it were day ... but its night, and my conscience wouldn't let me leave you here. A hundred other men would ask you what I did. I've told you what I think is the best. The rest is up to you." Kaja lit a bidi.

Can I trust him, wondered Bhagyam. If I go on standing here, won't other men make the same mistake he did and trouble me, as he says? What will I do, then?

Frightened at the prospect, Bhagyam enquired about Kaja's family; she asked him about his household. At last, it occurred to her that regardless of what transpired, no man could violate a woman's modesty unless she consented to it.

"You can spend the night with my mother," Kaja assured her. This instilled some confidence in her, and she agreed to accompany him to his house.

Kaja began his enquiries about domestic help that very night, and continued them for the next few days. His efforts yielded practically no results, and finally, he built a hut for her by the drain. She stayed in his home until this was ready for occupation. There were not as many huts or people at that time as there were now; the area had been used as a kind of roadside urinal by passers-by.

It was there that Bhagyam first met Chinnapponnu. Chinnapponnu, unlike other women, was a person of few words and calm temperament: honest and straightforward. There was no hanky panky about her; stealing and lying were foreign to her. Impressed by these qualities, Bhagyam allowed Chinnapponnu to make her home with her.

"What does it matter how she earns her living?" she argued with those who asked her why she had let Chinnapponnu in. "She's company – and I have help at home."

A few years of running a stall in Chekkumedu enabled Bhagyam to buy a piece of land in Mutthamizh Nagar, and build a hut there. She gifted the hut near the drain to Chinnapponnu. Off and on, Bhagyam would also give Chinnapponnu clothes, mutton curry, and dosai. Countless were the number of times she had had her released from police custody either by bribing the police, or by getting bail in courts. Whenever Chinnapponnu was ill, she would have her admitted to the hospital and pay the bills herself.

"Listen to me, woman," she would chide Chinnapponnu fondly. "Your naiveté will land you in trouble some day, if you're going to let men have a free rein – they'll bloat up your belly like a fluffy, fried paniyaaram," she warned. "As if anyone has any idea of right and wrong, these days! Other women manage their affairs so cleverly – why can't you? Every other woman's careful to see that the oven's burning bright at her home. Draping a sari around you doesn't make you one, eh? Or is it enough if you show off your body?"

Bhagyam took a sari or two as mortgage when she gave loans, but never did she ask such a thing of Chinnapponnu. Chekkumedu women often borrowed fifty or hundred rupees from Bhagyam, paying an interest of three or four paise. Bhagyam lent only to trustworthy women and permanent residents of the locality; she refused loans to anyone with the reputation of a troublemaker. If they persisted, she asked for their nose-ring or earring in mortgage. If the worst came to worst, she took two or three saris. In Chinnapponnu's case, however, the thought of charging interest or getting a mortgage never crossed her mind.

Bhagyam wailed and lamented as though she were at home instead of the hospital, completely oblivious of her surroundings. For all her grief-filled sobs, however, she did not spare Dharmamoorthy. "Call yourself a man, do you? You, who didn't know how to control your woman? Thoo! Ah, look at the imbecile, with his long moustache. Lying, cheating and talking filth all hours of the day ... why couldn't death have taken this ruffian, instead of her? Why doesn't it ever visit fellows like this one?"

Dharmamoorthy peered in longingly and then began to leave, whereupon Arumugam asked Vasantha to give the man five rupees.

Vasantha turned to Bhagyam, who said, "I'll give him money only if he takes me home in the rickshaw. It's a sin to give money to people who won't even feed their mothers, my girl."

Sometimes, Dharmamoorthy came to Bhagyam's stall, timing his visits so that they coincided with her absence. Arumugam usually gave him five or ten rupees, and even mutton curry and dosai, on occasion. Dharmamoorthy would not even peep in if Bhagyam happened to be in. He had come over thrice, ever since Arumugam had been admitted in hospital.

Bhagyam had never really liked Dharmamoorthy, and after Chinnapponnu's death, her dislike for him turned into full-blown hatred.

"Go home; it's getting late," Vasantha told Bhagyam twice or thrice.

Bhagyam insisted that she come with her too, whereupon Vasantha said, "You'd better go, first; I'll come later. Why do you want me now?"

Bhagyam insisted that she must, but Vasantha refused. By and by, her features took on a frigid expression, and her tone turned harsh.

Eventually, Bhagyam gave in, realizing that she could not change Vasantha's mind. "Don't dawdle about here; you'd better come in time. Ah, if my daughter were alive, why would I put up with you and your absurd moods?"

Vasantha heaved a deep sigh as soon as Bhagyam went out, as though relieved of a heavy load. She loosened her sari, adjusting the folds over her breasts. Then she gulped down water, as though possessed by an unquenchable thirst.

In a little while she relaxed, and the rigid tension lining her face disappeared. She sat on the floor, and rested her head on the edge of

Arumugam's cot. He could only see the back of her head, and wondered why she looked so thin and dark.

The riots and commotion that had torn through Chekkumedu the other day, came to his mind.

It had all happened last Sunday – a day which was always terribly crowded in Chekkumedu. It was eight at night, and Vasantha had gone behind the hut to answer the call of nature. Bhagyam had chased after a fellow who'd gobbled up a dosai but had not paid for it, and was haranguing him with all her might. Arumugam was in charge of the oven; sales was brisk.

Suddenly, a wild shriek erupted from somewhere to the north. Before they could find out what it was all about, all hell broke loose.

Arrack and soda bottles flew through the air; broken bottles were strewn all over the place. Bamboo staves were ripped off roofs. Stones and mud were flung about in all directions.

Arumugam began to pack away the articles in the stall hurriedly, determined to close shop. A cry rang out from somewhere in the eastern direction and he turned that way. Abruptly, a big stone landed in the pan containing the dosai batter; the vessel tipped over, and the dough spilled onto the floor. He bent down to pick up the pan as a crowd of people came rushing in, pushed Arumugam and rushed out to the south. A log of wood landed near Arumugam when he hastened to recover whatever was strewn all over the stall, and he escaped by the skin of his teeth.

Bhagyam came running in, shrieking, "Oh my god, the scoundrels ...!" She grabbed the cash box and began to put away the rest of the articles, assisted by Arumugam.

It was at this moment that a large stone found its target on

Arumugam's head. Simultaneously, a soda bottle sliced through his ribs. "Amma ...!" shrieked Arumugam, as he collapsed onto the floor.

Vasantha gave a screech of terror, dashed towards him, lifted him as though he were a baby and begun running. "You old hag – leave everything alone and come quickly! Let those vessels go to the dogs," she yelled to Bhagyam. "You chandali, come on now ...!"

She ran out and tried to stop passing auto-rickshaws at the Newtone Theatre corner. They, however, were hastening to escape the riot; none of them stopped for her. She carried Arumugam on her shoulder as far as the Cuddalore Road, and there, was able to get an auto. She took Arumugam to the Jipmer Hospital and got him admitted straightaway.

"What're you looking at me for?" asked Arumugam.

"I was just ... looking."

"Think you want to see your face in mine? How can that happen?"

"Quiet."

"You'd better push off."

"I'm not going to."

"Why not?"

"I don't like it there," murmured Vasantha.

"That's wrong."

"What's wrong?"

"Everything is."

"What's right, then?"

"Everything is."

"Well, then, tell me why you left the company. I'd been chaste until that day. Curse me, why did I ever see Bhagyam? It's my fate to slog in Chekkumedu ..."

Vasantha broke into heaving sobs, as though someone had slapped her. Arumugam tried his best to console her, but she could not stifle her cries, and continued to cry like a small child.

The two or three months following Arumugam's departure from the cardboard company had been enough, it seemed, to make way for all sorts of horrible events to occur.

The manager's molestations had gone beyond tolerable limits as the days passed. Vasantha was trapped. The watchman, an accomplice of the manager, informed a Krishnapuram youngster of what had occurred. The boy, in turn, threatened Vasantha that he would expose everything to her family, writing it out on the walls of the village, to boot. Vasantha had yielded to him too, helpless, giving up her body to him like a toy in the hands of a child.

News of her transgressions reached the village, nevertheless. Vasantha's brothers, sisters-in-law and relations erupted in anger.

"Cut her up and bury her, the brazen little bitch. How dare she, and at her age, too?" "You can't rest well enough without bedding a man, can you?" "Shave her head – stick her face with black and red dots, and throw her out of the village – the blasted whore's thrown the honour of our Nayudu clan to the winds! Our girls will be ruined if she isn't taught a lesson. How can we all walk the street wearing a veshti, then?" They thrashed her. They spat on her. "Go hang yourself."

The villagers vented their anger and disdain too, and beat her up. "Don't you dare walk the streets with this wretched body of yours, you shameless whore, you."

Utter misery choked Vasantha's words. She could not complete what she had begun; her words were broken, amidst cries and sighs. Her cheeks twitched; everything still stayed vividly fresh in her mind, as though it had happened just moments ago.

Had all this truly happened to Vasantha? Why? How had one blow followed the other, so perfectly orchestrated, as though predetermined?

She slapped herself. Arumugam did not stop her. He closed his eyes; images of Vasantha passed through his mind like a procession. Her eyes are sunken and her cheeks shriveled, now. She looks emaciated. Lifeless.

She had never refused a pail of water to any villager who needed it, back home, he reflected. It wasn't in her nature to be disobliging; she would even assist old women who owned no pails by lending her own. "It's a great merit, a punyam to satisfy anyone's thirst," she would explain, as she poured out buckets of water into the cupped hands of youngsters. "What have I got to lose by drawing a bucket or two more? How can you call yourself a human if you don't do even these little bits?"

Was this the same Vasantha? Arumugam wondered, with a heavy heart. What did she do to deserve her fate?

"How can I ever tell you what I've gone through? It's etched on my forehead that I'm going to die, slandered and despised. I haven't killed myself yet, because my self-respect won't be restored to me just because I do," she sobbed.

Arumugam sat up with an effort. He gazed at Vasantha, at a loss to find words to console her. All that he could say, after a brief struggle, was, "What's the use of crying, now? You can sob all day and night if that will achieve something. Forget everything, and let go." Still, she continued to weep.

A nurse came in after a long time. "Get out. Do you know what time it is, now? You can't stay here any longer, do you hear me? Get

out, now," she shouted at Vasantha, and walked out. Vasantha followed
the nurse at a run.

"Go away, you filth," the nurse abused her so loudly that Arumugam
could hear her. "What do you think this place is? Yei, yei ... what do
you think you're doing in a place like this?" Long moments passed
before Vasantha returned to Arumugam's side. She looked at him,
her gaze frozen. "I was denied all four, and was thrown in a four way
junction. When will I lose all ten and be carried in a paadai, I wonder?"
she murmured. "I can't think straight. My mind's still seething – I've
lost all hope about everything. I'm a fool, Arumugam. I've been a fool
all along. Life has betrayed me ..." she turned away from Arumugam,
and wept.

Her sorrow and tears wearied him. "It's late," he told her again
and again. "Bhagyam will yell at you," he reminded her.

Vasantha did not even turn towards him. Her unwillingness to leave
suggested that her most valuable possessions were in that room. She
sat glued to her seat, as though aware that she would find no place or
time to pour out her feelings this way. Arumugam, however, was bent
on dispatching her.

She turned to him. "I'm bothering you, am I? Does it all make you
want to throw up? You people won't let me in peace – you won't let
me share my feelings – my sadness ... what've I done to you, to
deserve this treatment?" She began to cry again.

Arumugam shut his eyes tight.

What a prosperous, noble village! A charitable village which had installed
drinking water booths and established rest houses for long distance
travellers. Doubtless, he thought, someone in the village might have
argued on Vasantha's behalf. "How will she survive, the poor girl?

The eyes have seen nothing; the ears have heard naught. Forget everything and find a way to get her married to someone who mightn't have heard these tales. She didn't do it willingly, did she, the artless, innocent girl? A woman's curse will dog at your footsteps not just for seven, but seven by seven generations. Something similar happened in a village I know – worse, in fact, because it was a low-caste fellow and an upper-caste girl – but did they cast her out?"

Hadn't it occurred to anyone that she might throw herself into a well, or hang herself? How she would have suffered – sobbed, wailed. How had she borne the thrashings, kicks and slaps, the abuse? Would her parents have allowed any of this, if they had still lived? There had been no earthly reason for Vasantha to leave home whether she had one meal a day or three, if it hadn't been for that wretched company. Why did she have to suffer such a fate? Tears filled his eyes.

When the nurse entered again, Arumugam wiped his tears, and looked at her. Her face appeared serene now; she did not ask Vasantha to leave. And was that a glimmer of a smile on her face?

Vasantha went with her when she walked out, and returned after a little while. "I'll be back early next morning." She left half-heartedly.

Arumugam was exhausted. He sat up and switched on the light, but could not bear the glare it cast. He closed his eyes and lay down, and immediately felt as though he had been pushed into a phantom world. His whole body hurt; the pain was intense along his spine. It seemed as if he was carrying the weight of two bodies. He wanted to sleep. The fan carried the breeze over to him, swathing him in waves of fire. How could he stop it, though? It would be his only companion during the long hours of the night. And if even this sound wasn't there ...?

Nurse Pushpa Mary came in. She spoke calmly now, for the first time, and Arumugam liked the way she did. She administered an injection, and wrote a note in the patient record sheet hanging from the cot. She explained to Arumugam about the medicines he had to take, articulating each word slowly, as though speaking to a toddler. She stayed a little while, surveying the room as if she were new at work.

"How are you feeling?" she asked, unusually, for her. "Tell me if you need anything." Then she went out.

Arumugam was afraid to be alone. He shouldn't have asked Vasantha to leave, he thought. He didn't quite know what to do. A strange doubt rose in his mind. Was he alive, or dead?

He looked at the fan revolving above him. His mind went back to the Chekkumedu riot, and he wondered what might have happened if he'd died in it. The thought was frightening. He perspired heavily, imagining himself lying dead with wounds and blood all over, while flies and ants crawled over the body. Would he have shared Chinnapponnu's fate if he'd died, with his corpse rotting in a drain? Chinnapponnu had had Dharmamoorthy, Bhagyam and the women of Chekkumedu to mourn her ... who would mourn him?

He was an orphan, he realized. Sobs suffocated him, blanking his mind and thoughts. How could you live without a single soul related to you?

After a few moments spent in tears, he remembered all the gods he'd ever known. He began to murmur their names one by one.

Vasantha was attending to the oven as Bhagyam made preparations to leave for Chekkumedu.

"Don't dawdle," instructed Bhagyam. "Wind up the chores here, and come over quickly." She left, taking a few essential articles with her.

Arumugam came over to light a cigarette in the oven fire.

"What more do you want, now? We lack nothing, no?" Vasantha murmured, laughing. "We've got a windfall waiting at our doorstep, haven't we?" The rigidity that had lined her face while Bhagyam was present had vanished; now, she was smiling.

Hearing a shout, she went to the door. A few boys had come calling on Arumugam to paste cinema posters. "He won't be coming," Vasantha informed them. "He hasn't recovered completely, yet. Don't call him out for such jobs, anymore. Go away, Thambigalaa, he's not coming."

Arumugam took a good look at her when she came back in. She had been working in front of the oven fire, and perspiration drenched her body. Her blouse clung to her form, damp and sticky.

Arumugam edged closer to her. "May I ask you something?"

"What would you want to ask a wretch raped by the whole wide world?"

"Very well, then. I won't."

"Why do say that? What're you going to ask that others haven't, already?"

"All right. Why don't you go to Chekkumedu during the day?"

"I won't."

"Why not?"

"I never will," Vasantha said firmly.

"That's exactly what I'm asking. Why do you say that you won't go?"

"Imagine the reactions of the people from my village if someone happened to see me there ..."

"Ha-ha."

"What're you laughing at?"   ⁹

"Ha-ha."

"You sound like a dog barking."

"Ha-ha."

"Why, you disgraceful fellow." Vasantha dealt Arumugam a few sound slaps on his thigh, pinched his cheeks, hands and stomach. He did not stop laughing even then; her mood changed as she watched his amusement, and she began to laugh, too.

They laughed together for a long time. Vasantha began to cough, the effort bringing tears to her eyes. For all that, she could not stop chuckling along with Arumugam.

"What would it matter if somebody did see you?"

"Wouldn't they go back and report that they saw the prosperous Nayudu house's daughter in Chekkumedu?"

"Which Vasantha would they say they saw?"

"How many Vasanthas are here, anyway?"

"So you're Vasantha?"

"Who else is?"

"Are you the only Vasantha, hereabouts?"

"Yes."

"What about Saanthi, Punniyavathi, Selvi, Sasirekha, Meenakshi, Manjayee, Mariamma, and all the rest of them?"

"I shall always stick to my given name, no matter what."

"Why do we people need names at all?"

"True, we don't, really."

They elbowed, beat, and pinched each other like a newly married couple, laughing together for a long time.

Suddenly, amidst all the laughter, Vasantha began to sob. It seemed she could not stop. Arumugam looked at her, bewildered, regretting having been so outspoken. He wanted to stop her tears somehow, and touched her gently. "Don't cry. What's this? Why're you sobbing for every little thing that happens?"

He held the lamp in front of her face and looked at her eyes intently. Perspiration had stuck strands of hair on her forehead and cheeks in a beautiful pattern, much like the kolams in front of houses.

Vasantha raised her head and looked at Arumugam, staring at her. She took the lamp from his hand and placed it aside. Then, she tried to take his hand and fold it in hers. Arumugam withdrew his hand abruptly.

"Why not?" she asked.

"It's wrong."

"How?"

"It's just ... wrong."

"What's so wrong about this?"

"Sit away from me."

"Why should I?"

"There's no reason."

Arumugam moved away by himself and reclined on the wall. He looked at Vasantha, whose face was covered in darkness; only her back could be seen. He felt like talking to her, but did not know what he could talk about. What would he do if she began to weep again? Once she started, she would not stop easily. But unless she cried, she wouldn't be able to talk.

Now, more than ever, he thought her extremely beautiful. He wanted to tell her so, but bit his lips. Vasantha, however, questioned him:

"What're you thinking about so deeply?"

"My grandfather."

"Your father's father or your mother's father?"

"My Pootthurai grandfather."

"Was he a good man?"

"I don't know. But he was good at telling stories."

"What kinds of stories?"

"All kinds. Ghost stories, stories about spirits, stories about gods ... he knew plenty of good ones. But what's the use?"

"Why do you say that?"

"He used to say often that my mother was Pootthurai soil ... but you know what my mother became, don't you?"

"Leave it."

"Why did I run away, that day?"

"That's fate. Such things do happen."

"Will our village be the same now, as the day we left it?"

"Why not?"

"You're lying."

While working in the factory at Mettuppalayam, Arumugam had access to plenty of news about Krishnapuram. Vasantha would tell him the latest as soon as they met, first thing in the morning. He ceased to get any news of the village, however, once he left the company. Occasionally, when he came across someone from Krishnapuram, his mind would go back to it – the cheri houses, the streets, the people, their speech, laughter, play, their threats; those who had beaten him, those who had fought with him, those who had pushed his head into the water in the tank ...

He had forgotten nothing. How could he forget the whistles he used to make out of Poovarasu leaves? The toy cars fashioned out of jowar stems, and how he used to drive it through the streets? Making a train out of jowar stems, sitting on a bullock cart's yoke and swinging it up and down, imagining that he was going to another village to conclude a marriage, to convey the sad news of a death, or the glad news of a girl coming of age, or even to invite people to the temple festival ... which of these memories could he give up?

Loading sand on plantain stems and dragging it through the streets, yelling out, "Here's the lorry, here's the lorry!"

Swimming in the lake endlessly, frolicking through the golden hours of day.

Screeching, "Sweet potatoes! Sweet potatoes, a kilo for a Rupee!" as he saw the sweet potato cart, and gorging himself on them, finally, the reward for his services as a middleman.

Selling Dhanabhagyam's pair of chappals to the dates vendor when he came announcing, "Dates in exchange for brass and lead, dates for iron vessels, dates for plastic buckets!" ... oh, how she had thrashed him then, and indeed, hadn't given up beating him the whole day and even all the following week. "You dratted boy, it was a new pair, not even four months old ...!" How could he ever forget that trouncing?

All the trees and plants of Krishnapuram still lay fresh in his memory; he could describe and list them all as though he had seen them moments ago. He could tell plants and trees even before they came within his line of sight.

Blooming flowers, insects and beetles that hovered about ... he could tell them all, just by inhaling their distinctive scents and smells; Kizhavar had taught him all of it. He knew all about the flowers over which golden beetles, dragon-flies, and black beetles hovered; the beetles that rolled ballsout of cow dung, and the one that made an areca-nut sized ball of night soil; he knew where one could find the anthills of red ants, black ants, and the mounds of winged white ants and snakes ... he knew all this too.

And he wondered if the Krishnapuram of his memories still remained the same.

Arumugam reminded Vasantha that they had to go to Chekkumedu.

Well aware that Bhagyam would scold her if she was late, Vasantha completed her make-up quickly. Taking the articles meant for Chekkumedu, Arumugam locked the stall door, and they began to walk.

Vasantha looked pretty, like a small, well decorated chariot. She knocked him on his head fondly when he told her this.

"True, Arumugam, I'm just a painted doll now. My stupidity led me to this," she sighed. Her sincerity and intimate tone appealed to him; Arumugam walked closer to her.

There was only thing that he didn't like and this, he told her candidly.

"Why've you cut up your hair? And the eye-liner ... you shouldn't have applied so much."

Vasantha walked silently, not taking her eyes off Arumugam. "Do you think I've caked myself up because I like it?" she said dolefully, after a while. "That woman's the reason for all of this. Tell me, can we ever do anything the way we want to?" Arumugam made no comment.

The road was crowded. Traffic was heavy; it was becoming difficult to walk.

Arumugam was allergic to crowds on any given day; he always felt an urge to throw up in the midst of one. He avoided crowds as much as possible, and always walked with his head bent. One had to wonder if this *was* Pondicherry, to look at the crowd. What was the hullabaloo for? Why this swarm of people? What part of it was after the wine and women?

Pondicherry, it seemed, had become the byword for liquors and women. Half the shops in any street were wine shops. As for women, the first grade would be found in hotels, the second in lodges and the third in areas like Chekkumedu, and the locality near the drain where Chinnapponnu and others had their huts. Aside from this gradation, there was a region-wise classification in the hotels and lodges as well. The women in hotels and lodges were the ones sent to people who asked for call-girls.

When those who hired rickshaws for journeys asked, "Can I get a party?" Dharmamoorthy would describe the grades and quote the rates.

"Ah, the kutti's a wiggling coquette, and asks for the coins in your pocket," he would chuckle in a low, singsong voice.

Arumugam himself had taken whoremongers to Chekkumedu, lodges

and hotels quite often. He was tipped very well, and he often got
more by raising the rate for the rickshaw rides.

Pondicherry was swelling with crowds of people in recent days;
regardless of what street you went to, you could see not less than ten
white folk. Why did so many foreigners flock to Pondicherry?

"Look over there, Arumugam ... what's that? Why's such a crowd
over there? Oh, look at the people walking over there! Why's that girl
swaggering along?" Vasantha kept pointing out something, or asking
questions as they walked.

She began talking of many things when they had passed the
new bus stand: she hated Chekkumedu. She would get a job
through Pushpa Mary, somehow. She smiled as she praised herself
for having had the forethought to bring her tenth standard
certificate with her when she had left home. She talked about
Pushpa Mary in the same breath as wanting to run away from
Mutthamizh Nagar.

"I pity her. We're comparatively lucky. So many people in the
country are in such a miserable condition," she commiserated. "Their
fate's so much worse than ours." Then, she continued to talk about
Pushpa Mary.

Pushpa Mary was thirty eight years old. Unmarried, she had no
relations, and was a refugee from Burma. A Catholic Sister had raised
her and given her an education. Six months after Pushpa Mary took
up work, the Sister died.

In the course of her duties, Pushpa Mary developed intimate relations
with a Doctor, making her resort to abortions four times. The doctor
transferred himself and was now married to someone else.

"Now she hates men as a whole," explained Vasantha. "Oh god, why must these things happen? But there are all kinds of people in the world. The things one has to do to make a living, and keep body and soul together!" Vasantha lamented, as tears filled her eyes.

That was Vasantha, all over. She usually shared everything about her life to anyone, if he or she spoke to her for a scant five minutes. She kept back nothing, and listened without a hint of boredom to everyone's stories. Having listened to their woes, she would grieve as though it had happened to her own with kith and kin. This was what endeared Vasantha to people.

Three weeks after admission into hospital, Arumugam had recovered completely. Vasantha had made arrangements with Pushpa Mary, passing him off as her relative, and had had him admitted into the "A" ward. Likewise, she had arranged through Pushpa Mary for Arumugam to remain in the hospital even after he had recovered.

Arumugam was not in favour of this.

"There's nothing for you in Chekkumedu, is there?" argued Vasantha. "Do you have a family waiting for you? You talk as if your money would be looted, if you stayed here. Lie quiet for a few days. Is your whole world in that pig sty of a hut?"

Soon, Vasantha became an intimate friend of Pushpa Mary. This was very convenient, as the shops in Chekkumedu had not reopened after the riots, and Vasantha did not have to go to Bhagyam's stall.

Pushpa Mary dragged Vasantha along, to a number of places, promising her the sweeper's job she wanted.

Vasantha stopped Arumugam at the Newtone Theatre corner with a word of warning: "Go back. Bhagyam won't leave you in peace if you come into Chekkumedu."

She thrust a ten rupee note into his hand. Barely three days had passed since he had been discharged from the hospital; she insisted that he should not come to Chekkumedu. She herself went there, however, carrying the basket containing provisions and food items.

Arumugam stood looking at her, watching until she vanished out of sight.

Arumugam walked to the beach and stayed there until around midnight, having left Vasantha on the outskirts of Chekkumedu. When he finally returned home, he found that Vasantha had reached there much earlier. He heard voices inside as he approached the door; there appeared to be a conversation between two persons. He hesitated a little before entering.

He went in, but found no one inside except Vasantha, and looked confused. "Who was here with you?" he asked her, smiling.

"Why do you ask?"

"No reason."

"She who has no lord and master, may stay or gad about, what's it matter? Who's got the right to question her, anyway?"

"What's that supposed to mean?"

"I've got no one. Who'll want to be with me?"

"You're answering a question I never asked."

"Can't you see the mirror in my hand?"

"Ah. I see."

"Why are you standing? Sit down, won't you?"

Vasantha resumed inspecting her face in the mirror. She lay on her
stomach, resting her elbow on the ground and her chin on her palms,
and stared at her reflection in the mirror as though peering at something
vastly important. A kerosene lamp burnt steadily, to her right. Her
cheeks, neck and chest were damp with perspiration; strands of hair
stuck to her forehead, drenched in sweat. She closed and opened one
eye after another alternately. She screwed up her face, closed both
eyes, then opened either one or the other, and chuckled at her reflection.

Then she parked the mirror at various angles, pulling it nearer or
pushing it to a distance, and admired the image it produced. She
bared her teeth, stuck out her tongue, tweaked her nose, and swung
her plaited hair in front. She tried to touch the tip of her nose with
her tongue, and giggled at the mirror. It seemed there would be no
end to her antics; she did not seem conscious of Arumugam,
beside her.

Vasantha's pranks amused and irritated Arumugam in equal measure.
Feeling a prick of emotion at her silence, he snapped:

"Why don't you have a photograph taken?"

"Why would I?"

"Then you'd be able to stare at it to your heart's content."

"I'd hate that. How can I go on seeing a single expression all
the time?"

"What does it matter if you do?"

"I won't like it."

"Why not?"

"Today's Vasantha isn't the same as yesterday's, no? My face lost
its life a long time ago."

Arumugam wanted to laugh at her words, but he watched her calmly.

He regretted having left the beach and returned home. What could he do, however?

He took Vasantha's hair in his hands, unbraided it halfway, and braided it, again. He liked the fragrance of the jasmine flowers she wore; though a short strip, the perfume pervaded the entire house. He wished that the fragrance alone remained, without her presence. He gazed at Vasantha, who sat the mirror, repeating, "Vasantha, Vasantha," over and over again.

He too laid himself on his stomach by her side, resting his elbows on the ground, his chin on his palms and smiled, looking at her. She continued to stare at the mirror.

"Arumugam, is this Vasantha really myself? Is it me and nobody else? Who's fair and who's not, in the darkness? What's the use of a glowing skin for outcastes like me? My life ended overnight. Why does a bat hang upside down? Because that's its fate."

Arumugam turned away from Vasantha and closed his eyes. Then, he opened his eyes and looked at the house and Vasantha. The light of the lamp flickered; he sat still, not knowing what to do.

She was looking into his eyes intently. "In whose face can I go and see my own? If it weren't for this mirror, I'd be as good as dead. Those who have nothing should have at least a mirror, for themselves."

Arumugam snatched the mirror from Vasantha's hands and put it away. He then turned over and looked at the ceiling, feeling an urge to walk somewhere. He lay on his side, resting his left elbow on the ground and his chin on the left palm, and looked at Vasantha. She had covered her face with her palms. Anger and pity consumed him at the same time. What was she saying? Why was she talking like this?

How many Vasanthas were there with him at the moment: the one who'd fed him, making him sit in the cattle shed in her home at

Krishnapuram? The one who had taken him to the company and got him a job? The one who had rushed him to the hospital all by herself, when he had been wounded in the riot? The one who, a moment ago had been talking like a melodramatic actress in a cinema ...? I could talk to her, he mused. But what could I say?

He thought of going out ... but if he did, Bhagyam, who slept at the doorstep might wake up and tick him off. "Where've you been wandering about, without coming to the stall?" He would not know what to say.

He sat up, lit a cigarette and inhaled the smoke deeply.

Vasantha sat up along with him, and spoke in a broken voice. "Whose food did I fling mud in? Whose drinking water did I poison, whose path did I wreck with thorns? What's my crime?" she lamented. "When have I ever been happy, with a man of my choice? Why did they thrash me black and blue, trampling me like threshed paddy? I never sleep – I can't sleep. Will the shit inside disappear if you wash your asshole?"

She bent her head. "Oh, curse my fate," she whimpered. "Why did I ever come across Bhagyam that night?"

For an instant, her first meeting with Bhagyam came to mind.

She had come away from home, and having arrived at the Pondicherry bus stand, had not the ghost of an idea about where to go next. She did not have the courage to go to the homes of relatives or friends; if her brothers were to get wind, they would drag her home by force and thrash her.

She stayed in the bus stand all day, shifting from one place to another. When darkness fell, however, fear had crept up on her; she began to wish that somebody did come to fetch her, that she could go home with them ... for if she went back on her own, she would lose what little self-respect she had.

The traffic grew light as night advanced. People stood about only in the bus stops. The Police had begun patrolling, since it was past eleven; they warned those who were sitting alone or dozing off about thieves, and began interrogating those who seemed to be staying on, despite their warning.

Vasantha grew frightened when they started questioning someone near her, shuddering. What could she say if they asked her for her name and her destination? They would take her to the police station, if she did not give a satisfactory answer.

She started walking on the road briskly when this occurred to her, as though going on an urgent piece of business. When she reached the end of the main road, she proceeded where her feet took her. Once or twice, she turned back to see where the police were.

It had been barely a minute since two auto- rickshaws coming from the direction of Pillai Chavadi in the west nearly collided and went past her, when a female voice screamed, "Ayyo, my god!"

Vasantha looked back. Twenty or thirty feet behind her lay a woman, screaming, vessels lying scattered on the ground.

Vasantha rushed to the woman and helped her rise and sit up, asking what had happened. Seven or eight passers-by had collected in the meantime, berating the auto drivers, with no intention of seeing to the victims. It was only Vasantha who examined the wounded woman, gathered the scattered vessels, and arranged them in the bamboo basket lying nearby. She tried to console Bhagyam too, who was wailing, shrieking, and abusing the auto-rickshaw drivers.

"Quiet, now," comforted Vasantha. "Let's be thankful that what might have been a bad accident turned out to be only a few bruises."

Bhagyam got up, shook her hands and legs to make sure that there was no serious injury, adjusted her sari and felt the bruises on her

knees, hands, hip and shoulders with her hand. Her tears had
not been so much for her wounds, as for damaged vessels and their
scattered contents.

As the crowd dispersed, Vasantha instructed Bhagyam to "go
carefully," and began to leave, when Bhagyam called to her.

"Could you just carry this basket up to my house? I'm finding it
difficult to walk," she lifted her sari and inspected the bruises on
her thigh.

Vasantha hesitated. This is uninvited trouble, she thought.
Why should I get involved in it? Who's she, and why's she asking for
my help?

She did not, however, have the heart to leave the woman helpless.
"Well then, come quickly." She hefted the basket.

Bhagyam walked alongside, limping as she cursed the auto drivers.
"Let the sun come up, they'll come to know what's in store for them.
Won't I get hold of them ...?" When they had gone a little distance,
Bhagyam asked Vasantha who she was.

Vasantha volunteered no answer, and broke into sobs.

"That night was the beginning," Vasantha told Arumugam. "Where
else could I go? I stayed with Bhagyam – that was my fate, I thought.
All that I knew about Pondicherry, before this, was that the sea was
close by. Only after I began to stay with Bhagyam did I know that
there was a place called Chekkumedu, too."

Arumugam was drowsy, but Vasantha was talking to him.
He could sleep in peace if she stopped talking and put out the
lamp. Why was Vasantha talking on and on? Her words aroused
all sorts of memories; memories of events he had been trying to
obliterate forever.

Agitation gripped his mind as never before. He closed his eyes, wondering how he could find release from such torment.

Vasantha shook him up, asking the reason for his silence. Then, she stood up and gulped water noisily, giving some to Arumugam too. She scrutinized him intently, holding the lamp in front of his face.

Arumugam snatched the lamp and put it away. "What are you searching for, in my face?" He asked.

"Without doubt, it's beautiful."

"Whose face are you talking about?"

"Your face, of course."

"Ha ha. There're many faces ... which one do you like? Which one is the most beautiful?"

"If you had thousands of faces, all of them would be beautiful. They would all be dear to the eyes and mind."

"Would any woman like a man who had just the one face? And would any man like such a woman too?"

"Have you ever cried?" asked Vasantha.

"I don't know."

"You're lying."

"Fine, then. What're you crying for?"

"There's only one thing I cry about – how all of them thrashed me, one after another, aiming at my private parts," Vasantha murmured. "I wish I didn't have It in my body. I don't know how I held on to my life those eight days in the village. How they thrashed me, battered and kicked me, trampling me, threshing me underfoot like paddy in the fields ... it's a wonder that I'm still holding on to life."

"Don't cry."

"I'm not."

"I see tears in your eyes."

"I won't keep anything from you. Even those who pretended to console me looked only for what was below my waist."

"You mustn't cry."

"No, I won't. I tried to humiliate others, but I ended up humiliating myself. That would have been the picture, even if I'd given up my life. I realize that only now."

"Why're you digging up all that now?"

Vasantha's tears broke free. She beat her hands and forehead on the ground, in a frenzy. A wild swipe of her hair extinguished the lamp.

Arumugam stopped her from knocking herself senseless, whispering, "Don't cry," as he clasped her tightly to himself. In return, she threw herself into his lap, face down, and sobbed as though her heart would break.

Arumugam placed his hands on her back, and looked around. He stared at the house plunged in darkness, himself, and Vasantha lying on his lap.

Fear gripped him. He moved away and lit a cigarette. Barring the twinkling tip of the cigarette, it was pitch dark.

A little later, Vasantha wiped her face, and stretched her legs, reclining on the wall close to Arumugam.

"Arumugam," she whispered.

"Vasantha," he whispered back.

She continued to repeat his name. He responded, turning her name into a mere sound.

Doubt grew in him, suddenly. He stopped murmuring, "Vasantha," and thought of all the other names he knew. What was the meaning behind all this? Why had Vasantha poured out to him all that happened to her? Would she have told this to others? Or am I the only one she's told it to? Why does she still guard all that happened in the distant past, events that have nothing to do with the present?

He, on the other hand, had forgotten everything. Or had he? What about the memories he could not afford to let go? Journeys in the village to cut nocchi twigs, his days at school, the days of mapping roads, days spent pedalling a rickshaw, Mettuppalayam, cooking assignments, Bhagyam's stall – so many more ...

Arumugam lit the lamp again; light spread in the room, accompanied by a smoky, acrid smell. The light threw their shadows on the walls and floor, the images swaying strangely. An interesting sight.

A black beetle was hovering around the lamp. Then, it flitted over to the trunk kept in the room, the saris hanging on the pole and the smoke charred rafters. Arumugam and Vasantha watched the beetle. It approached them one moment and then flew away. After a little while, it flew upwards, went up a hole in the rafter, and disappeared, its drone dying away gradually.

Vasantha asked Arumugam to fetch water, and drank it.

"I thought so," she said, as soon as he came near her and sat reclining on the wall, stretching his legs.

"What about?"

"Just ... something."

"Tell me."

"That you would come, now."

"How did you know?"

"How can I explain if you keep asking for a reason?" she said. "My heart told me so."

"Raise the wick of the lamp a little."

"No, I'm afraid of the light."

"But I'm afraid of the dark. The whole locality's deep in sleep. Let's go to bed."

"What does it matter if the whole locality's asleep? Listen to this ..."

"Listen to what?"

"Yesterday, I dreamt a strange dream," Vasantha began. "Listen, and tell me if it's a good omen. In the dream, first, it seems that I'm comfortably asleep, stretching out my legs. After a while I look down, and my legs are missing below the knees. When I look again, I can't see either my legs or my hands, and I'm just a trunk without limbs. And then, suddenly, my body's sinking into the ground. I try my best to move about, but I can't ... and when I finally look up, a mesquite tree stands where I lay sleeping. I pat the ground, trying to search for myself, wondering where I'd disappeared to ... and that was when I woke up."

B arely eight months after Arumugam had been discharged from hospital and had begun to go to Bhagyam's stall along with Vasantha, Pushpa Mary got a job for her in the hospital. The next day, Vasantha left Bhagyam's house.

Three months had passed since Vasantha began to stay with Pushpa Mary. She insisted on Arumugam also staying with her, but Arumugam continued to stay with Bhagyam in spite of her pleas. Vasantha was displeased with him; she did not look him up at all.

Even if she doesn't wish to meet me, thought Arumugam, why mustn't I meet her?

He visited her. He was returning after a four-day stay, when, even at a little distance from Mutthamizh Nagar, he could see the area where Bhagyam had had her hut. It resembled the epicentre of an earthquake.

Alarmed, he came running. Barring the signboard reading Mutthamizh Nagar, there was no sign of there having been a habitation in the area, at all. What had happened to the cluster of hundred odd huts? Whom could he find out the details from? He rushed to Chekkumedu, searching desperately for Bhagyam, and met her, Thangamani and Sekar along the way.

As soon as she saw Arumugam, Bhagyam came running, grasped him, and cried her eyes out.

"Look at this," she showed the wounds inflicted by the police. The police had demolished the hut Bhagyam had built in Mutthamizh Nagar, along with the other huts. The land was purampokku, not private property, and had promptly been cleared by the Government.

Offered no other alternative, Bhagyam had repaired the hut that Chinnapponnu had occupied, and they had been staying there the past three days. It was when she had refused to vacate her Mutthamizh Nagar house, asking the policemen, "I've lived in this house the past ten years. Don't I have the right to live here?," that the policeman had beaten her up mercilessly. Hospitalized for two days, she had been discharged only that very day.

She cursed Vasantha for having gone to stay with Pushpa Mary. "I can't even think of her as a woman. Would you look at the way she struts about, showing herself off? I don't know what black magic that Pushpa Mary employed to seduce my daughter." She cursed Arumugam also. "Why didn't you discipline Vasantha? Why did you stay with them four days, for no reason? Poda, you imbecile. Don't have any idea about how to keep a woman in his pocket. Why does a fellow like you need a moustache?"

Malar had run away, she lamented, taking with her three saris and one hundred rupees belonging to Bhagyam. She had also cheated Bhagyam in a loan transaction of hundred rupees.

"It's time to go to the court," Thangamani and Sekar, who had been standing aside, reminded Bhagyam. Bhagyam dragged Arumugam along with her.

Sekar kept grumbling throughout during the journey to the court.

"It's not even been two days since I brought those three women," he complained. "And already the police are demanding cuts. Sons of bitches. That fair girl isn't well – she hasn't been able to entertain even a single party. How am I going to make any money with them?"

"You go out to get girls, but can't bother to make sure that they're good quality," Bhagyam told him off. "You haven't got the right to complain." Sekar walked along, head bent.

Once they reached the court premises, Sekar and Thangamani went to the lawyer's chamber. Arumugam stayed outside.

When they finally paid a fine, got the eight girls they had come for released, and walked up to the Law College opposite the Court, Thangamani and Abidha began to quarrel. Abidha had returned only yesterday, having stayed in Salem for a week, and had been arrested the very day she had returned.

Thangamani objected to her having gone to Salem in the first place, while Abidha snapped back at her, not even considering that she was speaking to her mother. "I'll go where I like, and stay as long as I like. That's my affair. Did I ask you to get me released?"

The two began a shouting match right in the middle of the road, and eventually, it was Bhagyam who pacified Abidha. "Go and sit on the beach till the evening. You can come back when it's dark," she advised, and sent her with Arumugam. Sekar hurried away to Chekkumedu with the four girls he had brought along for business.

Thangamani left, taking Prema, Valli and Manjayee, and abusing Abidha, all the while. Bhagyam went with them.

Abidha walked by Arumugam, eyes firmly fixed on the ground.

Arumugam looked at the French buildings on both sides of the road as he walked along; he did not speak a word to her until they reached the beach road.

He bought tea for both of them in the Le Café on the beach road. It surprised him that Abidha had not spoken a word to him on her own. Walking out of the Le Café, Arumugam sat on the bench on the opposite side adjacent to the road. Abidha sat by him.

Arumugam looked out at the sea about thirty or forty feet away, throwing sidelong glances at Abidha all the while. She, however, merely crossed one leg over the other and looked at the bicycles and pedestrians going about, as though not even aware that someone sat by her. Although Arumugam tried to divert his mind by looking at the sea, the dark blue colour of the vast ocean did not attract him today; he did not know why. The sky was cloudless, and the men working in the harbour could be seen clearly. Lots of people stood about in groups where the waves broke onto the shore. The largest crowd was near the Gandhi statue. But how long could he look at the sea?

Arumugam began to talk to Abidha. "Why did you quarrel with your mother like that?"

Her face hardened the moment he said this, and her eyes turned bloodshot. He was afraid that she might start crying.

"I'll run away again," she replied. "She won't let me live if I don't." She resumed staring at the road.

Arumugam turned his gaze towards the road too. Pedestrians walked in both directions. A boy coming alone from the southern direction walked step by step over the white line in the middle of the road, as though measuring the distance. A lean white man with a fully shaven head gleaming in the sun, walked past that boy with long strides, on wooden sandals that sanyasis wear, making a tak tak noise. Arumugam watched the white man, astonished. After the white man went out of sight, Arumugam turned his unenthusiastic gaze towards the sea again.

Were it night, it would be a wonderful sight. The lights in the boats would twinkle in the sea, creating a beautiful pattern against the background of the dark sea, urging one to drink in the scene. Cars, motorcycles, even cycles and rickshaws were banned on the beach road after four in the afternoon. Watching just the pedestrians was boring. He had had no food, and an empty stomach created a headache.

"Shall we make a move?" he asked Abidha, but she did not reply. She was bent on looking at the people moving about, as before. The things she had gone through ... arrested by the police at eleven the previous night, no sleep or food throughout all that time and standing in court the whole day on legs throbbing with pain, had exhausted her. Normally a cheerful person, she was now sullen and taciturn. Her face wore a jaded look as though she had starved a whole week, and her eyes were sunken. Noticing Arumugam's gaze on her, she turned towards him.

"What're you looking at?"

"Just looking ... no reason."

Abidha gave a scornful laugh. She called the ice vendor, bought two pieces of ice cones and gave one to Arumugam, sucking on hers with relish. She was regaining her enthusiasm gradually. She rose up to get another ice-cone, but Arumugam stopped her.

"I want one," Abidha said, adamant.

Arumugam sat closer to her, and asked why she quarreled with Thangamani and left for other towns so often.

"I hate it here," she answered curtly.

"Why?" he asked.

She stared at him. "I hate it, and that's it," she snapped.

Suddenly good-humoured, she began to pat Arumugam's cheeks, and pinched his thighs fondly. Arumugam experienced a sudden urge to crush her into a hug. He was silent for a little while.

"Will you come away with me?" he asked, abruptly.

Abidha looked at him as though startled. Suddenly, she burst into laughter. She laughed for a long time. It seemed that she was laughing at him, the way she was shaking with mirth, clutching her stomach.

It appeared she could not control her amusement. The more she laughed, the more did Arumugam hang his head, speechless, looking at his toenails.

"What did you just ask?" she asked, still laughing.

"Forget it. Let's go."

"I won't. Not until you repeat what you just said."

"Nothing."

"Are you going to tell me or not? I'll strip you."

"It's getting late. Get up."

"I won't. Tell me."

"What do you want me to tell you?"

"What you said earlier."

"Leave that. Let's just go."

"I won't. Tell me," persisted Abidha.

"I asked you if you'd come away with me."

"Why did you?"

"I just ... felt like it."

"Why must I come with you?" she gurgled merrily. "Are you going to marry me?"

"Yes."

"I don't want to marry you."

"Why not?"

"There's no reason. And even if there was, I wouldn't tell you."

"We could live together."

"Chi poda, you and your insane wife crazes ...!" Abidha began to laugh again.

Arumugam began to stare at the sea vacantly, realizing that she wouldn't stop. He regretted having asked Abidha what he had. His agitation grew, unable as he was, to understand the meaning of her laughter.

He felt like screaming aloud. He wanted to sob without reserve. He wanted to get away from there. The salt laden breeze of the sea made the atmosphere damp and sultry, matching his mood. The sun's fierce heat had subsided. He looked at the pedestrians on the road, the waves and the isolated boats far out in the sea.

When he finally said, "Let's go," Abidha rose, stifling her chuckles. She walked, keeping herself two feet away from Arumugam. They proceeded towards Chekkumedu, having reached the Gandhi statue, passing the old light house and the shops selling paani poori, vadai, ground nut, mango slices and tender coconut, going through Nehru park and passing the main hospital. Arumugam walked, looking at the shops on both sides.

It was Abidha who finally broke the silence. "Why did you ask me that?"

"Just a casual question."

"Why would anybody want to marry a Chekkumedu woman who doesn't even know her father?"

"Where's your father? Did he die before you were born?"

"Chi, go on. Even my mother doesn't know who my father is."

"Leave it, then. Come on. "

She was now walking close to Arumugam. Suddenly, she stopped right in the middle of the road and hiked her sari up to her knees, showing him the bruises and contusions caused by the police.

"What do you expect me to do?" she spoke. "The beatings I got yesterday will ache a week. On top of all this, I'll have to go and grab Parties in Chekkumedu and earn something for a meal tomorrow. Those fellows snatched away the little cash I had, last night. And where are the Parties coming in as before, even in Chekkumedu?" She went on. "Haven't they filled the lodges and hotels with Kerala items? How can we expect them to come to Chekkumedu?"

Arumugam walked, forgetting the pedestrians and shops on both sides, his mind dwelling totally on Abidha's predicament. Abidha talked quite a lot. She spoke of her stay in Salem, her earnings there, and of the harlots of that place. She talked of her stay at Ulundurpettai, Athur and Tuvarankurichi.

Night had fallen by the time they reached the outskirts of Chekkumedu. As they passed Newtone Theatre, a woman selling food called out to Abidha, and began asking about her arrest.

Arumugam told Abidha that he would go ahead. As he walked further, the urge to make a full tour of Chekkumedu overwhelmed him, and he walked, taking in one place after another. Nausea rose in him, and he felt giddy. The place reeked horribly; it seemed to him that all the filth of the world had settled in Chekkumedu. Two people passed by, brushing against him.

By the time Arumugam came to Bhagyam's stall, having sight-seen Chekkumedu, the loathing bubbling up by what he had seen had turned into anger at the whole of Chekkumedu. He wanted to get away from it. His face seemed to be covered by a sticky, stinking substance, and he wiped his face again and again. A headache began to gnaw at him;

it seemed it would not go away. For the first time, he felt a revulsion — as though he had been lying in a sewer all this while.

The very thought of Chekkumedu was frightening, somehow.

Bhagyam made him sit at the cash counter and banged on the dosai pan, making a tada tada sound with the spatula. He could not bear to look at her; she was terribly emaciated, looking terrible with her shrunken cheeks, and dark circles around her eyes. He was surprised that she had not found fault with him and scolded him for his absence. He had also expected her to lambast Vasantha. "Is she still guarding the honour of her clan and caste? I don't know where she's going to end up, the haughty, florid slut. She's virtually lopped off my hand. When will they learn, these tramps? They've been in this business far too long. How can a tongue that's tasted sweets, and a body that's known the pleasures of bed not hanker after them? Try and ask these people to stay put in one place. If they do I'll cut off my ears." But today, she did not say a word.

During the first week of Vasantha's stay with Pushpa Mary, Bhagyam had abused her vulgarly. "I was foolish enough to give her, a woman standing helpless and perplexed on the road, shelter in my house. It was I who saved her that day, from being stripped naked in Chekkumedu. If it hadn't been for me, wouldn't fellows passing by have raped and ruined her in a single night? And now, what's my reward? I'm ruined, like a home without a door."

Abidha approached Bhagyam, asking about the sales. "Why don't you take over the oven department for a while?" she asked Arumugam loudly. Then she edged over to him and whispered into his ears, "Well, Mama, still want a wife?" and winked at him. Arumugam sat like a doll, still and lifeless.

A girl came running from the northern direction and dragged Abidha away. "Come quickly. The party might leave." Abidha rushed away with the girl, not losing a moment. Arumugam stared at the way Abidha went. People were walking about in all directions. The police-inflicted wounds Abidha had shown him came to his mind.

"Wait," he told Bhagyam. "I'll come back in a minute." Barely listening to Bhagyam's, "Why're you rushing out?" he ran in the direction Abidha went, to catch up with her.

People thronged about him. Men were flashing torches on women standing in groups, to see whether they were old or fresh arrivals, curled their lips in derision if they were the old ones, bargained for lower rates. Some women shut their eyes tight at the torches flashing, and stood still. One or two abused the men: "Chi, get lost."

All of them wore make-up, but it did not suit everybody's face. What could make-up do to faces drained of blood, wrinkled, dry, pock marked and pale? In fact, the face powder, eye-liner, and even the flowers only accentuated the age and haggardness of the women. Make-up suited women when about twenty or thirty years old. If they were they past fifty, the clever ones generally gave up selling their own bodies, and instead, plied the trade by gathering two or three younger women under their helm, and earning through them. Those who were sick or ill often took to begging in Chekkumedu itself, or earned by nabbing Parties on behalf of newly arrived young women, and by fetching tea, et cetera, for them.

They might be alone or move about in groups, but one generally had no problem recognizing Chekkumedu prostitutes or the women connected with them. The colour of the sari, the way they wore it, their blouses and the cut and stitch of it, the overdone, powdered face, the discoloured patches on their cheeks, a particular way of combing hair, the style of wearing flowers, the hair on the forehead,

snipped away and trimmed, their very walk with legs splayed apart ...
what would not reveal them for what they were? However intimately
acquainted one Chekkumedu woman was with another, she never
revealed her trade secrets to that other. Only some women were
permanent residents of Chekkumedu; the rest came to ply the trade,
stayed only for a week or ten days, and went back. What kept them
from staying on? The Police? The woman who employed them for
the flesh trade? Not enough money?

Sometimes, whores who met for the first time quickly made friends
with each other, yet, at the same time, something might lead to a
quarrel the next minute, and one would see them fighting and rolling
on the ground. The disputes would not end even when a crowd
gathered. Oftentimes, it would have begun on a very flimsy pretext.
One woman may have asked the other to give some her flowers for
free, or borrowed an eye-liner or face powder from the other's place
without asking. Or a woman may have taken on loan a hairpin, hook,
the forehead pottu, hair oil, petticoat, sari or blouse and failed to
return it. Perhaps they might not have repaid a loan in time. The
most violent quarrels erupted only if one crossed the other's path in
the trade.

People were criss-crossing Arumugam's path in all directions. He
found it difficult to go fast. For a moment, he felt that he had arrived
newly at Chekkumedu; so difficult did he find negotiating the crowd.

Night had fallen by the time he had completed two rounds of
Chekkumedu. He had peered at each passing face on his two trips
through the area, to see whether it was Abidha. Where would Abidha
have gone? Which hut would she have entered?

Two figures went past him. One of them came back, peered at him
and asked, "Looking for a woman?"

He was considerably embarrassed when he recognized that it was Thangamani, and began to turn back. Thangamani stopped him, and dragged him by his hand.

"I was just passing by," he tried to explain. "Listen, I'm not used to this. I don't want to."

He tried to wriggle out of her hold, but Thangamani was insistent. "You don't have to pay. Just enjoy yourself," she pulled at him. "It's a new party. She's arrived only today. Enjoy yourself if you like her. Leave if you don't." She stopped in front of a hut nearby, and called out to someone.

A man and woman walked out. The man ran towards the arrack shop; the woman squatted down right in front of the hut to urinate.

The woman who had accompanied Thangamani for the trade was standing by the side of the hut. Thangamani told her to go inside, then dragged Arumugam, and pushed him inside too. She thrust a hand into his pocket, pulled out whatever money was in it, and walked away to the arrack shop with a snigger.

Pushed inside against his will, Arumugam felt giddy. He thought he would faint; he wanted to get away from there. Wouldn't Abidha have returned to Bhagyam's stall by now? He wondered. I needn't have gone in search of her. She would have come back on her own. Why the hell did I come out here and get trapped into this by Thangamani?

The walls were just waist high in that hut, and there was room for just three people to lie down. He felt a wave of disgust just standing there, and recoiled. He began to walk out and had taken just two steps, when he felt something sticky under his feet. He bent down to see what it was.

It was too dark. He could not make out anything clearly. If it had been a Chekkumedu woman, he mused, she would have slipped her hand into his pocket as soon as he entered, nagging him for tips, would have finished the job hurriedly, and driven him out. Maybe Thangamani had been right: "It's a new party. Just for you. Take your own time."

Sensing the way the figure squatted in a corner, waiting patiently, he wondered whether the woman was new to the town, or merely to the profession. He shook off what was sticking to his legs with disgust, struck a match and brought the light to the face of the figure near his legs.

There, like a statue made of stone, sat Dhanabhagyam.

D hanabhagyam was clasping Arumugam, hugging him tight. Her face suggested that she would tuck him back into her womb, if she could. Arumugam gave himself up to her completely, yielding to her embrace like a baby clinging to his mother.

Abruptly, she sobbed aloud, not really caring that it was Chekkumedu.

Mother and son walked together, passing many lanes, roads and streets. The moon was as bright as a sunlit day, gliding along the sky, floating in its own pearly light. The night was bereft of clouds. The characteristic noise and demoniac pandemonium of Pondicherry had abated. A strong breeze blew in from the sea, chillingly cold, making one shiver.

Dhanabhagyam and Arumugam walked at leisure, like travellers going on a long journey, silent. Their walk seemed to indicate a pleasantly dreamy state, and a fear that the dream would be lost forever if they uttered a word aloud.

Every step Arumugam took was agonizing. It had shattered his heart, discovering Dhanabhagyam as he did, in that place. Breathing became difficult, buffeted as he was by waves of strange, indescribable emotions. His gait was unsteady and listless. Every hair in his body felt as though it was a poisonous snake, gouging out his skin, and every drop of blood was evaporating through each breath he took. His body seemed to have dissolved, and he felt like a speck of dust, flying about without settling on the ground.

Pondicherry had sunk into sleep; darkness now guarded the slumbering town. Arumugam walked, staring into the sky, while Dhanabhagyam walked three feet away, her eyes riveted on him, chanting "Arumugam," with every breath she took.

The moment he saw Dhanabhagyam, Arumugam had decided that they would go only to Pushpa Mary's house, in Kurichikkuppam. Midnight was upon them when they reached her home, and it was Vasantha who clasped Dhanabhagyam to herself as soon as she saw her, with a loud cry. Dhanabhagyam wanted to return the embrace, but sat silent instead, face pinched and drawn.

Pushpa Mary looked at her with awe. Dhanabhagyam's countenance left her speechless. She could only imagine how beautiful she must have been as a child, later, at puberty, still later, pregnant and glowing, and even when she had been living with Jerry Albert. Having sat in a stupefied silence for a long while, she suddenly took Vasantha out into another room, leaving Arumugam and Dhanabhagyam alone, seated at a little distance from each other.

Dhanabhagyam had been sobbing silently for a long time. Now, she beckoned to Arumugam, as though wishing to confide in him a secret.

"Arumugam ...?"

"Yes? What is it?"

"Nothing. I just ... spoke your name. I want to keep repeating it. How many years has it been ...? The past has taken birth again, I think. All this is god's will – and everything that went wrong before this was god's fault too, not mine. Great god above, what a proud, chaste woman I was … and now, I'm nothing but scum floating in a pond, Thambi."

Sighs and tears were all that came out of Dhanabhagyam. She wished to say so much, yet, seemed to be able to only sigh. What's left now, her despondent manner seemed to imply.

Arumugam wondered how she could slump this way, as though unaware of her own presence in this room; as though she had been living for ages in a place empty of human habitation, of human voices, of human presence. How much longer could she sit this way? Was she, maybe, reliving the whole of her past, dreaming of all the yesterdays, while still awake?

Dhanabhagyam wept in the meantime, hating herself, feeling orphaned. She lamented the days when all things had claimed her gladly, when all had existed within her, and had then left forever, nevermore to be claimed. Was she willing herself to die a death of tears? Arumugam was at a loss. All he could do was stare at her. Even as he did, he had the impression that he was looking not at Dhanabhagyam, but at somebody else.

Dhanabhagyam dragged Arumugam down and settled him on her lap. She caressed his face, chest, stomach, hands and fingers. Bending down, she placed her face on his, and cried a little. She parted her lips to say something, but he closed her mouth with his hand as though he were the elder, advising a child.

"There's no need to say anything. What's happened has happened. You're alive, and that's all that's important. This is all that I want. Nothing else matters. Nobody bundles up their bad dreams and carries it around on their heads. Yesterday's a corpse, and no one keeps a corpse at home. Uproot the past and throw it all away. Don't we bury dead bodies in the earth? Spit on everything, all the yesterdays, and bury them." Arumugam hung his head as he finished speaking. He felt like sobbing aloud – he wanted to talk to Dhanabhagyam endlessly.

"I held on to my life only because I wanted to see you at least once," she murmured. "That was all I wished for – to see you, to speak your name in your ears, and then die, looking at you. I prayed endlessly, just to lie at your feet, like soot clinging to a vessel. The last time I ate food as a woman worth the name, was the day before you ran away. The last night I slept as a woman, was the night before, when I slept by your side. And here you are, in front of me, like god. Ah, only tonight will I sleep. My eyes haven't rested in years. I depended on my body – I thought I *was* my body ... but my body's made me live on shit. I realized that it wasn't difficult to push the breath out of my lungs and stop it forever, the very day your father died. Do you think I went with your father to lead a happy married life? No, it was nothing less than exile. I've kept some life in this log of wood, only because I wanted you to light my pyre."

Why was Dhanabhagyam saying all this? Why was she crying her heart out? There had been no deity in those days she had not prayed to, that Arumugam should excel in his studies and rise to a great position. Silk skirts for Sengeniyamman, arrack and hens for Ayyanar, a day's folk drama performance for Mariamman during the festival, the ceremonial tonsuring by the whole family for Mailam Murugan ... but what did all that achieve? Now, Dhanabhagyam merely slumps like an old woman. All her dreams are wisps of smoke.

Hadn't the whole village assembled and watched with delight, when she had arrived at Krishnapuram with a glittering taali around her neck? Had there been a single voice that did not praise the sari she wore, the blouse she had on, her nose ring, ear-studs, anklets, her hands, legs, height and complexion? Had there been any Nayudu, eligible in the whole village and the neighbouring ones, who had not sought her, either directly or through messengers? And hadn't she sent back all such discreet inquiries with a curt reply: "You'll wait for the sea to dry up, and then eat fish, will you? You and your useless desires!"

What has become, now, of that pride? Now she droops, as though caught red handed while stealing.

How long can anyone sit in darkness without even a lamp? What would it be like, to be blind? How long can one bear to sit in front of an endlessly tearful Dhanabhagyam?

"There's no doubt about that, Thambi — I've lost all my honour and respect, but I'm still holding on to life. I didn't go along willingly. If anything, it's society that's to be blamed. I let myself be a feather, buffeted along by the wind. Days and events were mixed up. One thing led to another, hopelessly twined like the ropes of a temple chariot ... I couldn't accept that life, but I couldn't cut myself away. What could I do when the heat rose up in my blood?"

"Thambi, my family was scattered like clouds blown apart by the wind. You people have played with my life, making me a stone-pawn in a game; a game of goats and tigers. Why've you conspired against me? Why've you reduced me to this? What wrong did I do? You've turned me into a shrivelled kernel — you've left me alone. Deserted me as Rama deserted Sita — disgraced me as Duschasana did Panchali. My life was a beautifully plaited hair, but now its soiled and matted. Merciless god, don't let me be born again in this world, or lead another miserable life like this! Everything's turned out to be a role in a street play. Is that all I am, a street entertainer? A gypsy? I've had to bear barbed words and insults from everyone, because I've heaped dishonour onto my caste and clan. It's the same everywhere ... there's only darkness, whatever I see, wherever I go. Why am I still alive?"

Arumugam looked at Dhanabhagyam intently. She shakes her head violently, as though somebody was swinging it from behind. She had sat the same way, like someone insane, the day Raman's dead body had been brought in. She had wailed day and night a whole month after Raman's burial, slumped in the middle of the house, limbs stretched out. She weeps the same way now. Shedding silent tears, staring at the lines in her palm.

Arumugam felt a desperate urge to talk to her, but he did not know what he could speak about. His hands yearned to touch her, but he pressed them down on the floor, and restrained himself.

"Thambi, Arumugam," she murmured, "My thoughts have always been about you. You're the apple of my eye. You're the red of my blood. You're the earth under my feet. You're everything to me. Not for a moment has your image left my eyes, in all these years."

Dhanabhagyam crushed him in her embrace. Suddenly, for some reason, she began to sob more loudly than ever before.

The wind lifted her grief-laden cries, carrying them unto the heavens. Above them, night seeped away.

"Y ei Dhanabhagyam, how could you die when your master's daughter is still alive?" Vasantha was wailing aloud. "What's happened to you that you must kill yourself? Wasn't I there for you, always?"

Arumugam woke up, startled by the sound of her hysterical cries. Vasantha's screams from the kitchen left him in no doubt as to what had happened.

Dawn had broken by the time Dhanabhagyam and Arumugam finished their conversation. He had fallen asleep, slumped against the wall. When, he wondered, did she bathe, comb her hair, deck herself out like a bride, and tie his shirt around her waist? When did she string her sari to the hook in the kitchen's ceiling, and hang herself?

Vasantha came to Arumugam, asking him in broken tones to help her untie the sari and lower the body.

He stared at her as though caught in a frenzy of madness.

"I won't come over there," he screamed, beating the floor violently. "That body died a long time ago ... why must I see a corpse that's given up its life – that's died without anybody to mourn it, without anybody to bathe it – no one to follow it to the cremation ground? Nothing's ever happened in my life the way I wanted it to – nothing that I hated stopped happening. What's going to stop happening if I'm not there? Tell me, tell me ..."

BIO NOTES

IMAYAM (V Annamalai), teaches English at a high school in Vridhachalam, Tamilnadu. He made his mark on the Tamil Literary Scene with his very first novel, *Koveru Kazhuthaigal*, published in 1994, which created heated debates on issues like the role of a Dalit writer in the context of oppression seen within the Dalit community.

He is a recipient of the Agni Akshara Award, the Tamil Nadu Progressive Writers' Association Award and the Amutham Adigal Award.

Arumugam is his second novel.

D Krishna Ayyar has, for the past decade and a half, been devoting time exclusively to the study of Advaita Vedanta under a traditional preceptor, after an active career with the central government. During the freedom struggle he was inspired by the nationalist spirit and throughout his life by leftist and Gandhian ideologies.

BE A FRIEND OF KATHA!

If you feel strongly about Indian literature, you belong with us! KathaNet, an invaluable network of story and translation activists, is the mainstay of all our translation related activities.

Katha has limited financial resources; it is the unqualified enthusiasm and the indispensable support of nearly 5000 dedicated people out there which makes our work possible.

We are constantly on the lookout for people who can spare the time to find stories for us, and to translate them. Katha has been able to access mainly the literature of the major Indian languages. Our efforts to locate resource people who could make the lesser known literatures available to us have not yielded satisfactory results. We are specially eager to find Friends who could introduce us to Bhojpuri, Dogri, Kashmiri, Maithili, Manipuri, Nepali, Rajasthani and Sindhi fiction. And to oral and tribal literature.

BE A FRIEND OF KATHA! Do write to us with details about yourself, your language skills, the ways in which you can help us as a writer, translator or editor. In case you have any material that you already have please do let us know, so we can together forge an active partnership for the greater benefit for language development and survival in India. As a Friend of Katha, we would like to offer you a discount of 30% on all our publications.

For details, please write to us at kathavilasam@katha.org. Or call us at 2652 4350, 2652 4511.

WHAT PEOPLE SAY ABOUT US

"... an extraordinary non-profit company called Katha ... has begun to salvage the lost classics of modern India, translating them into English with flair and publishing them in beautiful editions."

— The Independent, U.K.

"Katha is doing an incredibly heroic work. By making available in English translation the best of Indian short fiction. Katha is presenting the "real" India to English readers across the world ... Katha is a celebration of the diversity of the Indian experience."

— The Indian Express

"... the first independent publishing house to insist that translators are as important as writers."

— The Business Standard

"Katha has been able to incorporate tremendous variety in tone, structure, and themes ranging from the absolutely contemporary to the timeless."

— The Hindustan Times

ABOUT KATHA

Katha, a nonprofit organization working with and in story and storytelling since 1988, is one of India's top publishing houses. Focusing on quality translations – our list includes more than 300 of India's best literary talents from twenty one languages – we showcase contemporary Indian fiction like no other publisher. Katha also introduces an array of writings from the many oral and written traditions of India to children, ages 0 - 17. Classy productions, child-friendly layouts and superb illustrations go in tandem with excellent writing. **Katha Indica**[R] is a leading edge series that brings the best of India to children.

Katha's major activities include the **Katha Awards for Literary Excellence** that are considered national recognitions; and the **Katha Festivals** and utsavs that bring literature into the public ken. These create open meeting places for writers, translators, scholars, critics, storytellers, folk and contemporary artists and community activists from India and abroad.

Katha works with 6,000 Friends of Katha and a growing pool of writers, translators and literary enthusiasts. Our constant striving is for greater reach and impact amongst teachers and students, policy makers and the corporate sector.

In the areas of education, Katha, with five international recognitions to its credit including the **NASDAQ STOCK MARKET EDUCATION AWARD** for 2002, is internationally known for its endeavours to spread the joy of reading, knowing, and living amongst adults and children, the common reader and the neo-literate. Story pedagogy[R] is an innovative classroom practice in Katha schools that work with communities in Delhi and other parts of India – helping more than 8,000 children and 250,000 adults across 57 communities bring themselves positive change.

Our mission: Enhancing the joys of reading. Our belief: Stories help create friendships of a rare kind to culturelink people, faiths and creative impulses. Stories are the life-savers of future nations. Our credo: An uncommon education for a common good.[R]

Katha . A3 Sarvodaya Enclave . Sri Aurobindo Marg . New Delhi -110 017 . India
Ph: (91.11) 2652.4511, 2652.4350, 2686 8193, 2652.1752 . Fax: (91.11) 2651.4373
E-mail: info@katha.org
www.katha.org

Help shape my future!

Doctor, engineer, policewoman, computer specialist ...

what will I be?

What happens when 1300 children, a determined Katha team of teachers and activists, and a whole community come together? Yes ... Sheer magic! You'll find this excitement in the air when you enter our school, a brick low-cost building.

We, the children and women of Govindpuri, a large slum cluster of more than 1,50,000 people, have come a long way in more than fourteen years with Katha. But there are excitements ahead. Small but sure steps towards self-confidence, self-reliance touched by the power of self-esteem. Many of us are working today to support our families in ways we could never have dreamt of! Many of us have finished our BAs and BComs from Delhi's colleges. We once didn't even dare to dream ... today dreams coming true, we talk of what Katha's goal of an uncommon education for a common good can help us all achieve. We are fun-loving dreamers-doers at Katha. And we'd like you to join us in our fight against poverty.

Be our special friend! Sponsor quality education at Katha. Giving has never been so easy, or with so much impact. It costs you just Rs 250/month to provide basic quality education to one of us. That's Rs 3,000/yr. Include computer education for a child with just Rs 1,800/yr more!

Please send your cheque/DD in favour of Katha Resources to Educate a Child (REACH) Fund to **Katha, A3, Sarvodaya Enclave, Sri Aurobindo Marg, New Delhi 110017**. For more details visit us at **www.katha.org**. Or write to us at **networking@katha.org**.

Donations to Katha Reach Fund qualify for 100% tax exemption under 35 AC of the IT Act. Registered under FCRA, Katha can receive donations in foreign currencies.